The FOURTH FATE

The Fourth Fate
Text Copyright © 2018 by Rebecca Casselman
Cover Illustration © 2021 by Chas Coffman

ISBN: 978-1-7363918-2-2

Bright Eyes Publishing is an imprint of
Cassel Core Industries, LLC
Bright Eyes Publishing name and logo are trademarks of
Cassel Core Industries, LLC

For information contact:
Bright Eyes Publishing c/o Cassel Core Industries, LLC
721 Depot Drive
Anchorage, Ak
casselcore.com
First Edition: May 2021

For my girls.

Always let your light shine; and when it's too hard to follow, lead.

I believe in you.

- Mom

THE FOURTH FATE

REBECCA CASSELMAN

Bright Eyes
Publishing

Chapter 1: The Girl Who Ran Away

Mrs. Dallape droned on, squeezing out any remaining attention from her seventh-grade class as the minutes counted down to the last bell. "Mitochondria! It is the mighty mouse powerhouse!" A wide, triumphant smile stretched her thin face as she tapped the screen hanging at the front of the classroom, displaying a blurry picture of a multicolored bean with squiggly lines inside it. "Without this, you wouldn't have energy or be able to breathe." She sucked in a huge breath, resembling a blowfish, and then blew it out to demonstrate. "This little guy converts oxygen into ATP which is..." the bell rang loudly, and everyone grabbed their backpacks, frantically stuffing them full of books and loose papers, the last of her lecture overruled by the din.

Heaving a relieved sigh, Rachel Soarenson wedged her worksheet into her Biology book and slid it heavily between her English and Math books nestled inside her teal bag. She looked forward to completing her homework in the peace of her room at home. Rachel enjoyed science and math more than some of the other girls in her class, who were primarily concerned with their appearance and boys. At home, she could concentrate without their note passing and giggling distractions.

Pulling either side of her curly ponytail to tighten the band, she stuck a pencil through the base near her head before zipping up her bag. She slung it over a shoulder and headed out of the lab with purpose. Little did she know her purpose was about to change . . . drastically.

A large, sunny courtyard separated the Cape Cod middle school from the elementary school, and Rachel squinted, searching for her younger sister. At times like these, it was handy she stood a head taller than most of the kids in her class. It was her responsibility to collect Morgan at the end of the day and head straight home to meet up with their mother, who was usually late. She always got stuck in traffic on her way home from work as a marine robotics specialist. Rachel was used to it, and carried a house key so she and Morgan wouldn't be stuck outside waiting on her.

Just then Rachel spotted Morgan trotting into the courtyard from the fourth-grade wing near a big aspen tree with its cheery yellow leaves dancing in the autumn breeze. As usual, Morgan's hair looked like a squirrel had been nesting in it. Her jacket hung halfway off a thin shoulder and one of her shoelaces, dark and frayed from being walked on, was trailing along the pavement. She was a joyful girl with a palpable energy that exploded when she saw Rachel. Morgan darted between groups of kids to greet her big sister with a lunging hug.

"Hi, Rachel!"

"Hi, Morgan. Do you have your backpack?"

Morgan glanced over her shoulder, saw she wasn't wearing her backpack and raced off, back to her classroom. Rachel followed behind, shaking her head. "Don't forget your water bottle!" she called to Morgan, who was pulling her purple cheetah print bag off a hook outside her classroom. The main zipper gaped open, a wide mouth stuffed haphazardly with colorful papers.

Rachel wondered if birds ever found snacks in it. Entire fowl families probably survive off goldfish cracker crumbs in there, she thought, and her lips twitched, revealing a dimple in one light-brown cheek.

Morgan dashed to the little table outside the room's door, snatching her pink water bottle dotted with pink hearts, and jammed it into the mesh pouch on the side of her backpack. "I've got everything now, I promise!" She grinned up at Rachel, her chestnut eyes wide and full of spunk.

Rachel had the same warm eyes, only hers were more thoughtful. They'd inherited them from their father, who was currently deployed out of the country. It comforted Rachel to know she had a part of him always with her, and it made her smile anytime she looked at her own reflection. He called her "Bright Eyes" as a term of endearment. Since his absence, she'd started using the nickname for her sister.

"Alright, Bright Eyes, zip up and let's go."

The girls walked off the now deserted campus, across the empty parking lot, and hopped onto their regular sidewalk home.

Morgan liked to jump the cracks. She giggled, singing, "Don't step on a crack! Or you'll break your Mother's back!"

That's when Rachel noticed a girl she had never seen before across the street. She only noticed her because the girl was standing stock still and staring at them.

3

That's odd, thought Rachel, her smile fading.

The girl looked older, like maybe she was in high school. She had long brunette hair pulled back into a thick braid. The braid fell over the front of her dark green jacket that paired neatly with brown riding boots.

Something about the way the girl watched them gave Rachel a chill. With a shiver, she took Morgan's hand and walked a little faster. The sidewalk declined, and they were nearly trotting down the hill where they usually crossed the street. Rachel didn't want to cross the street because the strange girl was following them. She was at a distance now, but definitely tailing them.

Before Rachel could think of a plan, Morgan tore her hand free and raced down the hill with her arms shot out like wings.

"Woo Hoo!!!" Morgan shouted as she neared the base of the slope where the crosswalk was. Normally they both liked to race down the hill to see who could get to the bottom first, but Rachel had been distracted and didn't realize exactly how close they were.

"Stop, Morgan!" shouted Rachel, but she was too late. Morgan reached the bottom of the hill and started across the crosswalk just as a red SUV rounded the bend too fast. Morgan didn't see it barreling toward her, but Rachel did. She screamed at her sister.

The vehicle slammed its brakes, tires screeching as it swerved, knocking Morgan to the ground and jerked to a stop directly on top of her.

Rachel ran toward her sister as fast as she could with tears streaming off her face, littering the ground like tiny raindrops. She could see the top half of Morgan sticking out from under the tire, and she wasn't moving.

The driver jumped out, cell phone in hand.

"Oh, no. Oh no, no, no," he said repeatedly while giving directions to a 911 dispatcher.

Rachel glanced up the street to make sure no more cars were coming and vaguely noted that the mysterious girl was standing a ways back, watching them. "Morgan! Can you hear me, Morgan!?" She knelt next to Morgan's head, staring at her lifeless face. "Please don't die," she whispered.

Wailing sirens grew louder as an ambulance rounded the bend. The rest happened rather quickly, but time slowed down in those moments for Rachel. The driver backed up his SUV, its tire inching slowly off Morgan's abdomen. The instant she was free, EMTs slid a board under her, lifted it on a gurney and in seconds, loaded her into the back of the ambulance. Rachel looked at the man who'd been driving the SUV with blank eyes. He wept freely, blubbering incoherently about how sorry he was. An EMT's kind face floated in front of hers. He asked Rachel a question and she stared at his lips, trying to focus.

I must be in shock, she realized, her eyes drifting to a mustard stain on his white uniform.

He asked her again if she was going to ride with them and if they should call someone. Rachel mumbled her mother's phone number and clumsily climbed into the back of the ambulance. It was disconcerting how the red and blue flashing lights kept changing the colors of everything. It made her head spin. Nausea bubbled up her throat, threatening rupture. The sudden crash of the back doors jarred her out of the brain fog. Rachel's dilated pupils snapped back to pinpoints and she cringed, swallowing the bitter water brash accumulating in her glands.

EMTs pummeled her with questions, working quickly and efficiently on Morgan, inserting a needle into her small, limp arm, starting an IV for fluids.

And hopefully pain medicine, Rachel thought. She answered them as best she could as the shock wore off, replaced with something worse. Fear.

She couldn't stand to see Morgan this way! Tearing her eyes away, she looked out the back window. Rachel narrowed her dark eyebrows when she saw the strange girl at the scene of the accident. The girl rose from where she'd been kneeling next to the SUV. She was holding Morgan's backpack, the purple cheetah print stained dark with drying blood.

The girl's head snapped up, making direct eye contact with Rachel through the ambulance window. A waterfall of chipped ice flooded down Rachel's spine when she looked straight into the girl's face. Rachel's mouth went bone dry, she could scarcely breathe, and her hands felt cold and clammy.

Petrified, unable to move or advert her gaze, Rachel's eyes remained locked with the girl's. The seconds ticked by like molasses as the ambulance gained distance, racing to the hospital. The figure of the girl faded when they turned a corner, and the connection broke. Rachel's breath rushed out, her lungs deflating like popped balloons. Warmth flooded back into her, and she sagged against the interior wall of the ambulance.

Screeching to a full stop at the hospital, the ambulance doors flung open and emergency workers hastily wheeled Morgan into the hospital. Rachel could see Morgan's eyes fluttering in the commotion. She prayed it was a good sign.

Jumping down, intending to follow her sister, a stout woman in colorful scrubs wearing a face mask stopped Rachel, directing her to a waiting area instead.

Rachel felt numb. She rubbed both hands over her face, smoothing the skin still taught from dried tears. What was she supposed to do now? She sank heavily into a hard leather-covered chair with wooden armrests and wrapped her arms around herself. Had anyone called her mom? She couldn't remember if someone had called her mom or not.

Rachel stood back up to ask the receptionist if she could borrow a phone. All the other kids in school had their own cell phones, but her parents seemed to think phones weren't a necessity for middle school children. They refused to give her one, no matter how much she begged.

I bet they'll give me one now, she thought, her heart sinking low. Just then she heard her name shouted from across the waiting area.

"Rachel!"

Emily Soarenson spotted her eldest daughter the moment she stepped through the automatic sliding glass doors. Above average in height and weight, she had a fluffy red halo of hair that blew back from her shoulders as she charged into the waiting area, a force of nature in panic mode.

"Mom!" Rachel fell into her mother's arms, her sobs muffled between them. "I couldn't stop her, I just . . . I'm so sorry." She let it all out, clinging to her mom, her knees going weak.

"Oh, Rachel. Honey, I'm so sorry I wasn't there!" her mom cried, squeezing Rachel, supporting her weight and kissing the top of her head several times. "It's not your fault baby, it was an accident!" She hugged Rachel tight, rubbing her back reassuringly. "When they called me, I headed straight over. I haven't even contacted your father!"

Emily strode toward the emergency waiting room's front desk with Rachel glued to her side. "Hello. I'm Morgan Soarenson's mother and I need to know if she's okay, and if I can see her." She sniffed loudly.

The receptionist looked up from his computer. He had a clean face, and gel styled hair combed to one side in a blond wave.

"Yes, Ma'am. Let me just check," he said in a southern drawl. His warm accent stood out against the crisp East Coast dialect Rachel was used to hearing, and it soothed her.

The receptionist put a phone call on hold while simultaneously clicking buttons on his keyboard. "It looks like we've admitted Morgan. She's finishin' up her CT scan, and will be moved to a room in the ER soon. I can escort you to the room where she'll be, if you'd like."

"Yes, thank you." Emily produced a crumpled tissue from her coat pocket and began vigorously rubbing her nose as she looked down at Rachel. "Would you like to come back with me, or would you rather stay here? I can ask our neighbor to come pick you up. I have to call her anyway to hurry and pick up your brother from daycare; Luke can't stay late again or they'll charge extra."

Before Rachel could answer, the receptionist interrupted.

"Oh! I almost forgot. An item was dropped off for your daughter."

To Rachel's astonishment, the receptionist lifted Morgan's backpack out from under his desk and handed it over to her mom.

"Some girl dropped it off just before you got here. She looked like a runaway if you ask me, all gloomy and such, but it was still nice of her to bring it by for ya'll."

"Oh, thank you so much." Emily took the backpack from him, stuffing the used tissue back in her pocket. "Why would a runaway have Morgan's backpack?" she asked Rachel, who was staring disbelievingly at the russet stained backpack hugged

8

tightly in her mother's other arm as if it was Morgan. The water bottle on the side was cracked through, and all the water had leaked out.

How in the world did it get here before they did? Rachel wondered. Could that strange girl have driven here that fast? Rachel didn't know of any shortcuts to the hospital. It was totally bizarre.

"I don't know, Mom. There was a girl I've never seen before walking near us when the accident happened."

"Well, maybe she's new to the neighborhood and just wanted to help in some way. Two new military families have moved to our street this past week."

"Yeah, maybe."

That still didn't explain how she got to the hospital before the ambulance, Rachel thought with a shiver. Her legs were heavy and Rachel couldn't lift a foot, but it didn't matter because her mom dragged her along under a protective bear grip, following the receptionist through a set of double doors into the ER.

If the strange girl was a runaway, what was she doing at their school? Rachel thought about the way the girl had been watching her and Morgan, like she knew something was about to happen. It sent another icy shiver down her spine.

Chapter 2: Introductions

November was out of sorts with their dad gone. He'd been deployed with his Army unit about half a year, and Rachel wasn't excited to celebrate the holidays without him. People were gathering with their families, gearing up to share delicious food and traditions for Thanksgiving but it didn't feel right to Rachel without her dad home.

It had been six weeks since Morgan's accident. The doctors said she had a cracked pelvis but was otherwise, miraculously uninjured. Rachel was thankful for it, but lately, she felt annoyed helping Morgan with everything while their mother tended to Luke and worked all the time.

Halloween had been a disaster. Their mom fussed over Morgan having a costume to cover her walker so much, that Rachel ended up wearing a random blanket as a cape. Then she had to carry Morgan's candy bucket while they moved at a snail's pace, and she dropped her own, spilling loot all over the sidewalk. Other trick-or-treaters had pounced, stealing over half her candy. She'd only bagged a quarter amount of her normal treats before they had to go home because Morgan was tired. She'd long since eaten all the pieces and now it was the "holiday season" and Rachel felt extra moody about it. Normally she loved this time of year, but with her father gone, and constantly helping Morgan with recovery, she just couldn't shake her glum attitude. Everyone around her was growing more cheerful while she became more sour. It didn't help that she had to work on a report over fall break.

Rachel and Morgan sat on a tired grey couch in their living room going over homework. It was a neutral-colored room, with floral patterned curtains and neglected house plants wilting on various end tables and shelves. A large family photo displayed on the main wall promised a happier time when the family would be together again.

Morgan tossed her pencil at Rachel. "Sharpen that." It was a command rather than a request.

Rachel's lips tightened. "Do it yourself, Morgan. The doctor said you need to walk as much as possible to strengthen your muscles."

Morgan cocked an eyebrow at Rachel. "Mom! Rachel's not helping me!" she hollered.

"Come on, really?"

"Rachel! Help your sister while I get these side dishes ready!" their mother yelled from the kitchen. Rachel began to protest, but her mom cut her off. "Don't make me come in there you two!"

Rachel snatched the pencil off the coffee table and snapped it in half. "Oops. Guess I need to *help* you get a new pencil."

Morgan's eyes instantly filled with angry tears. "Moooom! Rachel broke my pencil!"

"It was an accident!"

"Was not!"

Their mother stormed into the living room, her cheeks full blooming roses from cooking over a hot stove. "Rachel Soarenson, what has gotten into you? Apologize this instant!"

"I'm sorry," said Rachel, embarrassed that she'd acted like a little kid. Somehow her mother always knew when she wasn't being truthful.

A smug smile crossed Morgan's face at their mother's harsh words. It felt good to get her way. But the smile vanished when their mother turned a scolding look on her as well.

"Are you causing strife, young lady?"

Morgan rubbed her eyes with the back of her hand. "No! I just needed my pencil sharpened."

Emily narrowed her eyes, but before she could say another word, Luke toddled into the living room. Noticing the tension and Morgan's tears, his little lip quivered. Without missing a beat, their mother scooped him up. "Look girls, I know Morgan's recovery has been stressful on everyone. You've done a wonderful job helping me, Rachel. And Morgan, you've been working so hard at physical therapy. I'm proud of you both. I just need us all to take a breath, so I can get these pies and side dishes finished for tomorrow's dinner."

Rachel restrained herself from rolling her eyes as her mother led them all in a breathing exercise.

"In through the nose, one- two- three and out through the mouth, one- two- three."

"Mom, do we have to invite a bunch of strangers over for Thanksgiving? It feels so weird without Dad here," said Rachel.

"You know it's our tradition to invite soldiers without family around over for Thanksgiving."

"I know, but you're doing all the work by yourself and it

feels like too much."

Her mother studied her a moment, then Morgan and then Luke, who was playing with her necklace, trying to get it into his mouth. "You're right, Rachel. It does feel like too much." She let out a sigh. "That's because it is. I have been asking a lot from you lately and I am sorry. Your dad's deployment will be over soon; I'm hoping he'll be home by Christmas. Until then, we've got to pull together to get through a few more weeks." She shifted Luke to her other hip. "It's important that when struggles come our way, we remain steadfast. I know siblings can be taxing, but we need to remember our love for each other, and that we're a team."

"Yes, Mom," said Rachel, giving Morgan an apologetic smile.

"I don't want to sacrifice our family traditions while your dad is away. Believe it or not, keeping our routines as normal as possible helps us. Think of how much you miss Daddy. That's how many of these young soldiers feel during the holidays. We must try our best to show them a kindness while we're stationed here. Do you understand?"

Rachel and Morgan nodded.

"Maybe you can help me think of ways we can help each other. Children often have the best ideas; you girls are natural problem solvers." She pulled her necklace away from Luke just as it touched his lips. "I can't wait to hear what you come up with! In the meantime, would it help if I ask for less hours at work, so I can be here when you get home from school? If you can't have your dad just yet, maybe more of me will be okay?"

"Oh, Mom! That would be great!" exclaimed Rachel, jumping to her feet and closing in for a hug. Morgan followed, lifting herself off the couch and using her walker to stabilize herself, rolled toward her mom and sister to join in a family hug.

* * *

The next morning, sunlight glinted through the blinds lighting up dancing dust particles and Rachel stretched awake in the cozy halo. The house smelled amazing! Her mother must have gotten up early to put the turkey in the oven. Rachel's mood lifted like the rising sun, driving away all shadows.

Quickly brushing her teeth and rinsing off her face, she chose a pretty, cabled green sweater to wear with her jeans. She knew it was polite to look nice when having company over for a holiday meal. Plus, it was what her mom expected and she didn't want to have to change later.

Trotting down the stairs, pulling unruly curls up into her signature ponytail, Rachel greeted her siblings already nestled around the table.

Her mom beamed at her. "Good morning, baby. You look so nice! You can watch the parade after you eat some breakfast." She slid a plate of eggs and sausage towards Rachel and kissed the top of her head before turning her attention on Luke.

Luke sat in his highchair wearing only a bib and a diaper. There were scrambled eggs mashed in his hair. Ignoring the baby fork, he grabbed at the eggs their mother spooned onto his tray with chubby hands, stuffing them into his mouth by the fistful.

"Mom, I'm not a baby," Rachel insisted, eyeing her brother's mess.

"I know dear heart, but you'll always be *my* baby," her mom countered, pointing the wooden spoon at her eldest. Rachel smiled and dug into her breakfast.

Early that afternoon, their first guests arrived. Rachel proudly set out a veggie tray, and deviled eggs she'd crafted. The young soldiers were shy at first, but after Rachel's appetizers they warmed up to the homy environment. Then Rachel turned on the traditional football game, and everyone relaxed. Only ten people showed up, but that was plenty in Rachel's opinion. They enjoyed an early dinner with conversations about favorite family memories and after the meal several board games started up, raising the noise level considerably!

The doorbell rang and Rachel frowned, guessing it was a latecomer. Well, they made it in time for pie, she thought, leaving a game of spoons and making her way to the front door. Rachel opened the door and her jaw dropped, her eyes growing wide in absolute shock. Her father was standing in front of her with a huge grin on his face.

"Happy Thanksgiving, Bright Eyes!" he said, stepping inside the doorframe, arms open wide. In one sobbing breath, Rachel reached him. He wrapped her up and stood to his impressive full height while she clung to him, her feet dangling. He squeezed her tight. "I missed you so much."

"I missed you so much too, Daddy," she sniffed, her head tucked in his neck. He smelled like sweat and pine.

"Come on in!" Rachel's mom called, marching into the entryway, wiping her hands on a festive, fall-colored tea towel. She stopped abruptly, thunderstruck at the sight of her husband standing there. He was broad shouldered, still in uniform and his dark head, recently shaved, was shining under the overhead light.

"What in the world? Lawrence?!"

"Surprise!" their dad said, and in two steps he pulled his

wife close, kissing her warmly. They both laughed and pulled apart. Rachel's mom placed a hand lightly on her husband's cheek and they gazed into each other's eyes, unspoken words passing between them.

Morgan came around the corner, pushing her walker in front of her, the front wheel squeaking. "Daddy! Daddy!" she shouted, overjoyed by the surprise.

A cloud of sadness passed over his face, but quickly disappeared as he knelt to hug his youngest daughter. "Oh, my baby girl! I'm so blessed."

"Luke! Come see who it is!" called Rachel, dashing away a few happy tears. Luke toddled into the entryway to see what all the fuss was about. He'd grown accustomed to seeing his father on a computer screen and was confused by seeing him so large and in person. It was more frightening than exciting, and he started crying.

Their mom picked him up making soothing sounds. "It's alright sweetie! It's just Daddy, see? Say hi Da da."

"Da, da?" said Luke, and they all laughed when he stretched out his little arms, wanting his father to hold him.

Inside, the soldiers greeted Mr. Soarenson with handshakes and several pats on the back. Everyone was in good spirits, and when Mrs. Soarenson declared it was time to cut into the pies, the doorbell rang again. This time Rachel let someone else get it. She didn't want to leave her father's side for the rest of the day!

The newcomer was ushered into line for pie. Rachel served up generous slices and Morgan handed out forks next to her, delightfully stabbing them into their guest's dessert.

Rachel was so happy she didn't recognize the girl holding out a plate in front of her at first. While sliding a wedge of pumpkin pie onto the festive plate decorated with fat turkeys,

Rachel's smile froze.

It was that same runaway girl from the accident! Her clothes and hair were different; she had a short blond bob now and wore a cutesy pink pullover, but it was the same face, Rachel was sure of it! Why was she wearing a disguise?

When they locked eyes, Rachel felt her legs freezing from the inside out. Unable to move, her heart raced like a wild train about to crash through her ribcage!

The girl broke eye contact when Morgan pierced her slice of pie, and Rachel sucked in a breath. Dizzily gripping the kitchen counter, her legs melted and she used the solid, cool marble to steady herself, while her runaway heartbeat returned to a normal speed.

The strange girl made her way down the line as if nothing had happened. Rachel daringly glanced at her, noting how she easily chatted with her parents. They didn't seem bothered by her presence at all. They laughed and joked around while loading up pie slices with clouds of whipped cream.

Who was this girl? Whoever she was, Rachel did not trust her. Especially after what had happened to Morgan the last time she saw her. Rachel wasn't about to let anything happen to her unsuspecting parents.

Passing the serving utensils to a helpful soldier, she walked up to her mother's side and brazenly stuck out her hand. "Hi, I'm Rachel Soarenson. What's your name?"

The girl looked like she would fit in anywhere. Her face was pleasant, with a high forehead and a wide amiable smile, but her dark green eyes held secrets.

Those eyes widened slightly at Rachel's boldness, but the girl smiled warmly, showing perfectly straight, white teeth. Rachel was not charmed. Wariness flitted behind the girl's eyes.

"I'm Arka," she said, clasping Rachel's hand.

Electricity rocketed through Rachel. She gasped as all her surroundings faded away. She could no longer see or hear anyone in the kitchen. Instead, she saw a dark hollow and three shadows bent together, whispering. Glittering light at the edge of her vision pushed the image away, and it faded back to Arka's face. She was studying Rachel, her dazzling smile now a slight frown.

Rachel blinked and pulled her hand free. Shakily, she wiped a bead of sweat away from her temple.

"Where do you live, Arka?" Rachel heard her mother ask.

"Oh, my family and I are new to this post. We noticed you were having a get-together. My mom saw you had a couple of kids and suggested I stop by to introduce myself and wish everyone a Happy Thanksgiving. She said I should offer babysitting services or try making new friends." Her gaze flicked toward Rachel, who was staring at her, mouth agape at the obvious lie. "I really should be getting back home though."

Her mom dug an elbow into Rachel's ribs. "Did you hear that, Rachel? Arka here is looking for new friends. Why don't you walk her home, sweetheart?"

Rachel looked at her mother with bulging eyes. Seriously? Did she not see what just happened?! Before she could think of an excuse, her dad chimed in.

"That's a great idea! You can also take out the trash, Rach," he nodded encouragingly, ignoring her gobsmacked face.

Rachel was about to argue when Arka spoke up. "That would be great! It will give us time to get to know one another."

Moments later, with a fake smile plastered on her face, Rachel followed Arka outside, lugging a bulging trash bag behind her. On the front porch, she tossed the trash at a bin and jerked upright, slamming both hands on her hips. "Alright," said Rachel, "you have some serious explaining to do, *Arka*, if that's even your real name."

Chapter 3: Answers

The mysterious girl stood with her back toward Rachel, scanning the street. "I have some questions to ask you, Rachel Soarenson. It would be better for everyone if we weren't overheard."

"YOU have questions? I have questions!"

Arka spun on her heel to face Rachel and that horrible frozen feeling washed over her again, but this time Rachel broke the connection by glaring at a spot on Arka's forehead.

Arka narrowed her eyes. "Good. Let's go." She spun around again, and her blond hair rippled, replaced by a dark braid that tumbled down her back instead. She marched across the quiet suburb street without another word.

Rachel blinked. How did she do that? Was it a magic trick?

Despite her better judgment, Rachel hopped off the porch and jogged a bit to catch up with the strange girl.

Arka's hair wasn't the only thing that had changed, she was in a completely different outfit. She had on tight jeans, the riding boots Rachel had seen before, and a brown leather jacket. There was a glow about her as well, like an afterimage that followed her as she moved.

Rachel shook her head. Maybe what happened in the kitchen had really messed with her mind.

A little way down the street there was a grassy knoll topped with a small community playground. It was vacant right then, with all the neighbors inside enjoying turkey and family time. Arka glided over to a weathered bench facing the swings and gestured for Rachel to sit.

Rachel, not wanting to look up at Arka from a seated position, stood still and crossed her arms defiantly, keeping the bench between them as a barrier.

"Mortals are impossible," Arka growled under her breath, but Rachel heard her.

"What do you mean, mortals?" she demanded, her eyebrows drawing together.

"Look, *kid*, I don't know how you can see me or why we seem to have a bond, but I need to find out what's going on here before someone gets hurt."

Rachel did not like the sound of that. She could feel adrenaline flooding her veins. "If you come anywhere near my family again, I won't be the one getting hurt," she said in a low threatening voice. It surprised her how the thought of protecting her family made her suddenly braver than she felt.

Arka chuckled. "Calm down. I'm hardly a threat to you. I've been trying to help you, you just didn't realize it," she said, and sniffed, looking down her nose at Rachel.

"You mean at the accident? Or bringing Morgan's backpack to the hospital?"

Arka's mirth blew out like a candle. She was suddenly very serious, and her intensity was frightening. "So, you did see me at the accident?" she asked, her eyes boring into Rachel's.

Rachel's tongue stuck to the roof of her mouth and she merely nodded, eyes wide.

Arka drew her shoulders back, causing the leather of her jacket to creak. "I admit bringing the bag to the hospital was an error, but I wanted to see how the little girl was doing, to make sure she was alright, you see?" She paused and when Rachel still didn't reply she continued, her emerald eyes shining freakishly bright. "I mean to get to the bottom of this right here, right now. Tell me who you are, *child,* and don't lie. If you do, I'll know."

Rachel stared at her incredulously. Was this weirdo serious? "Tell you who I am? I'm just a kid! Everything started going crazy the day *you* showed up!"

Arka studied her a moment, then nodded. "I believe you."

"Good."

Neither one knew quite what to do next. A swing shifted with the breeze, squeaking its rusty hinge. The sun dipped low and a cotton candy sky crept toward them like a lazy stream.

Rachel finally plucked up enough courage to speak. "Are you going to tell me who you are and what in the world is happening to me?" she asked, unable to keep desperation from creeping into her voice. She fidgeted with chipped paint on the back of the park bench, picking off a long sliver.

"You wouldn't believe me," Arka said, and abruptly turned to leave the park.

"Wait!" Rachel hollered, forgetting to keep distance between them and chased after Arka through the playground. "You owe me some sort of explanation! I mean, why do I feel frozen solid when I look at you? What happened when I shook your hand? It was like I was looking into a different room and I..."

"You saw something when you touched my hand?" Arka

22

interrupted, pointing a finger in Rachel's face.

Rachel stopped short, but her words tumbled out. "Yes, um, it was all blurred and there were these shadows, and then it just disappeared." She licked her lips. "No one noticed I seem to have, well, blacked out for a minute."

"Can you do it again?" Arka asked, leaning against a yellow ladder for the monkey bars. Her movements were fluid, and all around her silhouette colors were more vibrant. It was subtle, but noticeable to Rachel.

Rachel glanced at the worn play equipment that seemed livelier now. "I don't know. I didn't DO anything, it just happened."

"Has this ever happened to you before?" Arka asked, draping an elbow over a ladder rung casually, like they were old friends.

Rachel frowned. "No."

"Well then, take my hand again, and let's see if it was a one-time deal or not."

Rachel looked at Arka's outstretched hand and felt like she might throw up.

"Oh, come on! It will be like a science experiment. If nothing happens, I promise to leave, and you'll never see or hear from me again."

Rachel wasn't the type to back down from a challenge. She looked Arka straight in the eye and when she felt like she was turning into an ice sculpture, she reached out, firmly grabbing Arka's hand.

Shining gold light burned Rachel's retinas. The intensity grew and grew as it moved closer, engulfing her. Pressing through it was like passing slowly through several walls of Jell-O. Rachel wondered how long she could breathe while being squeezed from every direction. She could see delicate lines in the thick wall of gold and suddenly she popped through it, gasping. Rachel quickly looked over her shoulder, but the wall of light was gone. When she turned her head back around, she was in the park again with Arka staring at her without blinking, their hands still clasped. Rachel jerked her hand away, now slick with sweat, and rubbed it on her jeans.

"Well? Did you see anything?"

"Yes. Couldn't you tell? I mean, it seemed to take a while," Rachel swallowed. Her throat was so dry it felt like she was swallowing hay. She tried clearing it twice, but it didn't help.

Arka didn't seem to notice or care that Rachel was having some difficulty. "I couldn't sense anything. You grabbed my hand, looked over your shoulder, and then let go. What happened?"

"Um, I'm not sure. I think I walked through a wall. Or rather, it walked through me."

"What wall? Where?" Arka let go of the ladder. She brimmed with excitement, leaning forward.

"I don't know!" Rachel barked, rubbing her throat. "It's not like I stopped and asked for directions!" She slapped the little bouncy bridge next to the ladder that connected sections of the play equipment in frustration, and it bobbed in protest. "It was a thick wall thing and it was shining in my eyes, literally *in* them when I was in the middle of it. It felt like I was drowning!"

Arka's mouth hung slightly open and her eyebrows were lifted in astonished arches. She clicked her mouth shut and stilled the bridge with a finger. When she touched it, the little bridge became a happy brown, but when she took her hand away, it grew dull and lifeless once again.

Rachel tightened her ponytail. "I'm sorry. I don't mean to be

24

snappy. I feel like I've been squished and pulled and doused with ice water, and I'm really thirsty." She rubbed her face and crossed to the swings. Slumping into a black saddle, she leaned forward with an elbow on her knee and propped her head on a fist.

"It wasn't a wall. It was the Tapestry."

"The what?"

"The Tapestry of Life." Arka took a breath. "No mortal has ever seen it, let alone ever walked through it. I mean, I haven't even done that!" Her excitement bubbled, and she tugged on her braid. "Can you tell me if you saw anything else? Anything at all?"

Rachel lifted her head. "Well, inside the um, tapestry thing, there were all these little lines. It was almost pixelated, like when you look at a computer screen too close."

"A pixie-what?"

"Like a grid, with intersections all connected but overlapping each other."

"You saw the threads? You TOUCHED them?!"

"Shhhhh! Keep your voice down!" Rachel's eyes darted in every direction. What would people say if they saw her with this lunatic? There still wasn't anyone around, but dusk was settling and visitors would be returning home soon. "It was more like they tried to smother me." She shivered and rubbed her arms through her sweater.

"Remarkable," Arka said, pacing back and forth. "It can only mean one thing."

"What's that?" Rachel sat up, interested.

"You must be a seer!"

Rachel cocked her head. "A what?"

"You can see what is happening or what will happen to

25

certain people when they come into contact with you." Arka had a big grin on her face as if this was good news. She stood in front of Rachel with her hands on her hips like a superhero who'd just solved a crime.

Rachel threw up. The entirety of her Thanksgiving dinner spewed from her soul like an unchecked firehose.

"Gah!!!" Arka jumped back in alarm. A dark scowl replaced her grin when she saw her boots dripping with vomit and she glared down at Rachel in horrified disgust.

Chapter 4: Myth

Rachel gasped uncontrollably, gulping air. "Why is this happening to me? Why am I so thirsty?!" She forced herself to take several deep breaths, trying to calm the rising panic storm in her chest.

Arka shook the swing's chains in exasperation. "Get ahold of yourself girl!"

Rachel bobbled around before planting her feet angrily to stop the jerking. "Stop it! Let go!" A flash of anger pulled her out of the panic attack.

Arka let go, satisfied the girl had calmed down. "You should be grateful. Only a chosen few have had visions when in contact with gods." She moved to pat Rachel on the shoulder but thought better of it. She kept her distance, scraping splatters off her boots on the playground steps instead. "You're thirsty because you are a mortal who has had a supernatural experience."

Rachel hiccupped on one of her deep breaths and sputtered, "Contact with gods? You're crazier than I thought!" She stood up, awkwardly avoiding the puddle of sick, and backed away from Arka, keeping behind the swing set. It was a flimsy excuse for a barricade, but it was all she had.

"Grecian goddess, rather. I know it sounds ridiculous to you, but there are forces in the universe you can't even imagine, let alone understand, and somehow you're able to tap into them." Arka stepped over the stinking puddle easily, pushing the swings out of her way, advancing toward Rachel. "Think about it, *child*. What other explanation do you have? If you asked anyone besides me, they'd say you are the crazy one. They would lock you up in an asylum."

"Impossible," Rachel whispered, wiping her mouth with the sleeve of her sweater. "Greek gods and all that are just a myth." With more conviction, she said, "I believe there is only one God."

"Indeed," replied Arka. "Most myths are based in some sort of truth, are they not? One must only look for the truth and they will find it. All the best stories have some sort of truth embedded in them. That's why they are our favorites, remembered and retold generation after generation." Rachel eyed her suspiciously, but Arka continued unwaveringly. "Most gods live in a different realm than you mortals. Only a few reside here, as demigods or as some have called them, Nephilim. Their parents, lesser gods than the Creator, known to you as fallen angels, were cast down to Tartarus for trying to corrupt humans and generally making a mess of things."

Rachel pressed her lips together. She was not in the mood for a history lesson, and her mouth tasted awful.

"It's a pit of darkness deep below the Underworld where they stay bound with everlasting chains in an eternal fire," Arka explained.

"I know what Tartarus is. I learned about it in school."

Arka lifted a smooth eyebrow. "Well, your school sometimes leaves out important parts."

"You're telling me you're a goddess, but you admit there is a Creator?"

"Of course." Arka snorted at her. "I'm a goddess, naturally I would believe in a deity."

A car rumbled up the street, making Rachel jump. This was too much. She needed to get home, away from this crazy girl, or whatever she was. Rachel tried walking around her, edging to the rim of the park, but Arka blocked her path.

"Come now, Rachel, think," she gestured with her hands, "you've heard of Atlas holding up the sky? Well, his mother was an Oceanid." Arka saw Rachel's face scrunch. "It means fresh-water nymph," she said. There was no recognition in Rachel's features, so she tried again. "How about Hercules? His mother was a human mortal."

"Yes," Rachel said uneasily, "I know that story."

"Well, both were Nephilim or demigods. Heroes of old, warriors of renown. You've been taught about the Great Flood, right?"

Rachel nodded.

"Well, it nearly wiped out all the remaining demigods, but a few survived. They were often called giants."

"Like Goliath?"

"I'm glad you're following. He had a few brothers that aren't so famous, and they had a king named Og of all things. Even after the birth, death, and resurrection of the Messiah, there were demigods among you. There still are. In fact, I plan on meeting with one shortly." Arka stopped short, realizing she had revealed some of her plans to a mortal child.

Well, she thought, if she's a seer, it shouldn't be an issue.

"Anyway, you and I have our own stories, but their threads have become entwined."

"It's not because of me! You're the one who was lurking around when my sister got hit by a freaking car! It's because of you I'm having weird daydreams . . . this is your fault and if you're a goddess or whatever, you need to fix it!"

Arka was unaccustomed to being shouted at. Especially by a teenage girl. She blinked several times and rose to her full height, stretching a few feet taller than Rachel's dad. "I told you before, I was trying to help her, *child*! All I have done has been to help your family! Have you considered what would have happened if I had NOT been there to bend the strands of fate?!" Her cheeks glowed brightly with indignation.

Rachel gaped at her, horrified. Maybe this girl was a goddess. She definitely had powers of some kind. Rachel shook from head to toe, but she lifted her chin at Arka. "Your idea of HELPING is more like INTERFERING!"

Arka threw her hands up in exasperation. Struggling to gain control of herself, she pinched the bridge of her nose. After a momentary ripple, she was back to her previous height.

Rachel stared at Arka. Her ability to change her appearance was out of this world! She looked human again, but still out of place. The way colors grew brighter and more vibrant wherever she went wasn't natural. Slowly, the pieces connected. The accident, the strange connection between them, and how Arka seemed to be anywhere she wanted without any means of transportation. It was clearly an indicator of something. Rachel swallowed hard. "Okay, let's say I believe you."

Arka looked up, surprised. Perhaps this mortal child wasn't as dense as she'd originally thought.

Chapter 5: The Truth

"For the record," said Rachel, "you need to stop calling me 'child', it's annoyingly rude. Besides, you don't look much older than me."

Arka sucked in a startled breath and laughed out loud. "I am eons older than you," she said, still chuckling, "but I'll try to be more respectful. Come, let us sit."

She strode to the park bench with that warm glow around her and sat easily, patting the place next to her.

Rachel crossed her arms. This was the weirdest experience of her life! She cautiously approached Arka. "I have some questions," she said, trying to be assertive.

Arka's lip twitched, but she nodded encouragingly.

Rachel loved solving puzzles and this one was huge. She plopped onto the bench, crossed a leg and held up a hand, counting on her fingers. "So, who are you? Why did my parents buy your sweet neighbor girl story? I mean, babysitting? Really? Also, how did your clothes change like a mirage and why are things so vibrant around you?" Rachel pointed at the bench and the grass at their feet. Both were rich in color.

The bench, normally worn with peeling navy-blue paint, was a beautiful ocean blue where Arka sat, and faded into normal hues a few inches away from Rachel. The grass around Arka's boots was so green, it looked like artwork painted on a canvas, whereas the grass under Rachel's sneakers was half dead with cold.

Arka shifted in her seat before responding. "Have you ever heard of the Moirai, or Fates, from Greek mythology?"

"Erm, the old hags that share an eye and cut strands of people's lives?"

A fit of laughter escaped from Arka and she bent at the waist, clutching the arm of the bench to prevent herself from sliding off. "Does my appearance look hag-like to you?" she asked, looking up at Rachel, mirth dancing in her eyes.

Rachel's lips drew into a deep frown. "You mean to tell me you're one of the three Fates?" she asked, her tone skeptical.

"Yes, and no. The three Fates as you call them are my sisters. They are powerful goddesses. They do share a special eye, but it's only for certain occasions when they need to see something important in the fabric of time."

"Like a crystal ball?"

"Don't interrupt."

"Sorry."

"Yes, like a crystal ball. And they each have different responsibilities."

"Right, one measures thread, and the other one cuts it. I don't remember what the other sister does." Rachel thought hard. She'd scored well on a test about Greek mythology, but that'd been a few months ago. She picked at another flake of peeling paint on her side of the bench, trying to remember the third

Fate's job.

"Stop interrupting," said Arka, miffed. "My sister Clotho is whom you're referring to." Her voice darkened. "She spins the thread of life. Lachesis draws lots to measure the thread, and its Atropos who cuts it."

"But wait, there are only three Fates. If you're their sister, then that means…"

"There are four of us. See what I mean about myths only being sort of true?" Arka spread her palms. "I am often overlooked." She crossed her arms and toed a rock with her boot. It was speckled now, with crusted over splatters of puke she'd missed wiping off.

"That still doesn't explain why I am suddenly wrapped up in your affairs," complained Rachel.

"I'm trying to figure that out. You're obviously a seer. Your visions prove that, plus you can see through my weave of hiding."

"Your weave of hiding?"

"I can bend the strands of fate," said Arka, as if her explanation made sense. "I was pulled to your life thread the day of your sister's accident. That has never happened to me before. Our strands have synced somehow, but I cannot see how far, or for what purpose." She tapped her chin, staring into the distance. "I must figure this out properly. It is of the most importance, *chil*-Rachel."

"Well, you're the only god or whatever I've come into contact with, so if you leave me alone, everything should go back to normal." Rachel tightened her ponytail. "Look, I've been gone a while, and my parents will wonder what happened to me if I don't get back."

Arka gave her a sympathetic smile. "I wish it were that

33

simple. You have been chosen for a purpose, and it appears to be aligned with mine. As a seer, it is your duty to help the gods, to help me. When my sisters find out about you, it will be the end of you. They will not tolerate another with the gift of sight. They'll either use you or destroy you, and most likely your family, too. You need to come with me."

Rachel jumped up, alarmed. "No freaking way." She held up her hands, shielding herself weakly. "I didn't ask to be a seer. There's no way I'm traveling to other dimensions or whatever, having my atoms mixed up to help you do who knows what! Messing with space and time never ends well for anyone involved, everyone knows that!" A wave of fear washed over Rachel when Arka rose from the bench, her jaw clenched and face stern.

"Your understanding is limited. Human mortals can visit other realms when they intersect on certain days, possess a special artifact, or have a guide. The gods can come here whenever they like, which means you and your entire family are in danger. It is only a matter of time until my sisters find you." Arka stepped toward Rachel. "Come with me, I will be your guide. The universe is at a great tipping point, Rachel. Either for the good or the terrible. I'm working for the good, and I think you are meant to join me. We can help each other." Arka thought she was being inviting, but Rachel thought she was overbearing and felt trapped.

Rachel stumbled backward and fell, landing in chipped mulch. Scrambling up, she rubbed fresh scrapes on her hands, breathing fast. Why was it suddenly her responsibility to help the universe? This was too much pressure for a girl in middle school! "No. This is crazy. You're crazy!"

Arka clenched her fists. A seer was supposed to work with

the gods, but asking a child for help was highly irregular! Crickets started singing, and Arka suddenly wondered how long they'd been outside. This mortal girl was wasting her time! She blew out her lips in frustration.

A rubber band snapped inside Rachel. All she wanted to do was enjoy time with her family in the comfort of her home. It was Thanksgiving, and her dad had just come home from overseas! Maybe this girl is a psychiatric patient who escaped from a hospital somewhere, she thought, her mind racing for a rational explanation.

The idea didn't explain what Rachel had witnessed, or her newfound visions, but she didn't care. She wasn't about to get kidnapped by this crazy person. "I am not leaving with you. You can't force me to go with you, so don't even try!"

Arka shook with fury. How dare this mortal refuse a goddess! She fixed a look on Rachel that could have melted the polar ice caps and clipped in a low voice, "You will regret your choice." Her nostrils flared. She's lucky I'm not Nemesis! Arka thought, but imagining how the goddess of retribution would punish a human for such insolent hubris did give her some satisfaction.

Both girls stared each other down, refusing to yield.

Just then a dog ran across the street. Rachel recognized the chocolate lab, Marco. He belonged to a neighboring family, and she'd watched him a few times when they'd been out of town.

"Here Marco! Here, boy!" called Rachel, urging him out of the street. He bounded up to her, tail wagging and his pink tongue lolling. She knelt, scratching behind his ears, and caught his collar, thankful to have a distraction and some protection against Arka.

Arka kept her focus on Rachel, ignoring the dog but

relenting a fraction. "If you change your mind, you just have to say so, and I'll find you. I won't force you to help me, but there's more at stake than you know," she said the next bit through clenched teeth, "please think about it."

Rachel rolled her eyes and ruffled Marco's neck. She meant to say something intelligent, something to make Arka see that she was asking too much, but when Rachel looked up, Arka was gone. She'd completely vanished!

Goosebumps sprang up on Rachel's arms and Marco's hackles rose, a low growl rumbling in his chest. Rachel shot a look around the park, but Arka was nowhere to be seen. It was dark now. She hadn't noticed the sunset because of Arka's glow. Everything was still. Even the swings refrained from showing any sign of movement. Rachel held her breath in the eerie silence of early nightfall, and Marco lifted an ear.

The streetlights sprang into brilliance. "Oh!" cried Rachel, and Marco barked madly in her defense, searching for danger. Annoyed at being frightened so easily, Rachel shook herself and pulled Marco toward his house. "Come on boy, let's go home."

She dropped him off with praises and many thanks, then sprinted down the street to her house. She couldn't shake an uneasy feeling in the pit of her stomach and checked over her shoulder several times before reaching the front porch. Pretty molding over the heavy front door stood out in a light blue with a contrasting S for their last name painted in the center. Rachel licked her lips, eager for a glass of water. She turned the knob, letting the warm smells of Thanksgiving melt away the troubling conversation, and forgot all about Arka the minute she heard her dad laughing in the kitchen.

Chapter 6: Nightmares

December was delightful. With their father home, the Soarenson girls were spoiled rotten and their little brother was treated like a tiny prince. It was also when the frightening dreams started. January was joyful. They made wishes and plans for the new year, settling back into a family routine. Morgan was completely healed and back to her exuberant self, but nightmares plagued Rachel every night, growing out of control, and by February they became detrimental.

"Noooooooo!" Rachel lurched upright in her twin-size bed, sweat matting curls to her face. She fumbled for the lamp on her nightstand, clicking on the little bloom of yellow light. She held a hand over her racing heart and pushed her wild, damp hair back. Even when she napped on the couch, she was afflicted by these awful dreams! She'd dreamt about that blasted tapestry again. This time it felt like it was drowning her for real! Rather than being gold and warm, it was dull, grey and freezing. She shivered, remembering it.

The last dream she had, the tapestry pressed into her but

instead of passing through, it crushed her. The dream before that, the tapestry was made of thorns and it scratched her skin into ribbons. She didn't know how much longer she could go without sleeping well.

Shakily, Rachel pushed the suffocating covers off, swinging her feet over the bed onto the hardwood floor and let the cool wood planks chill her overheated feet.

Shuffling out of her bedroom, down the dark hall to the bathroom she shared with Morgan, Rachel flicked on the light. The lively green wall paint and fun mermaid pictures didn't help energize her. A jaw cracking yawn proved it.

She squinted at her reflection, drew a steadying breath into her lungs, and blew it out at the mirror. It fogged up a moment before revealing her lethargic face. It was obvious she hadn't slept well for several weeks. Her eyes were sunken and shadowed with dark raccoon circles. Her face drooped, and her shoulders sagged.

Wow, thought Rachel, I didn't know middle school kids could look so haggard.

Rachel splashed cool water on her face to help revive herself and let go of the dream. Getting ready for school was drudgery, every movement adding to her fatigue. Her arms were heavy lead dumbbells, and it made brushing her teeth a chore.

Back in her bedroom, dressed in a soft blue t-shirt and jeans with her hair in a sagging ponytail, Rachel puttered around her room collecting schoolbooks that'd been scattered around. She was stuffing them in her backpack when it finally registered with her that the rest of the house was quiet. She stifled another yawn and squinted at her alarm clock through gritty, sleep laden eyes. It glowed an angry red 3:00 a.m. Groaning, Rachel dropped her bag, collapsing back on her bed. She was asleep instantly.

A fire roared all around her, the smoke blinding her eyes. Choking, Rachel covered her mouth and nose with her elbow, the other arm frantically waving thick black smoke away from her face. The flames grew, intensifying the blazing heat! She saw the tapestry a few feet away completely engulfed, and it was creeping toward her like lava. She wanted to run, but she was immobile. There was no escape!

It inched closer and Rachel whimpered, helpless. Jumping embers caught her hair on fire and blistered her bare arms. In seconds it would burn her to ashes! Then she heard a faint voice calling through the blaze. Rachel squinted through smoke-heavy eyelashes and saw that mystery girl. No, that *goddess*! What was she saying? Tears streaked down Rachel's soot-covered face and she listened hard, desperate to catch the words as her clothes smoldered and her shoes melted to the floor.

"Join me!" Arka yelled over the deafening roar of the flames. "You have to make the choice!" Her arm stretched through the inferno, miraculously unscathed by the fire. Rachel coughed uncontrollably. Sobbing with unbearable pain, she fumbled for Arka's outstretched hand.

She was too far away! The fireball tapestry touched Rachel's outstretched hands instead, and her scream of agony disappeared in a bomb blast.

"AAAAaaaaaaarrrrrg!" Rachel slid off her bed, thudding to the floor in a tangle of blankets, still in a coughing fit. She lay huddled in the pile, gasping for breath.

I can't keep having these dreams, she thought. I need help. "Arka," she whispered, "I'll help you. I will. If you'll help me. I can't… I just can't…"

"We'll help each other," said Arka reassuringly, suddenly there, kneeling beside Rachel in real-time on a soft yellow area

39

rug covering a small portion of the wood floor. The room was tidy. Several drawings, posters and encouraging quotes were pinned to the walls and taped to the mirror of an antique vanity along with a few photos of smiling faces. Its top was littered with small jewelry boxes, lotion bottles, hair-ties and a large brush. Arka smiled at the innocence of it. "But first, you need to rest child, you look like death."

This time, the term *child* was said endearingly, and Rachel didn't have the strength to argue about it anyway.

Careful not to touch Rachel, lest she accidentally threw her into a vision while in a weakened state, Arka guided her back into bed and tucked her in. It was the early hours of morning, but the entire room glowed like midday at the beach.

Rachel was too exhausted to care. She drifted into a dreamless, coma-like sleep that was sheer bliss.

* * *

Stretching awake feeling glorious, toasty warm, and rested felt amazing! Rachel kept her eyes closed, reveling in the feeling until she heard a soft chuckle. She peeked open one eye and started when she saw Arka leaning against a corner wall in her bedroom, a smirk playing on her face.

"Morning, sunshine," said Arka, that knowing smirk lingering on her lips. Her riding boots were clean, with leggings tucked snugly into them and her dark braid rested over a shoulder, reaching down the front of a hunter green jacket, brushing her waist.

"You!" said Rachel, propping herself up on her elbows. "What are you doing in my room?"

"You asked for my help, so here I am." Arka straightened up, worried. "You don't remember?"

Rachel thought about it, and the dreadful memory of the nightmare flooded back. She shuddered. The warm blankets enveloping her lent some comfort, but it was Arka's presence that felt the most reassuring. *She looks like a female Robin Hood*, thought Rachel, nodding. *All she needs is a bow and arrow set.*

Arka spoke, quite somber. "I would have come anyway, you know. Not only because you agreed to help me. I'm not as uncaring as my sisters and don't operate on a *quid pro quo* system."

"A what?"

"You know, tit for tat? Only helping you because I'm getting something out of it."

"Oh. Well, thank you. Really. I feel wonderful." Rachel stretched again and sat up fully.

Arka shrugged, moving away from the wall and her thick braid swung off her shoulder, trailing down her back. "Why didn't you call for me sooner, Rachel? You looked awful when I stepped here."

"Stepped here?"

"I step through the fabric of space."

"Right." Rachel looked guiltily at her hands and folded them in her lap. "I don't know. I thought I could manage by myself, I guess. Then I think I wanted to ask for help, but it was like living in a dream world or something and I couldn't even remember your name. I sort of forgot about you." She chewed her lip, eyes downcast, and fiddled with the lavender comforter pillowed around her.

"Just as I suspected," Arka said, sitting on the edge of the bed. "There must be dream weavers hunting you in the dream realm. They probably followed me the last time came here. They obviously don't know who, or what, you are yet because you're still alive. For now, anyway. Being in their vicinity causes dreams to be more realistic than normal."

"Well, I think these dream weavers or whatever, deserve a punch in the face," said Rachel, angry at the unknown villains for her months of torment.

"It's a good thing you called for me when you did. They are vile creatures. Look at your forearm."

Rachel rotated her arm and gasped when she saw several little blisters fading there. She looked up at Arka with wide, questioning eyes.

"Dreams twisted by the dream weavers become real to the dreamer. Eventually their victim succumbs to the dream." She went still, her eyes serious. "Mortals die in real life if they perish in a twisted dream, and immortals are driven mad."

Rachel was too stunned to say anything. How close had she been to dying?

"My sisters must know I'm finding others to help my cause, and they've deployed tools to thwart me."

"Can't your sisters see you with their magic crystal ball eye-thing?" Rachel asked, her anger shifting toward the real culprits. "Should we just poke their eye out?"

"No. You can't reach it, and they can't see me. I bend the threads of fate, remember? I can make different weaves and use them at will. Mostly I use them for travel, hiding and safety. If I don't want to be seen, even they can't find me." Arka stood and padded to a little bookshelf near the door, scanning the titles.

"It's why I was so perplexed when you *could*." She spoke over her shoulder a little louder, "I can't tell you what my sisters have planned, but you need to know that the universe is in peril. You may not have asked for the gift of sight, but that's beside the point. What matters now, is how you use it." She dusted her hands and turned around, staring matter-of-factly at Rachel.

Rachel felt that some sort of response was required, so she nodded, murmuring, "Alright. Um, why don't we ask an oracle what to do? Aren't they prevalent in Greek mythology?"

Arka snorted. "Oracles work for the Fates. How do you think they tell the future? Only if they're allowed to see it of course." She eyed Rachel shrewdly, deciding whether or not to trust her. "I'm on a quest to stop my sisters' meddling with lives, cutting threads too short or at the wrong time, in *all* realms. No one holds them accountable, and they need to be stopped!"

Rachel's eyebrows shot up. "That sounds like an effortless task," she said sarcastically.

"I'm trying to find gods and creatures who will support my quest. The only problem is, there are those who oppose me and others who are simply indifferent. They cause trouble for the fun of it, just like my sisters. It's creating chaos in the universe!"

"And you've been trying to stop them by yourself?"

"I have to be discreet with who I ask to join me. It is an important mission, and for some reason the universe led me to you." Arka's hands balled into fists and she jammed them into her jacket pockets. "It hasn't been going well and judging by your dreams, the tapestry is more distorted than I thought. If it is destroyed, everything else will be too."

Rachel pulled her blanket to her chin. "If I go on this mission with you, how long would I be gone?"

Arka was less than impressed. She had just poured her heart

out and Rachel was worried how long a quest would take? Still, the girl *was* contemplating helping her, after nearly dying in the dream realm no less. She hunched her shoulders. "Any quest takes time, chil-I mean, Rachel. I cannot say how long, exactly." She stepped forward and knelt, eye level with Rachel. "But, I can bend the strands of time into a curved path, creating a heavier gravity that would pull us at a greater velocity. It would be like you never left when I return you. I won't lie, you'll be in danger, but hopefully no more than you already are."

"Where would we go?"

"Well, for now to my hideout so we can forge a plan. Then to the realm of the gods, I imagine."

Rachel tucked her knees up and hugged her arms around herself. She didn't speak for several moments. She was good at puzzling out problems, but this was bigger than anything she'd had to work at before.

Arka rose and tapped her foot impatiently. "Well?"

"I don't know."

"What else is there to know?! If this quest isn't successful, we will cease to exist."

Rachel thought about her family. Then she thought about what it would be like if everyone just ceased to exist. She looked at the fading marks on her arms and her eyes welled with tears.

Arka shuffled her boots. "Hey, I'm not trying to pressure you. I've, ah, been managing on my own so if you don't want to use your new abilities . . ."

"I'll do it. I'll help you on this quest, or whatever. I'm only doing it to protect my family, though," said Rachel defiantly, dabbing at her eyes with her shirt collar.

"Great! I mean, thank you." Arka said, not wanting to show how elated she was to have the first seer in over two thousand years join her quest. She tossed back the fluffy bed covers, ignoring Rachel's squeal. "I'll take us to my hideout."

Rachel slapped the comforter back, and it poufed around her in a purple cloud. "I can't leave right now, I have school! And what am I supposed to tell my family?"

"You *had* school, three days ago. Today is Saturday."

"What?! I've been sleeping for three days?"

"I put a protective weave around you, so you could rest as long as needed. I snuck a note onto the secretary's desk. You're excused," Arka said grinning, her perfect teeth a brilliant white. "I also put a deception weave over your family. They thought you were going through your normal routine, but it was me posing as you!" She beamed, pleased with herself.

Rachel flung her covers off and shot out of bed, seething, and jabbed a finger at Arka. "Don't use your witchcraft on my family!"

"I do *not* perform magic tricks. The very idea!" Arka stood back, incredulous. "I think what you mean to say is, 'Thank you, Arka'."

"Look, I didn't mean to offend you. I just don't want you messing with my family."

"It won't happen again," said Arka stiffly.

"Good." Rachel nodded sharply, her fury waning and she paced across the little area rug thinking hard.

Arka noted how worn it was in the spot Rachel walked back and forth over.

"Okay, I'll need to tell my parents that I'm going somewhere. We're supposed to have a Bar-B-Que this weekend," she paused, "today, I mean." She wanted to spend time with her family, especially if she might not see them again. "I can tell my mom and dad then." She flushed suddenly and rushed the next sentence out of her mouth. "Tuesday is Valentine's Day, so I have to go to school. I have, um, plans." Her face burned even brighter at the admission.

Arka raised an eyebrow into a question mark. "We wouldn't want to ruin your plans."

With too much gusto, Rachel tugged a heavy drawer in her dresser open, nearly pulling it out of the case. She avoided eye contact and began rifling through the shirts folded tidily there. Hers was wrinkled, and she needed a distraction. "I can leave after that," she said. "So, what should I tell my family?"

Arka thought Rachel's effort to change the subject was commendable, and she chose to go along with it. "Not a thing. I can make it so they don't even know you left. Pause them if you will, by speeding us up."

Rachel looked up suspiciously. "You can stop time?"

Arka shook her head. "Only the Creator can do that. No other god is as powerful as He. I can't step through time in the tapestry, but I can follow certain threads at a quicker pace and then loop back around." She shrugged. "Like I said, everything we do will be at an accelerated pace compared to the mortal world. We can be gone months and it will seem like days to them."

"Months!!" Rachel dropped her fresh shirt on the floor. Before she could argue, Arka pressed on.

"We only need a week. Maybe two. Tell your mom you're going on a camping trip for school or something."

"I can't lie to her."

"Can't, or won't?"

"Both. I won't lie to my own mother. She'd be able to tell, anyway. I'll tell her I'm helping a friend and need to stay over the weekend, to work on a big project."

It annoyed Arka they weren't leaving immediately, but she found herself admiring Rachel's honesty. It had been a long time since she'd been around someone with so much heart and conviction. "Very well," she nodded. "That's the closest to the truth you can get, for their own protection. I'll draw off the dream weavers and give you a few days with your family and, er, friends while I gather allies. There's no guarantee we'll succeed in our quest anyhow, so I understand the value in spending time with them."

"Wow. Thanks for the build of confidence, Arka."

"Seeing the future isn't my department," she looked pointedly at Rachel. "My sisters' meddling has taken a toll on the tapestry, and it is dimming. If my guess is correct, it's only a matter of time until it unravels. If that happens, our worlds are doomed. I aim to stop them before then, with your help." Arka watched Rachel struggle with the weight of new responsibility. She hesitated, annoyed at postponing her quest because of adolescent worries, then patted Rachel on the shoulder awkwardly in an attempt at reassurance. They both inhaled sharply, realizing there could be a vision, but nothing happened and they exhaled, relieved.

"Maybe I only have visions if *I* touch someone?"

"Perhaps. We can test your theory later, I need to go."

"Hey! I'm not frozen solid when I look at you."

"Probably because you've agreed to the quest, and no longer need a sign of its importance. Take care of yourself, Rachel."

"It's freaky how you just pop in and out of thin air like that," complained Rachel, shrugging off Arka's hand and scooping up the shirt she'd dropped.

Arka wondered what it would be like having someone so young as a quest companion. "See you in one week," she said,

barely keeping disdain out of her voice. "After your Valentine's
Date." The sudden flush in Rachel's cheeks made Arka chuckle.
Maybe it wouldn't be all bad. "If you need anything, call for me
and I'll be there." The air grew a bit brighter, and then Arka
faded into nothing.

Rachel watched Arka dissolve away in wonder. She'd
always been more of a nerdy girl, enjoying physics and learning
how the world operated, but this was like nothing she'd ever read
about. It was unreal! It's like when you look at a light and then
look away, but the glow is still in your eye, she thought, and
blinked several times until the afterglow faded.

Chapter 7: Family First

Grilling in the snow during the coldest month of the year was rather eccentric. 'Celebrating Summer in Winter' is what Rachel's mom called it. It wasn't very creative, but the idea was. "To get us through the last couple months of cold!" she'd say. It started one year as a joke and had continued as a quirky family tradition ever since.

Their dad loved to grill. He spent hours preparing special meats and marinades. The only problem was, it never tasted very good. Although several Bar-B-Que competitions had been entered, and none of them won, he was unwavering. He'd received a new grill from Santa that Christmas and was looking forward to trying it out.

The ladies of the Soarenson household found it endearing and hoped someday he would stumble upon a winning recipe. In the meantime, they covered their hockey puck burgers, with extra toppings and condiments.

Each family member worked on something to make the meal a success while music sang from a portable speaker in the dining room. Morgan fussed over setting the table perfectly, complete with a festive, red-checkered picnic tablecloth, while Luke followed her around stealing the napkins she'd just placed. He dropped most of them on the floor before Morgan noticed.

"Luke!" she gasped. "No, no." Morgan tried to pull the last napkin out of Luke's hand, but he held on, giggling at their new game. "Mom! Luke is messing up the table!" she yelled, but she couldn't help laughing with him and ended up playing, forgetting her job entirely.

Their mom was in the kitchen stirring two pitchers of sweet tea with a wooden spoon, humming to herself a beat behind the music. Her happy vibe was enhanced by bright white cabinets, and a fresh potted plant sprucing up the windowsill overhanging a cluttered sink, framed with a striped valance. The kids' artwork, pictures, and old holiday cards were plastered all over the fridge, stuck there with unique magnets of various shapes and sizes. Their mom enjoyed filling her house with love, and that meant it was full of family photos, bright colors, and leftovers.

Rachel stood next to her mom helping chop up lettuce, tomatoes, pickles, and an onion for the burgers. She couldn't cut the onion without weeping, and grabbed a paper towel to press against her stinging eyes.

"Oh honey," said her mom, "I know my singing is beautiful, but you don't need to cry." She hip-bumped Rachel.

"Funny, Mom. You should be a comedian," said Rachel drily. They both chuckled, enjoying each other's company.

"Dad is probably ready for the cheese. Be sure to take him the extra sharp cheddar, we need that added flavor."

Rachel shared a knowing look with her mom and pulled open a package of pre-sliced cheese singles. She walked them out to her dad through a sliding glass door across the dining room. He was overseeing the grill wearing an apron over his coat like a grill master marshmallow man.

"Hey, Bright Eyes. Got too much onion fever? I have some medicine for that," he said, and threw a premeditated snowball at her. Rachel squealed, blocking it with her forearm.

"Ha-ha, Dad," she said. "You and Mom are killin' it tonight." Her breath came out in little puffs of steam against the frigid winter air.

Her dad's rich laugher rang out, and he turned some hotdogs over with chrome-plated tongs held awkwardly in gloved hands.

Rachel set the cheese on a tray he'd wedged onto a snow-dusted patio table. "Can I talk to you?" she asked, fidgeting with the tray.

"Of course," he looked up, inquisitive. "What's up?"

Rachel inhaled the crisp air and blurted out, "I have a friend who needs help with a big project. We're working together and I, ah, really want a good grade so can I stay at her house next weekend?"

Her dad adjusted his wool hat. He always wore one in winter, but it slid around on his bald head. "Rachel, you know we don't allow sleepovers at people's homes we're not acquainted with."

"I know that. It's just Vlair," she lied, her stomach in knots.

"Vlair? Why didn't you say that in the first place silly? You and Vlair can always work on a school project. Do you want to have her come here? We don't mind. Course I'll have to ask your mother. She might have plans." He looked through the sliding door into the warm house where his wife was fixing napkins.

"I'd rather go to Vlair's house. We don't want Luke and Morgan bothering us too much," rushed Rachel, following his gaze. "I'll check with Mom." She darted inside before her father could ask any more questions.

The pitchers of tea and condiments were set on the table, and her mom had returned to the kitchen for cups. Rachel scurried after her. "Hey, Mom, can I stay at Vlair's house next weekend to work on a school project?" Before Rachel got to the kitchen, her mom came back out and handed her cups to help set out.

"What did your father say?"

"He said to ask you."

Her mom rolled her eyes, but she smiled, arranging plastic cups with characters on them for her younger children. "It's fine with me as long as her parents are on board."

"Thanks, Mom," said Rachel, placing the other cups around the festive table. It really did look like a summer picnic spread with plastic bowls full of potato salad, chips, and coleslaw crowded in the center. Rachel studied her mother a moment, feeling guilty about not telling the whole truth. She was always honest with her parents, and her heart was heavy with the thought of leaving.

She smiled then, as her little sister and baby brother ran around the table chasing each other, laughing hysterically, and bumped into her legs. Rachel gazed out the glass doors at her dad cooking out in the snow like a crazy person. He opened the grill lid and frantically waved an oven mitt in the air to dissipate the smoke wafting out. Rachel laughed. A little guilt was better than never seeing her family again, she decided. And after nearly being burnt to a crisp while dreaming, she was willing to do whatever it took to rid herself of this connection to Arka. For her own sake, and her family's.

Her dad slid open the glass patio door, stomping snow off his boots and pushed the pan loaded with charcoal-ized meat on the table, jumbling the already crowded setting. "Dinner is ready!"

"Get those wet boots of the carpet!" hollered Rachel's mom as the kids rushed to their seats. Morgan scooped a heaping spoonful of potato salad onto her plate with a plop. Rachel buckled Luke in his highchair, fitting a bib around his neck, and eagerly waited for the spoon. No one could make potato salad like their mom. It was something about dill pickle juice as a secret ingredient. Rachel loved pickles and was dying to know, but her mom said she had to wait until she was *sixteen* for the family recipe.

"Morgan, you wait until everyone is seated," said their mother in a warning tone, catching Morgan with a forkful halfway in her mouth.

"No, Daddy! It's yucky!" shouted Luke when their dad tried to put a burger on his highchair tray.

"Just try it, bud. You might like it. I seasoned it with my special spices."

"NO!" Luke threw the patty over the side of his tray. It landed with a thud on the floor, without rolling. It just sat there like a rock.

Morgan snickered, and Rachel bit her lip, trying not to laugh. Their mom covered a smile with her napkin. "I'll just cut up some hotdog for him honey, I don't think he likes burgers."

"You're missing out," her dad cajoled Luke. Luke didn't care, he'd moved on to squishing the potatoes between his fingers. Rachel's dad sighed and took his place at the head of the table. He prayed over them and their meal before they hungrily dug in.

Rachel shot her own silent arrow prayer. She prayed Arka would know how to fix her, and the tapestry she'd talked about, and that it wouldn't take too long. But mostly, she prayed for the safety of her family.

Chapter 8: The Dream Realm

Arka stepped into the dream realm through the gateway she'd woven in Rachel's room. She was on high alert the moment the gateway laced shut behind her. She could tell the dream weavers had been highly active, their energy left a residue, and they were close.

The imagination of all creatures sustained the dream realm. It was always in constant flux, like an ever-fluid watercolor painting. Arka stood out in her solid form, blurring the air with each step. As a material figure in an imaginary world, her thoughts could manipulate the setting more effectively than if she were sleeping. She pictured her desired surroundings, imagining herself standing inside the Parthenon, and the structure appeared, its giant white marble pillars dwarfing her, as if it had always been there. The temple dedicated to the goddess Athena was enormous, yet simple in design. Seventeen columns decorated the outer length, and the interior rectangle was divided into two rooms. Arka was in the larger room, that split into three isles, also lined with columns. It housed a colossal golden statue of Athena at its center. Arka snorted at the sight of it, standing two stories tall. While ostentatious, it *was* beautiful for being built four hundred and thirty-eight years before Christ.

There will never be a statue like that built in my honor, Arka thought, morosely. Humans don't care that I exist. The new seer had even forgotten who she was, proving her obsolescence.

A loud hiss sounded to her right, pulling Arka from her darkening mood. She pictured the statue's shield, enormously round and shining gold above her shoulder, and it sprung into existence, just in time to deflect a rain of black arrows from stabbing her face and torso. Arka spun around the wide base of a column, pressing her back against the marble for protection.

Two great big black things grew up on either side of her. The dream weavers! They were massive blob figures that dripped hateful oil, distorting the artificial dream Arka had constructed. Black stains warped the imagery as they swung hulking fists at her. Arka ducked, and the dream weavers smashed their fists through the column in a thundering crash. Their tarnished ink splattered all over the white marble, burning through it like acid.

Arka sprang up and bolted for the outer steps as the temple crumbled from the top down like a sandcastle doused in water, reforming into an open field with no cover. She was flung off the last step when the Parthenon vanished, and hurtled across the grass, now stained with black tar, twisting the dream.

The dream weavers used their treacherous mind manipulation to thought press panic into Arka's brain, inhibiting her ability to think clearly.

Arka grunted from the impact of the fall and mental attack. She ground her teeth, fighting to block the dream weavers from her mind. "Not today!" she shouted at them, jumping up, working her hands quickly. Between her palms, a ball of glowing thread appeared, and she pitched it like a fastball at the dream weavers.

The creatures shrieked and dissolved into bubbling puddles to avoid it. It was the break she needed. Arka slammed an invisible barrier in place at the forefront of her mind. The thick puddles oozed together and roared out of the grass, morphing into a giant rolling pin covered with spikes thundering toward her.

Arka sprinted in the opposite direction, her long legs carrying her lightning-fast, but it wasn't fast enough. The spiked roller gained on her like a deranged porcupine bent on murder.

I must get out of here! Arka thought, running with all her strength across the never-ending field. She was growing tired, and that was dangerous. Most gods who lingered in the dream realm became obsessed with creating their own universe. If they fell asleep, they forgot reality entirely, and never found their way out. Arka knew if a dream weaver captured her, she wouldn't just forget reality, she would be trapped forever in tormented nightmares.

I need time to weave! Her thoughts screamed at her, while her mental barricade chipped away, under siege from the dream weavers. If only I had help! Arka grinned at the idea.

Ares, the god of war, appeared, running at Arka's elbow. He was over ten feet tall, every muscle in his body chiseled, and a dark beard was trimmed to a point at his chin. He wore full battle armor, complete with a helmet, and shining breastplate. He gripped a spear in his left bear paw of a hand, and a lethal sword swung at his hip while he ran next to Arka.

"Greetings Fate! What battle lies before us?"

"Can you buy me some time, Olympian?"

His laughter boomed. "Easy!" Ares dug his heels into the turf, skidding to a halt. He took aim and flung his bronze war spear laden with a heavy leaf-shaped point and capped with a doru spike at its end. It whistled through the air, straight at the dream weavers. It wedged under the roller for a beat, only to snap like a brittle twig underneath the powerful rotation.

"Oh, you've asked for it!" Ares roared. "That was my favorite spear!" He drew his sword with a hiss from the sheath, charging headlong at the rolling pin of doom. He leapt over the churning spikes, flipped in the air, and drove his sword into its center with all his force, planting his feet on the other side. "Ha ha!" Ares cheered in triumph when the pinned dream weavers howled in torment.

The rolling pin separated where the sword pierced it and the dream weavers snarled, enraged at being cleaved in half. Now there were two spiked rolling pins, and one reversed its course, rolling backward after Ares. It was faster now, separated from its counterpart and Ares battled with it, striking at its spikes, but the moment he cut one off, it grew back instantly. The other dream weaver circled around the skirmish, waiting for a moment to strike. Ares knew they outmatched him.

"I tried!" he called to Arka, and bowed regally as they pulverized him into the ground.

"Come on!" Arka said, frustrated. "The god of war didn't have victory?"

As if summoned, the goddess Nike rode into the dream realm, driving a chariot pulled by two immortal Hippoi horses, her honey brown hair and feathered wings streaming behind her.

"How can I be of assistance?" called Nike, guiding the reins of her golden chariot with ease at their breakneck pace.

Arka's jaw dropped. Had she imagined the goddess of

victory? Her leg muscles threatened to seize up. Whether she'd imagined her, or the goddess had entered the dream realm while sleeping made no difference, Arka was desperate for help. "Anything you can do is welcomed, Nike!"

The chariot pulled around, pivoting in a tight circle, taunting one of the dream weavers to keep up. It ploughed after Nike and her horses. They snorted, hooves thundering, elated to be racing.

"Follow me, you wretched creature!" Arka bellowed over the hole punching earthquake at the other dream weaver and ran full tilt ahead. The moment she thought of it, a waterfall appeared, rushing and splashing over a cliff. Arka leaped as high as she could over the waterfall. With arms spread wide, she welcomed gravity in a graceful swan dive.

The rolling pin chased her right over the edge, hissing through the air. A pointed spike snagged the back of Arka's jacket, ripping a jagged line in the material, nearly stabbing her in mid-air but Arka pictured herself landing on the back of Pegasus.

She soared out from under the spikes on the back of the majestic, winged horse. His massive, snowy white wings beat powerfully, lifting them into the watercolor sky, above a lush valley she imagined below. For a moment, Arka's light merged with the dream realm and the effect was breathtaking. The sky shone with radiance as beams of every color stretched into the horizon. Pegasus nickered, tucked his wings and twirled them through the air.

Arka let out a whoop of excitement and just like that, her mental barrier wavered, and the dream weaver soared right behind her. Pegasus whinnied in alarm, pawing his hooves in the air to gain momentum.

Arka berated herself for enjoying the dream realm, even for

a second. She twisted in her seat, searching the cliff behind her just in time to see Nike's golden chariot with horses galloping wildly, career over the edge. The horses and cart plummeted down, but Nike leapt free, rising to safety, fiercely beating her wings. The dream weaver chasing her stretched into a great buzzard, lifting into the air, dripping black grease as it extended enormous talons to crush her. Larger and faster, it easily closed in for the kill.

"Best of luck, Arka!" Nike yelled across the sky and winked out of existence, just before the talons smashed tight. The buzzard screeched with rage at being robbed of its prey and snapped its beak, spraying black spittle, muddying the watercolor sky.

Arka suddenly felt an overwhelming temptation to fall asleep. She pushed it firmly away, forcing her heavy eyes open. Nike had not been her imagination! The goddess of victory had visited the dream realm to help. But without her presence, Arka's stamina was rapidly evaporating and with it, her chances of success.

Gripping Pegasus' silky mane to prevent herself from sliding off his back, Arka focused her mind. The two dream weavers were gaining on her again and she was running out of time. The closest one turned into a mirrored image of her steed. It became a midnight black stallion with blazing blood-red eyes and wings that stretched wide, dripping black oil like its brother, distorting the air. It snorted, eager to capture a victim.

No amount of dodging and weaving could shake the ominous shapes pursuing her, but Arka knew if she could keep them mimicking her, she could control them. She squeezed her knees for balance and quickly wove a clumsy net from the strands of fate she saw all around her, casting it at the closest dream weaver with her remaining strength. The evil horse swooped to avoid it, but the net caught one of its wings. The dream weaver roared, changing back into a black blob, straining at the net. In doing so, it fell dramatically from the sky, forever trapped in the strands of fate.

"Yes!" shouted Arka. She immediately regretted doing so. Suddenly dizzy with sleep and weak limbed, she fell forward onto Pegasus' neck. He neighed loudly and banked left to keep her from falling off.

With Arka's defenses down, the second dream weaver was at an advantage. A dark storm billowed into the sky, dumping buckets of rain and cracked lighting all around them. A hard wind pushed Arka and Pegasus to the ground in a crash landing. Pegasus disappeared, blending into the scenery and Arka tumbled in a ball across rain-soaked mud.

A funnel cloud formed in the sky and Arka looked up, fatigued and dazed. The water splashing her face felt refreshing, and she was content to sit in the muck and wait for the wind to sweep her away. Then something unusual happened. Arka felt an internal tug from the strands of fate so strong, it yanked her to her feet. A sense of urgency to finish the fight rushed through her, lending strength and clarity at that moment.

The dream weaver circled with the clouds like a giant dragon and then it dove, becoming one with the funnel, heading straight for her. It meant to sweep her into an endless cycle of spinning horror.

"Come on! I see you!" shouted Arka at the storm, her braid a dancing snake flying violently behind her. "This realm is under my protection now!"

Thunder answered her, and a gust of enraged evil rushed to knock her backward. Arka stepped aside, revealing a gateway resembling a giant golden dream catcher she'd woven behind her back. It sucked the horrid dream poison through, instantly dissipating the storm as it fell into the mortal world.

Arka stepped through after the dream weaver, landing on a sidewalk in front of a gas station, soaked to the bone, caked with mud and panting. Two more minutes in the dream realm would have been the end of her. She weakly shielded her eyes from the glaring afternoon sun. The solid shapes and harsh lines were startling after the fluidity of the dream realm.

The dream weaver loomed in front of her, a dark shadow in the mortal realm. It growled and clawed at her face, but Arka knew in this reality, it held no power. It melted into the cracked sidewalk, leaving behind an impressive stain.

Arka sat down abruptly. Her hand darted to her stinging cheek and when she took it away, she saw bright ichor on her fingertips. "What in the gods?" she whispered. "This cannot be."

Chapter 9: The Crush

Kevin Cardeaux was the best-looking boy at school. He was a grade older than Rachel, but she still planned on sending him a candy-gram. The only question was whether to put her name on it, or send it anonymously. She was agonizing over this very dilemma, standing in front of a row of bland, orange lockers when he walked by with his gaggle of friends tagging along.

Rachel caught herself before she let out a sigh and straightened the zipper on her well-loved hoodie. What was happening to her? She never bothered with boys before! Well, none of them were ever Kevin Cardeaux before, she told herself irritably, re-scrambling the combination on her locker.

"Hey Rachel," said a voice behind her, making her mess up the combo again. Rachel huffed and glanced over her shoulder. It was Vlair, her best friend since pre-K. Vlair stood too close, ignoring Rachel's personal space, like always. Her round blue eyes set in her round face, framed by straight blonde hair gave her the appearance of a startled emoji. She had on a shirt that matched her eyes, a cute plaid skirt paired with cropped leggings and ballerina flats. She enjoyed fashion and was a preppie compared to Rachel's casual comfy. "Do you have the notes from history last week?" Vlair asked. She tended to daydream during history and regularly asked for Rachel's notes.

"Sure. You can borrow them, but you have to give them back this time." Rachel yanked open her locker in victory. "I also need you to cover for me this weekend because I told my parents that we're working on a project together and I'm supposed to stay over but I have, um, other plans." Vlair was staring down the hall in Kevin's direction, a far off look in her eyes. "V," said Rachel, proffering the notes in front of her dreamy face.

"Oh, right. I will. Project, sleepover, got it." The bell rang and Vlair snatched the papers from Rachel's hand. "Thanks!" She gave a cute, little wave and trotted into the sea of people in the hallway, her blonde head washing into the crowd.

It wasn't Vlair's fault she'd spaced out. Kevin was popular, good at sports and even better looking. He was also really smart. That's what Rachel liked about him most. He wasn't just a pretty boy, and he wasn't conceited either. She had toyed with the idea of joining the math club he was in, but now with the fate of the world hanging by a thread, she had to put her life on hold.

Rachel slammed the locker with more force than she intended, and she heard the magnetic mirror crash inside. Groaning, she hefted her binder and books in her arms and marched with determination to the candy-gram line. She only ordered one, her hand shaking the entire time –

To: *Kevin Cardeaux*
From: *Rachel Soarenson*

- to be delivered before lunchtime.

The whole morning kids buzzed about the candy-grams. The air floated with speculation and rumors about who liked who, and who had a secret crush. Rachel felt sick to her stomach. At lunch, which Rachel only picked at, Vlair returned the notes. She sat across from Rachel at the brown, foldout cafeteria table and noticed her friend wasn't eating.

"You okay?" she asked over a mouthful of pizza.

"No. I put my name on a candy-gram for Kevin."

Vlair gasped and nearly choked. Coughing and hammering her chest, she took a gulp of soda. It didn't help. She gurgled, tears springing to her eyes. "No you didn't!" she managed to cough out, hacking into her slender hand.

The other students at the table, all talking and eating loudly, didn't pay any attention to them or Vlair's choking fit. She cleared her throat but her little bow of a mouth stayed stuck open in an astonished 'O', matching her features, making her look like a surprised owl.

"I did. And now I can hardly breathe. I was trying to be brave. Because what if tomorrow never comes, right? But now I think I might puke."

Vlair jolted back to life and scooched down the bench a bit, getting distance between them. She knew Rachel had a weak stomach. Admiration shone in her eyes, though. "That is *super* brave, Rach. I mean, wow. He might not care or have a clue who you are," she said, "but you'll know that you made a declaration!" Vlair shot her arms up like a cheerleader.

"Shhhh! You aren't helping."

"Sorry."

Rachel stood up and took her tray of leftover salad to the trash, dumping it through the lid's wide slot. She wiped her hands on her jeans and froze mid-thigh. Vlair had been following close behind and turned to see what Rachel was staring at. She gasped, tipping up the tray she held at chest level, causing the contents to slide back, splashing Pepsi against her collarbone.

Kevin Cardeaux was walking straight toward them.

"Hi. I'm Kevin. I asked around and found out you're Rachel?" A gentle smile rested easily on his face.

Rachel's heart stopped beating, she'd stopped breathing! She was sure she'd collapse from lack of oxygen and die of shock on the dirty cafeteria floor. Her obituary would read: Girl dropped dead in school cafeteria because a boy said hi. What a stupid way to go.

Vlair elbowed her in the ribs, pushing out the last remaining breath in her lungs and Rachel managed a wheezed out, "Hi." It sounded more like a dying accordion than a greeting.

"So, yeah. I just wanted to say thanks for the candy-gram. It's really nice and you're the only person who put their name on one. I got, like, fifty of the things." He unzipped his backpack, showing the girls a jumbled mess of valentines stuffed haphazardly around his binder and books. He pulled out two, handing one to Vlair, who took it without blinking, awkwardly holding her tray, and the other to Rachel.

"Thank you," said Rachel, her cheeks burning. She had never in her life received a valentine from a boy she liked in person. It was usually a class organized event. This felt incredibly different. Her stomach kept flip-flopping, but she didn't know if it was from excitement or nervousness. Maybe they felt the same? Just don't *puke*, she thought desperately, clenching her teeth.

"Sure thing. I have plenty." Kevin smiled at her and Rachel's heart dissolved completely. "Happy Valentine's Day, Rachel. I'll see ya around." He hoisted his backpack full of candy back over his shoulder and gave a brief wave to the girls.

As he turned to leave, Rachel struggled to make her voice box work again. "Bye. I mean, see ya," she said. Both girls stood rooted to the spot and watched him walk away. The entire cafeteria was hushed, and everyone was watching *them*.

"I can't believe Kevin Cardeaux knows your name, Rach!" Vlair squealed loudly when Kevin was just out of earshot, oblivious that the entire school was staring. All at once everyone started talking again, their voices thundering off the walls. Normally Rachel would have been mortified, but she was floating on a cloud. She gushed, looking down at the valentine in her hand.

Vlair sulked, looking at hers. "This is probably the one *I* bought for him." She pulled off the little chocolate heart candy and flicked the red aluminum wrapper in the trash with her lunch scraps. She tossed the tray on the shelf atop the garbage can and popped the candy in her mouth with a giggle. "I'll take it though!"

Rachel peeled off her chocolate and unwrapped it carefully, a slow smile growing at the corners of her mouth.

Vlair playfully smacked her arm. "You are so lucky!"

Rachel grinned wide and popped the chocolate in her mouth, intending to savor it. The whole world went black. Her ears started buzzing like wasp nests were packed in them. She saw three shadowy figures bent over something, whispering fiercely. Abruptly they stopped and in unison, the terrifying trio rose ten feet tall.

"I sense a presence," said one of the darkened figures in a deep, commanding voice.

"I, too, can sense it," agreed a second voice, beautifully melodious and higher pitched. The third figure remained silent. It

67

raised an arm, pointing a long shadowed finger in Rachel's direction.

Chapter 10: Discovery

Rachel woke up in the nurse's office at school and groaned softly. The buzzing in her head faded, winding down her ear canal, and she squeezed her eyes shut against the overhead fluorescent light. It persisted, piercing through her eyelids, hammering her brain, intensifying the headache that had already taken up residence there.

"Your mom is on her way," said the school nurse, sitting next to her, patting Rachel's arm reassuringly. Rachel risked peeking through her lashes at her. The nurse was a short round woman with a kind face and cropped hair.

She rattled on sweetly, without pausing for breath. "Your friend Vlair said you passed out and hit your head on a trashcan, and again when you crashed to the floor! You've got a large bump, but you're not concussed, which is good. You'll have a nasty headache, but you'll be alright." She patted Rachel again, pushing an ice pack into her hand.

"Thanks. I definitely feel the headache," croaked Rachel.

"Vlair and Kevin hauled you in like a sack of potatoes!" she tittered. "It took some effort, but we managed to lift you onto the exam bed here." She pinched the side of the world's most uncomfortable mattress pad. Then she pointed to a pile on the floor consisting of Rachel's bag and winter coat. "Vlair also brought your things, she's a sweet girl. I'll just let her and Kevin know you're awake and doing okay so they can go back to class." The nurse shuffled out of the room humming to herself, oblivious of Rachel's stricken face.

Kevin helped drag her lifeless body to the nurse?! Rachel checked her mouth, worried she'd been drooling. Thankfully, there was no saliva there. Holding the ice pack gently to her head, she pressed into the extra firm pillow, brooding.

"You don't look well," said Arka, waltzing into the room like she owned the school.

Rachel's eyes snapped open. "You can't be here!" she whispered frantically. "My mom will be here any second!"

"Don't worry. I look like your mom to everyone else. You are the only one who can see through my disguise weaves, remember? Just play along." She straightened up when the nurse bustled back in carrying a sheet of paper.

"Oh! Hello Mrs. Soarenson. I need you to sign this form acknowledging an accident involving a head injury occurred at school. Then you can take Rachel home."

"Of course." Arka stuck out her bottom lip at Rachel, imitating parental concern. "Do you feel okay, sweetie pie?"

"Er, Mom! Just sign the form, okay? I'm fine." Rachel winced, pulling the ice pack away. Then, talking in code she added, "I *am* feeling thirsty though."

The nurse hopped into action, filling a paper water cup. "Here, drink some water. We can't have you passing out again! You're most likely dehydrated."

"I agree," said Arka, catching Rachel's meaning. She handed the form back to the nurse with a flick of the wrist. "Rachel, you really should remember to pack your water bottle for school," she scolded. Arka took the empty cup from Rachel, crumpling it and deftly threw it at the trash without looking. It tipped the rim, landing in the plastic lined basket neatly. "Now, let's get you home to rest, and pump you up with fluids."

Rachel slid off the examination table, her sneakers squeaking on the tile floor. Arka snagged her bag, striding out of the Nurse's office with an air of authority.

"Thanks," Rachel murmured to the nurse and hurried to catch up, pulling on her coat.

Arka waited until they reached the parking lot before speaking. She tossed Rachel her bag. "When you said you had plans for Valentine's Day, I didn't think you'd be so dramatic."

"Not funny, Arka," said Rachel, following Arka until she stopped next to a motorcycle. "You ride a motorcycle?" Rachel asked, forgetting her annoyance.

"When I have to. Mortal transportation is rudimentary and clumsy. I might as well have a bit of fun." Arka handed Rachel a helmet. "Put this on, if you can fit it over that giant egg on your head and tell me what happened."

Rachel gingerly buckled the helmet in place. Several curls stubbornly poked out around the edges and she tried pushing them back in without much success. "I ate a piece of chocolate and had a vision. I didn't touch anyone, I just . . . blacked out. I'm sure I saw your sisters." She shuddered. "They knew I could see them."

Arka stared at her a moment, her green eyes darkening. "It sounds like the vision was forced by something in the candy. They must know I have a helper at the school and were trying to flush you out. I was," she hesitated, "on other business, when I had a powerful urge to check on you. Our bond is stronger than I thought."

"What happened to your face?" asked Rachel, noticing the large scratch across Arka's cheekbone for the first time.

"It's nothing."

"It doesn't look like nothing."

"What day is it?" asked Arka, turning aside, deflecting the comment.

"Tuesday. Why?"

Arka stiffened. She'd stepped out of the dream world that afternoon and followed the pull directly to the school. She had thought battling the dream weavers had taken less than an hour, but it had been over three days!

A thought struck Rachel. "Wait, will anyone who eats the candy have a bad reaction?" she asked, suddenly alarmed for her friends. She imagined everyone in the school dropping like flies all over the hallways.

"Only if they possess special gifts or talents like you, are a deity or some sort of creature." Arka eyed her a moment. When Rachel only stared back, she mumbled something about how Rachel better not be hiding other talented mortals from her. "A normal mortal wouldn't be affected. You, however, are not normal."

"Thanks."

"You are a seer, and your reaction to the candy has alerted my sisters to your presence. It will only be a matter of time before they find out who you are. We must leave this place."

"I can't leave yet!" Rachel threw her hands out. "I'm not ready!"

Arka bared her teeth, her temper sparking. "I realize you are struggling to come to terms with the severity of this situation, but I cannot keep waiting on the whims of a teenager!"

"I'm not a teenager yet, I turn thirteen this summer."

"What?" Steam pressurized inside her and Arka wrenched away from the bike, about to blow. This human is impossible! After everything I've gone through! Arka, stormed past three cars and caught herself before she threw her helmet into the snowcapped bushes. It would be uncouth to throw things. She was a goddess, after all. This is a cruel trick of fate, Arka thought, shaking her head. The fate of the universe was in jeopardy and she was waiting on a child. She hated waiting. She also hated needing help. "Why her?!" Arka shouted at the sky.

The clouds floated along lazily, ignoring her simmering rage. Arka knew in her gut she needed Rachel to complete the quest, and reason told her to be patient. The girl must be scared out of her wits, and she needs guidance, thought Arka, scratching her forehead, calming a little. Pushing only seems to make her dig her heels in.

Arka sighed, defeated. She walked back to her bike and swung a long leg over the smokey black seat, obscuring the shimmery gold pattern at the front. She motioned for Rachel to do the same, pulling leather gloves on her hands.

"Are we not going to talk about that little outburst?"

"No," said Arka, strapping on her helmet.

Rachel stood still, watching to see if Arka would explode again. "Look," she said, "I want everything to go back to normal sooner than later. I do. I'm just not the hero type, okay?" Rachel climbed on the back of the bike and fumbled with where to put her feet. "Maybe I have been putting it off. I guess, I was hoping you'd figure it out without me."

"Ignoring this will not make it go away. Things are . . .

getting worse."

"I've got everything squared away. I just have to say goodbye to my family." Rachel bit her lower lip. "I'll be packed and ready to go this weekend, I promise."

"You'd better be," said Arka, squeezing the handlebars, "we can't wait much longer."

The motorcycle roared to life before Rachel could retort. Its tires crunched little pebbles, scattering them across the icy ground as they rode out of the parking lot.

Mom would kill her if she knew Rachel was on a motorcycle! Dad would say how disappointed he was in her decision to behave in such a reckless manner, but boy was it fun! "Whoop!" cheered Rachel into the crisp wind stinging her cheeks.

It lifted Arka's mood. She smirked, gunning it faster, and the smell of burnt rubber and gasoline enveloped them. Neither girl was aware they were being watched as they flew over the pavement.

* * *

All three of Arka's sisters searched for her in the eye. They wouldn't have noticed the pair on the motorcycle except that Arka's weave of hiding only worked on herself. It appeared very odd that a young girl was sitting on the back of a motorized bike, riding along without touching the handlebars, shifting gears, or watching where she was going. It was the same girl whose life thread had thickened without their permission. The three Fates grinned in unison.

"Gotcha!" croaked Atropos, leaning over the eye, peering into its milky depths. Her black stringy hair covered the ball, and she hissed a laugh, showing rotted teeth.

Clotho pushed her back so she could lean in for a closer look, and Atropos growled at her. Clotho always called the shots and enjoyed lording herself over her sisters. "Knock it off," she rebuked, peering into the eye. "Curious," she said, tapping her chin with a curved white fingernail. Her skin swirled with Greek letters that moved as she thought. "Why would Arka choose a mortal child to accompany her? I would have thought she'd choose someone from our realm, or a creature with useful abilities." Rachel's name floated to the surface in Clotho's palm. Clotho studied it, making a fist around the letters, her long nails clicking. She grimaced. "There must be something we aren't seeing."

"Aren't seeing, *yet*," chirped Lachesis from an elegantly upholstered kline chair. She was busying herself, pinning large pearls in her red hair, and didn't care to look into the eye. It was boring, looking at other people all day. She preferred to admire the reflection in her own mirror. Lachesis took a sip of nectar from a dainty teacup decorated with a tiny painting of Eros, the winged Greek god of love, and went back to pinning pearls, saying absently, "We will simply follow them until Arka reveals her plans, then force her to return here. The girl is of no consequence."

"Perhaps," said Clotho, unconvinced. "We'll decide what to do with the girl later. For now, we will *persuade* our sister to take her place with us. Whether or not she wants to, Arka will prepare more threads for us." They all murmured in agreement, and Clotho watched the eye swirl until the image dimmed.

Chapter 11: The Crossing

Most girls in Rachel's seventh grade class enjoyed shopping on Fridays after school like it was a professional sport. Rachel wasn't that type. Four hours in a mall was torture. The only reason it was remotely bearable was because she scored a couple new shirts, and got to spend time with her mom. Time was precious to her now, but she was stressed to the max!

Rachel hated the idea of leaving work undone; and sneaking off wasn't something she'd ever considered. Her chewed off fingernails were a testament to how anxious she'd been all day. She tried working ahead on all her assignments, and still had to pack, but her mom pulled her away to go shopping and have an easy dinner at the food court. It would have been more fun if her little sister and baby brother had stayed home.

They sat on a bench in the mall's play area, her mom trying unsuccessfully to get Luke's attention on his chicken nuggets. He was more interested in watching the hoard of children sprinting around giant foam structures, climbing, and jumping off them in complete chaos. Luke strained against the buckles of his stroller, wanting to play with the bigger kids and Morgan.

"Oh, no you don't, Mister! You can't play until you've had your dinner." Their mother tried bribing him, waving a nugget in front of his face. "I'll let you slide down the giraffe if you eat three more bites."

Rachel lounged next to her mom, her hair up in a poufy ponytail with her signature pencil stuck through, sipping a soda. She knew her baby brother wouldn't finish his food and he'd still be allowed to play. Her siblings got away with everything! Just then Morgan ran up, her hair matted with sweat, and gulped her soda. The sugar was an instant re-charge for her.

"Want to play tag with me, Rach?"

Rachel scrunched her face. Her ears were ringing from playful screams and echoing noise from people dining at the food court. The decibel level was off the charts. "No thanks, Morgan. I'm too big to be running around in there. I'd knock someone over. You go have fun, though."

"Okay." Morgan was off like a shot, back into the fray.

Rachel checked a clock high on the wall behind a metal cage. It was nearing 6:30. She chewed a thumbnail. Her mom noticed her lackluster vibe and offered a solution. "Hey, why don't you look around that cool jewelry store for some cute accessories to go with your new clothes?" Rachel looked sideways at her mom, who pushed a little more. "I know you don't wear a lot of jewelry honey, but spring isn't that far off and maybe some fresh earrings or new hair ties would be nice? It would give you a break from all this noise."

Just then Morgan let out a high-pitched scream as a little boy tagged her shoulder. Rachel and her mom cringed at the same time.

"That's not a bad idea. I think I will, but then can we go

home?"

"Sure thing. As soon as Look finishes his food and has time to play. Here, take some cash in case you find something you like." She handed Rachel thirty dollars and smiled tenderly at her.

"Thanks, Mom." Rachel squeezed her mother's hand in thanks and pocketed the money. If she was stuck there, at least she could find something useful for her trip. What would she need for a quest anyway?

Walking through the mall was amusing. There were so many people on different errands. Some were trying extremely hard to pretend they were super important. One group of teen boys wearing sunglasses inside made Rachel chuckle. Maybe I should find some new shades, she thought. To be worn outside like a person with common sense, though.

While making her way to the end of the corridor, expertly avoiding kiosks with pushy salespeople, Rachel noticed a man keeping pace with her on the other side of the walkway. She paused, pretending to investigate a store's display window. In the reflection, she saw that he'd also stopped. She took a few more steps and smelled some lotions at a table near the entrance of another store. She stole a glance out of the corner of her eye and again, the guy paused when she did.

Suddenly uneasy, Rachel glanced around. The crowd bustled, unperturbed. Only she and the copycat weren't moving about. What if he's like Arka? Well, she meant for him to know she could see him plain as day. Rachel boldly faced the guy across the wide hall filled with shoppers. The guy stood near a fake tree in a giant stone flowerpot and stretched taller when she looked directly at him. Rachel felt tingly all over, but thankfully nothing like when she and Arka first met.

Rather than pretend he wasn't stalking her, the guy smiled sinisterly. He had pointed teeth! Goosebumps ran up Rachel's arms. She stared at the man as he rippled in a disjointed way, like he was underwater. It reminded Rachel of how Arka changed her appearance. With a creepy fang grin plastered on his face, he stepped toward her on what looked like hind legs and the rippling stopped.

Did he just step into my world? Rachel wondered, alarmed. She didn't have time to dwell on it though.

The man dropped to all fours, his body growing into the shape of a lion, and his clothes fading into red-brown shaggy fur. A scorpion tail with a giant stinger lifted into the air behind him, and Rachel gasped in horror, dropping the lotion bottle she'd been holding.

Is this for real? This guy is a freaking monster! From where, Rachel didn't care. She had to get out of there! She bolted, running as fast as she could through the mall.

Zigzagging through shoppers slowed her down, but she kept her legs pumping. Rachel knew the thing was chasing her. She needed to hide! She heard a whizzing sound and instinct caused her to duck. A black spike about a foot long flew past the spot her head had been. It lodged into a nearby wall with a solid thud, a hole exploding where the venomous point stabbed through the drywall.

Glancing over her shoulder, Rachel saw the beast level its tail and shoot another poisonous spike at her. With a cry she dove to the ground, rolling sideways, scrambling to get distance between them. Just ahead, she saw a sign for the ladies' restroom. She raced for the door. Nearly skidding past, Rachel caught the handle and threw it open. As she yanked it shut behind her, the beast thrust its head in, nearly chomping her arm off.

Its disconcerting human face was wedged between the door and the frame, with striking blue eyes that glared up at her. Up close, Rachel could see there were three rows of teeth in its mouth, all razor-sharp, snapping at her. She screamed and squished its head between the door and frame with all her might. The creature roared back at her, rattling her bones and splattering foul saliva. The rotten stench of its breath wafted up her nose and Rachel gagged.

Out of nowhere, a huge magenta handbag smashed into the creature's face! Its jaw snapped shut and the blue eyes widened, stupefied. Another *thwack!* The handbag smashed its face again, and before it could snarl at the assault, the purse struck it a third time, square on target.

"Take that, you brute!" shouted an elderly lady, her glasses askew from swinging her weapon. "Keep out of the ladies' room or there's more where that came from!"

The creature pulled its head back to avoid another hit and Rachel banged the door shut, slapping the lock into place. She braced her hands against the door breathing heavily a few moments before she realized the woman was speaking to her.

"There, there, honey. You just take a moment. Ain't nobody gonna mess with you while I'm here." She rubbed Rachel's back.

Rachel stiffened, worried she'd have a vision and be eaten alive by the creature while incapacitated.

"Now, now, you're okay. Everything is going to be okay."

"T-thank you," Rachel stammered. She pulled a paper towel from the dispenser to wipe the beast's spittle off her arms and face. "So, you could see that thing?"

"I've been alive long enough to know a creep when I see one, honey."

"Right. Just a creepy guy."

"Mm, hm. You should know better than to roam the mall by yourself." The woman straightened her glasses, looking over the rims at Rachel. She had curly grey hair, but that was the only dull thing about her. Her bright lipstick matched her purse, and she had navy blue eyebrows drawn on her forehead in peaked arches. Her fake nails shone bright red and several gaudy rings adorned her knobby fingers, the gemstones shining as she straightened her lemon-yellow jacket. "We'll stay in here as long as you need; go ahead and rest a minute, baby."

Rachel nodded in thanks, and leaned against the door, sliding down to the floor, every inch of her shaking.

A half-hour past and Rachel was thankful to have the tough, but sweet, elderly lady for company. The woman told stories about her life as the wife of a candy salesman and shared a couple homemade sweets from her massive purse.

"Well, darlin'," the woman said, "I suspect that guy is gone now. He found out you weren't an easy target." She chuckled, lifting her purse strap over a shoulder. "I'm going to head on out, but you can lock the door behind me if you need more time to collect yourself."

"I will, thank you."

After her protector had gone, Rachel tried processing the ordeal. No one else seemed to notice the lion scorpion guy like she did. There would have been screaming and chaos. The old lady had perceived him as a normal man, so he wasn't imagined. Rachel was unsure of what to do. Were there more monsters after her? She wanted to warn her mother, but if monsters were chasing her, she needed to lead them away.

Rachel turned on the cold water at the sink, splashing it refreshingly on the back of her neck. She leaned on the sink, looking at the mirror. "You can't stay in here forever," she told herself, pinching water droplets off her eyelashes. In the mirror, Rachel saw a bathroom stall door slowly creep open behind her. What now?! she thought, paralyzed by fear, holding her breath.

A girl stepped out. She looked like Arka, but Rachel knew it was not. The eyes were wrong, there was no vibrancy to her, and her smile was wicked.

"I thought that old hag would never leave!" said the fake Arka. In trance-like motion, she lifted an arm, her eyes never blinking and never looking away from Rachel. "Take my hand," she commanded. When Rachel didn't comply, the girl lunged forward to grab her.

Terrified, Rachel jumped back, letting out a scream.

The girl laughed at her, blocking the exit. "You can't escape me. You're trapped mortal," she sneered. "Now take my hand or I'll destroy you!"

"Arka!" cried Rachel in desperation. "I need you!"

"Then take *my* hand," said Arka's voice from the mirror.

Spinning, Rachel saw Arka instead of her reflection. The goddess' arm extended through the mirrored glass into the bathroom.

"NO!" the crazy eyed look-alike shrieked, diving at Rachel.

Rachel grabbed Arka's outstretched arm without hesitation. They locked wrists and suddenly Rachel felt like she was being pulled inside out.

Chapter 12: Breaking Bread

Rachel lay gasping for breath on the ground. The smell of grass and wildflowers tickling her nose. "What was that? OMG!"

"What was what?" Arka asked, poised and standing over her.

"Oh, I don't know. Um, how about the Scorpion King shooting death darts at me or the clone thing impersonating you in the bathroom?!" shouted Rachel, jumping to her feet, her hands balled up in fists.

"Calm down! There is no need to shout." Arka put her hands on her hips and said tersely, "I'm sure your encounter with a couple monsters was disturbing. Your ability to survive is commendable, but you do not get to yell at me. What is more important, is that your encounter confirms the veil between the worlds is thinning."

Rachel's voice rose an octave. "Ability to survive?! More like barely escaping without losing an arm!" She tucked an arm behind her back for effect.

"Rachel, anger is a secondary response. You are only angry

because you were scared."

"No duh!"

"Please! I need to think." Arka paced back and forth, biting her lip. "You escaped a Manticore. It's a creature with a lion's body, bat wings, a human head and poisonous darts that shoot from its scorpion tail."

"Yeah, I know," said Rachel, still fuming, roughly brushing grass off her pants.

"It has triple rows of teeth used for devouring human flesh."

"Oh, trust me, I got a good look at his teeth. He's keeping a dentist somewhere rich." She hugged her arms around herself despite the sarcastic joke.

"I'm sorry you went through a monster attack. As for the girl who looked like me," Arka shrugged, "I'm not sure what that was."

"They know who I am. I can't go home," said Rachel, her panic rising.

"Correct."

"My mom is still at the mall, my sister, my brother!"

"I'll take care of it." Arka rippled, disappearing. In two seconds, she stepped out of thin air in the exact spot she'd been. "I sent her a text from Vlair's mom saying she ran into you at the mall and asked if you could ride home with them, since you're staying there this weekend anyhow. Your mom said yes. She's heading home with your siblings."

Rachel just stood there nodding, holding her arms around herself, half hearing what Arka was saying. Distractedly, she wiped her mouth with the back of a hand.

"What is that awful smell?" asked Arka, wrinkling her nose. She glanced around and saw a puddle of vomit at Rachel's feet. She took a step back, protecting her boots. "Oh."

"Sorry."

"I also placed a weave of protection over your house."

"Okay."

Arka took pity on her. "Come on, I'll make you some tea." Arka headed for a thick tree line lush with pines and dotted with several birch trees.

"Hang on," said Rachel. "If you can pull me through mirrors and jump to different places, can't your sisters too? Won't they just pop out of the air and grab us?" Rachel's voice rose again, her wild eyes searching the woods.

"No. They don't have the same abilities as I do. I don't pop out of the air either, I weave gateways. You should pay closer attention. In any case, my sisters prefer to use others to do their bidding. Hence, the monsters." She lifted an eyebrow at Rachel.

"Right," said Rachel lamely, the knot in her shoulders unwinding a fraction.

They pushed through thick branches, following an unseen trail, as far as Rachel could tell, until they came into a little clearing.

Rachel assumed Arka would have a little cabin tucked in the forest. It seemed fitting because she dressed and moved like a huntress. But instead of a homey cabin, there was a low-lying pile of tree branches arranged in a sad lean-to, squatting in the clearing.

"Wow. Great place you have there."

Arka ignored Rachel and crouched through a small opening in the branches. Reluctantly, Rachel crawled after her.

I've had enough Alice in Wonderland experiences today, Rachel thought. If I tumble down a rabbit hole, I swear I'm going to flip out! She didn't fall, but felt the ground slope downward and after her eyes adjusted, Rachel saw a partially underground room with a dirt floor. A small fire pit waited in the center and primitive mats laid about on the ground.

Rachel was all for being one with nature, but this was roughing it a bit too much, and she *liked* camping! "You don't have company often, do you?" she asked. "Who's your decorator? I've got to get me one of these dirt floors."

Arka gave her a level stare. "Simplicity avoids notice." She knelt, and Rachel watched with fascination as she worked at starting a fire.

"It doesn't get any simpler than this. You're a regular girl scout, Arka."

Arka looked up, confused. "I rarely scout at all. Occasionally, I survey an area before making myself visible, but I leave scouting to the demigods."

Rachel rolled her eyes. "You need to learn how to joke around more. Are you always so serious?"

"Necessity makes me so." Gesturing towards the back of the lean-to Arka said, "Make yourself useful and look in those baskets for some mugs. I'll get some tea leaves."

Arka made delicious tea. Just holding the warm cup and smelling its steam was soothing. Rachel sat cross-legged on a mat near the fire and sighed in appreciation.

"Well," Arka broke the silence, "now that you're calm, we should make a plan, Seer."

Rachel frowned at the title. She didn't want to be referred to as a seer. She didn't even know how to control her visions, let alone be useful with them.

"I suggest we visit the god of secrets. There are rumors he knows where a special artifact is that can steal a god's power."

"Wow. Straight to the point, huh?"

"You've already wasted too much time. Harpocrates may be

able to tell us why you have developed abilities as a seer, and he will keep our quest confidential."

Rachel had no idea what to say or who the god of secrets was but felt a response was expected, so she nodded.

"We can journey there through a gateway tomorrow, but we should be prepared for another monster attack," said Arka, her face glowing ominously through the fire, "just in case."

Rachel gulped her mouthful of tea.

Arka chatted on about the special artifact and her plan to use it against her sisters while she made a second cup. She was more animated than Rachel had ever seen her.

"Do you always tell your plans to random kids?" teased Rachel.

"No." Arka sat down on a rugged grass mat by the crackling fire, crossing her legs easily. She gazed into her cup, swirling the umber liquid. "Honestly, I don't talk with people that often," she admitted, surprised by a twinge of embarrassment.

Rachel cleared her throat and changed the subject. "You drink a lot of this, huh?" she said, lifting her earthenware mug.

"It's ambrosia. Usually, we gods eat it, but I enjoy it as an infusion in tea to get nutrients into my body quickly. I also drink nectar, just not as often."

Rachel spat her tea out on the ground and coughed. "Are you trying to poison me?!"

"Certainly not!" Arka chastised her, "Do not waste it! You know, for a seer, you are quite naïve. You can partake of the same elements as I. They won't grant you immortality, like some humans believe, but perhaps a longer life thread. If you can keep away from monsters, that is."

"It's not like I've gone looking for monsters, Arka," said Rachel, "and I don't *want* to be a seer."

"Want has nothing to do with it. You'll have to accept your abilities if you have any hope of controlling them."

"Or maybe after this quest, everything will go back to being normal." Rachel sniffed her cup and took a little sip. It was good. It had a warmth and spice that reached past her stomach into her very bones. "I remember learning about ambrosia and nectar in school. Do you eat normal food too?" she asked, changing the subject.

"Of course. It isn't as energizing for me though. I need the foods grown at Olympus to maintain my power and strength, but I can survive on simple mortal food."

"Oh, wow." Rachel thought for a moment. "So, if I wanted to wipe out all the gods, or just weaken them, all I'd have to do is set some ambrosia fields on fire? Maybe dump out a bunch of nectar somehow?"

Arka stared at Rachel with blank horror.

"What? I thought we were planning to overthrow your sisters."

"It would weaken all the other gods who also need the enriching qualities of ambrosia."

"What if you just refuse to give power food to the evil ones? Then lock them up when they've been weakened by eating pork chops or something."

"How would you discern who is evil and who is not? Not all gods are warring with each other or the mortal world. It wouldn't be right."

"I guess it would be wrong to punish the peaceful ones," mused Rachel, "still, if the whole world is at stake, I wouldn't have a problem bringing all of Olympus down." She sipped her tea again, staring into the fire, attempting to process everything she'd been through.

Arka studied the mortal girl for a while and decided the universe had chosen well in making her a seer. She needed someone unbiased to aid her on the quest against her sisters. "I accede to your point. It is prudent for a seer to look at the complete picture, to weigh collateral damage and tend to the wellbeing of everyone. That way, you channel your abilities into actions that benefit all creatures, in all realms."

"Was that a compliment?"

"No. I merely agreed with you."

Rachel snorted. It was the closest thing to a compliment she'd likely ever get out of Arka. She decided to let it go and focus on the aroma of her heavenly tea, allowing it to melt away the day's terrors.

Chapter 13: Friendship

Tiny rays of sunlight poked through the thatched roof, glittering across Rachel's face. She turned her head, trying to ease a kink in her neck. She'd slept fitfully on an uncomfortable grass mat, tossing about on the hard ground. Dreams of horrible monsters dragging her through the woods made her jolt awake in fits and starts all night! It wasn't as bad as the twisted dreams, but she still felt awful.

Scrubbing sleep from her eyes Rachel looked around for Arka, but she wasn't inside the lean-to. Two little pancakes rested on a large flat stone in the circle around the fire pit. Gold embers smoldered in the center, keeping the cakes warm. Rachel inhaled them. "Whoops," she said, hoping one wasn't supposed to be for Arka.

Nosing around, she thought it odd Arka had no personal effects. Peeking in storage baskets at the back of the hideout, Rachel uncovered some dried meats and berries. She tasted a couple, grimacing at their bitterness and spat them out on the ground. She used a toe to cover up the evidence with dirt. A twig snapped outside, and Rachel froze.

She listened with all her might, her own breath loud in her ears. The makeshift door creaked open, and Rachel screamed, jumping back into the storage containers knocking several over, spilling their contents all over the ground.

Arka crouched halfway through the entrance and was so startled by Rachel's screaming that she too screamed, dropping the supplies she'd been carrying. "My gods! What is wrong with you?" she demanded.

"I thought you were a monster!" said Rachel, clutching her chest. She bent over, bracing her hands on her knees to take a few deep, gasping breaths. "You scared me to death!"

"Likewise," said Arka flatly, her lips pressed in a thin line as she surveyed the mess in her normally tidy dwelling. "Perhaps you were scared at being caught snooping."

"I wasn't . . ."

Arka held up a hand. "We don't have time for shenanigans. We need to pack and get moving before my sister's agents find us. I saw some tracks in the forest." She bent to collect the things she had dropped, among them a rope and a small knife. "Your screaming will have attracted the creatures who made them."

"Why are your sisters after us in the first place?" asked Rachel. "I mean, if you don't do anything important, why does it bother them so much you left?"

Arka stood, her face strained. "I do have a job," she admitted quietly.

Rachel waited a moment. "Well, what is it?" she prompted when Arka wasn't forthcoming.

"When new thread is being prepared for the tapestry, before it's spun and cut, I am supposed to handle it."

"What does that mean? Like, juggle it around?" Rachel

tilted her head, picturing Arka juggling puffy balls of yarn to carnival music. The image was so absurd Rachel couldn't help but giggle.

"Of course not. Don't be ridiculous," said Arka. "I breathe on it."

"What? You can't be serious. What if you had a cold or something? Gross!" Rachel laughed at her own joke.

Arka wilted. She unearthed a bag from a hole under her sleeping mat, and knelt down, brusquely stuffing the supplies she'd dropped into it.

"Sorry," Rachel bit her lip. "Um, why do you have to breathe on it?"

"The fibers are tied to mortals after my breath touches them. I card the fibers, then they're spun into threads and we all weave them into the Tapestry of Life. We are not supposed to alter the work of a sister unless we are all in agreement. Of course, my sisters don't follow this rule."

"Wait, where do the fibers come from?"

"From golden rams."

"Like the golden fleece in the story about Jason and the Argonauts?!"

Arka stifled a groan, sitting back on her heels. "Yes, but not *that* fleece. If you recall, Zeus gave the winged ram to Jason's father. I won't tell you precisely where the rams are, so don't ask." Arka shot Rachel an annoyed look over her shoulder.

"Okay." Rachel didn't mind. She didn't need to know every detail, but she did need to know the process, so she could puzzle out how she fit into it. "What does it mean to card the fibers?"

"I use two big brushes that look like, how would you understand . . ." Arka paused in thought. She'd never had to describe her work to someone, and Rachel had a lot to learn about the godly realm. Still, Arka wasn't keen on sharing everything with a sarcastic, mortal girl.

"They look like giant spatulas with bristles on them. They tear apart and mix the fibers, or fleece, as you say. This process gives the tapestry its sheen. It started losing its luster some time ago, however. I think it is because of my sisters' interference and our lack of agreement. There are a few grey spots and some threads have come undone."

"Wait. You mean, you're the reason it glows?" Rachel tugged on an earlobe, considering. It made sense that Arka gave color and light to the tapestry, since everywhere she went there was a vibrancy lent to the objects and people around her. "That's remarkable! Why did you leave then?"

Arka's shoulders had tightened substantially while Rachel peppered her with questions. Now they hunched up to the bottom of her ears.

"If the tapestry needs fixing, shouldn't you be there? It sounds like your job is really important."

"It's not, okay!" shouted Arka, her face drawn.

Rachel blinked in surprise.

"I've never been important, or wanted. I've spent my entire life watching my sisters scheme and manipulate other gods and mortals." Arka fidgeted with her braid. "I tried to reason with them, but they ignored me. I tried fixing their atrocities secretly, but they locked me up! I finally escaped and I'm not going back! I'm through with them." Arka's breath was heavy with emotion. She huffed past Rachel and rummaged in the overturned baskets, packing several snacks in her bag. "It's downright evil playing with destinies like that. They're only supposed to dole out consequences equivalent with actions and guide the threads, not punish whoever they want for no reason or create chaos just for the fun of it. It's so awful, Rachel. I've seen horrible things. Like what happened to your sister, and worse." Arka touched shimmering tears that welled up in her eyes with the tip of a finger. With her guard down, waves of frustration and sorrow threatened to bowl her over.

Rachel finally understood why Arka had been at Morgan's accident; to undo the damage caused by the three Fates. A grim determination to make them pay filled her soul. No wonder Arka is so abrupt and condescending all the time, thought Rachel. That's a lot of pain and hurt she's been carrying around. She's probably never even had a friend before. At least I can help with that. "I can see why you left, Arka. That must've been hard," Rachel said picking up a wicker basket and stacking it neatly against the sloping wall. "You need to talk about it, to get it out. I get it. Listen, when my dad was deployed the time before last, I talked with a counselor off and on for several weeks. I learned about grounding to help me when I'm overwhelmed. Stuff like that. Focusing on what I can see, feel, hear, smell- you know, the senses."

Arka looked up from where she knelt in the dirt, cleaning up Rachel's mess. "How many times has he been gone?"

"Three times for long hauls, and here and there for a few weeks at a time. My stress got really bad when he was gone during the pandemic though." Rachel knelt to help pick up the rest of the things she'd knocked over. "I try to keep it together for my sister, she needs the support, but it can be hard. Lately I've been working on breathing in and out for four beats when my stomach acts up. My mom even makes us do that as a family now." She smiled at the memory. "Sometimes I count back from a hundred to distract my brain and if that's too easy, I skip count backward, so I don't have to vomit. My point is, I understand your anxiety and that it can hit you anytime. Talking with someone can really help."

"I've never told anyone my story before," said Arka, rearranging the items Rachel had put back incorrectly. It was difficult to speak about her time living with her sisters. Powerful emotions threatened to choke her and didn't want to talk about it anymore. She stood up, ready to go, but Rachel was watching her with empathetic eyes.

"I can't say it's going to be okay, but I can say that I'm with you. I don't mind listening. That's what friends are for. I understand your choice to leave, but I do think you'll have to go back, eventually." Rachel gave Arka an encouraging, dimpled smile.

Arka stalked out of the little doorway with her bag clutched in a vice grip.

"So much for being friends," Rachel said sarcastically. "Meet my new BFF, a freaking stone-wall." She kicked dirt over the humble fire pit, smothering its remnants before making her way outside.

Arka stood just outside her hideout, stunned. This mortal child had just shown more grace and understanding toward her than she'd seen in her entire lifetime, and it was a long lifetime! The thought of having a friend, even for a short while, warmed her heart.

Rachel emerged from the lean-to squinting, her eyes adjusting to intense daylight. Her breath caught in her throat. It wasn't daylight, Arka was glowing like an angel!

"I am honored to have your friendship, Rachel. I will do my best to be a friend to you as well." Arka smiled tentatively the entire clearing around them growing brighter as she spoke.

"Oh, okay," said Rachel, shielding her eyes with an elbow.

"Sorry," said Arka. "I'll also try not being so serious all the time."

"Well, that's a relief," joked Rachel.

Arka chuckled and placed a few branches over the lean-to's doorway, hiding it from view. "You are right, I will have to go back and face my sisters. The tapestry must be repaired. If it is not tended to, eventually it will fade away to dust and so will the universe."

Arka's illumination dulled so dramatically as she spoke, Rachel thought rain clouds rolled overhead. She glanced at the sky, wishing for an umbrella, but it was a clear blue. She looked back at Arka and worry lines creased between her eyebrows when she saw the fear in Arka's eyes. "I guess we'll just have to fix it then," said Rachel, hoping to lend encouragement.

Arka smiled at her new friend. "I guess we will." She stuck her thumbs through belt loops already occupied with a sturdy leather belt. "Partners?"

"Partners." The moment the word passed Rachel's lips, the atmospheric pressure shifted, pressing her back a step. "Whoa. Did you feel that?"

Arka's jaw was slack and her eyes round. "Yes. I can see it too." She gazed in wonder at the strands of fate all around them shining and twisting on their own accord into new ropes. She'd never seen the strands of fate move by themselves before. Arka inspected them. They were thicker than she was used to, and several were now in little braids with three strands plaited together. They still formed the same designs as far as she could tell, but these cords were stronger and the weaves she saw were tighter.

"It feels like a piece of the universe just clicked into place," said Rachel, rubbing her temples. She didn't like the way Arka stared off into space like that. "Did you hear me?" she asked, frowning.

Arka's eyes snapped back, reflecting the green of the forest. "We are destined to be a team. I knew it! Nike is on my side."

"You mean our side?"

"Yes, of course."

Arka worked her hands in an intricate pattern, testing the new strands. Rachel detected a shimmer in the air and moved closer to watch her. Arka explained she'd created a protection weave and with a flick of her wrist, placed it over the hideout entrance. "If someone or something gets too close, it acts as a repellent. It's the same thing I used on your house, to protect your family. If the weave is tampered with, I will feel it. Like a spider senses an insect in its web."

It was fascinating, but Rachel couldn't help feeling like *she* was an insect, caught in a web of destiny that she desperately wanted out of. What exactly had she agreed to? Pushing the thought away, Rachel clung to the hope of their growing friendship instead. Suddenly, goosebumps sprang up on her arms, her stomach flip-flopped, and she shivered from head to toe. "Arka! I think there's a god nearby," she said, her voice hushed.

Arka quickly pulled Rachel behind a large tree trunk and with her fingers flying, created a gateway using the new strands of fate. They felt heavy and she was having some difficulty weaving them tightly.

It was the first time Rachel paid close attention to the way Arka made a gateway. She couldn't see the strands but swore she could feel them around her now. She imagined spiders crawling up her back and her shoulders twitched at the sensation. "I think I can feel the strands moving!" she whispered.

"Shh!" snapped Arka, but it was too late.

A noiseless figure stepped around the tree. "Not so fast, Arkaeivahina. Where are you taking this child?" A giant woman holding an enormous longbow pulled taught with an arrow pointed at Arka's chest stood perfectly still, waiting for a response.

Rachel thought Arka moved with grace, but this woman had her topped by a long shot. She carried herself like a queen and spoke with such a rich, commanding presence that Rachel suspected made everyone and everything obey her.

"I have been watching you, Fate. I allowed you to stay here for some time, but there are creatures in my forest tormenting my animals, and now you've abducted a child? My tolerance is at an end. Explain yourself, or feel my wrath. Your station will not preserve thee."

Arka kept every muscle still. To be pierced with the weapon of a god would cause unimaginable pain, but worse, it would end her quest! Very slowly, Arka opened her mouth to speak, but Rachel jumped in, interrupting as usual.

"She didn't abduct me! She saved me!"

The woman's stormy grey eyes swiveled, looking down at Rachel. Rachel's teeth made an audible *click!* from the force and speed used to clamp her mouth shut. She felt her legs ice up and her skin went numb. This was obviously a goddess she was supposed to encounter, but she was a hundred times scarier than Arka. Rachel would have whimpered under the intensity of the stare had her tongue not been glued to the roof of her mouth.

The goddess had black hair tied back in intricate braids and her clothes, made from a material Rachel had never seen before, matched the colors of the trees. Rachel shifted her gaze to the ground before she froze solid.

Arka spoke quietly, as if in a library. "Artemis, my apologies for disturbing the forest. It was not my intention. I require this girl for my quest. She is a seer."

"A seer?" Artemis flinched and loosed her arrow. It whizzed just past Arka, grazing her shoulder, and thudded into the tree trunk behind her.

Arka knew better than to move or comment that the great Artemis had mistakenly shot an arrow. Although her shoulder stung fiercely, she kept her poise and before she could blink, Artemis had another arrow knocked and drawn.

"Is this true?" asked Artemis. Her body relaxed a hair's breadth, but her arm muscles were still a taut extension of the bowstring.

Rachel realized the question was for her, and she risked a glance at the hostile goddess. Her skin was a deep sepia a few shades darker than Rachel's, that melded perfectly with the forest. Rachel nodded.

Artemis lowered her weapon, inspecting Rachel with her stormy eyes, leaning close. "The last seer was struck blind by Athena. Impertinence often ends poorly for mortals." She lowered her voice to a whisper, but every word hit their mark. "He maintains his gift of prophecy, in the Underworld, and is rarely sought out by the gods. It is a lonely existence."

Rachel's lip quivered. She didn't want to end up like the last seer.

Arka exhaled heavily. "We are leaving Artemis, and won't be returning. I vow our quest is honorable and once we're gone, the monsters will move on."

Artemis pursed her full lips. "I will allow your departure if the seer tells me her name."

Both goddesses looked at Rachel expectantly.

"Um. My name is Rachel Soarenson?"

"Do you not know your name? Are you toying with me mortal?" Artemis shifted her weight onto her back foot in a fighting stance.

"No! I mean, yes, I know my name. It's Rachel, I promise. And No, I would never toy with, or lie to you." Rachel crossed her heart.

The promise satisfied Artemis and she tilted her chin in acceptance. Straightening, she looked dangerously at Arka. "I shall dispose of the foul creatures hunting you." She dipped her head slightly toward Rachel. "Remember my kindness, Seer Rachel."

Rachel stood wide eyed until Arka kicked her with the heel of her boot. "Er, I will. Thank you too, lady goddess."

Artemis took three silent steps backward, never taking her eyes off them, and disappeared into the trees, expertly camouflaged. Arka resumed working on the gateway, grimacing at her stinging shoulder.

Rachel turned her petrified stare on her. "What in the world?! And here I thought *you* were too serious."

"Artemis is goddess of the hunt, forests, and protector of children. She is Apollo's twin and the daughter of Zeus. It would be prudent for you to show respect when in the presence of immortals Rachel, she could have ended the quest."

Rachel wiped sweaty palms on her jeans and whistled. "She's for sure the real deal. Are all goddesses and gods so terrifying?"

"Yes, and no. You gave your name to her, be prepared for her to call on you."

"What?! I'm at her beck and call?"

"It is your destiny to help the gods, Rachel."

Rachel reached up, pulling a handful of dried leaves off the overhanging tree branch above their heads. "That's all I need, another wackadoo immortal bossing me around." She crumpled the leaves in frustration and threw them on the ground.

"Be careful. I have known Artemis to shoot people for less offenses than disfiguring her trees."

"Whatever," said Rachel, but she stood over the fallen leaves, hiding the evidence. "So, your actual name is Arkaeivahina hu? That's a mouthful. I can see why you shortened it."

"It's not up for discussion," Arka said, stepping through her gateway, vanishing on the spot.

"Okay. Sorry I brought it up." The leaves rustled overhead, and Rachel glanced around. "Everyone has a disappearing trick except me," she grumbled and held her breath, cautiously following Arka's footsteps.

Chapter 14: Teamwork

Arka wouldn't tell Rachel exactly where they were. "In case you get captured," she reasoned. "You can't tell an enemy what you didn't know."

It made sense, but it made Rachel grumpy. "Whatever," she said, guessing they were somewhere North because it was freezing. Shivering in the cold also made her grumpy.

Arka pulled two fur-lined capelets from her bag and handed one to Rachel. "Here, put this on and stop glowering at me."

Appreciating how the short poncho covering instantly blocked the cold, Rachel shimmied. "We're cape wearing super twins!" she said sarcastically.

Arka stared blankly at her.

"Fine. We're still quest partners who keep secrets from each other. Is that more accurate for you?"

Arka ignored the barb, pointing past Rachel. "That's why we are here," she said. "It's a pretty big secret."

The girls stood at the base of a flat toped mountain dusted with snow. Rachel frowned skyward. "Are you sure a god lives here?"

"Yes, I am certain. When I lived with my sisters, I could see whatever they did when they used the eye. They keep tabs on Harpocrates. It took me a while to locate his mountain but, I'm sure." She sized it up. "It is no Mt. Olympus, but it is formidable."

"Won't they see us here?" asked Rachel, twitching her shoulders unconsciously, ruffling the capelet.

"No. My sisters watch him, in case he decides to leave, but they cannot see the specific goings-on at his mountain. This god literally cannot share secrets. If he does, he'll be cast into Tartarus." She paused, allowing the weight of that statement to sink in. Tartarus was no laughing matter to Arka. It was the worst fate imaginable to an immortal.

"To safeguard himself from that doom, there is a fog that surrounds this mountain if anyone looks too closely at it. It aids with guarding secrets, like the ones you're so worried about, and it keeps him from venturing out."

"Well, are you going to teleport us to the top?"

"I will do no such thing," said Arka indignantly.

"Why not? You don't expect me to hike up there." Rachel craned her neck back to see how far it was to the top.

"There is always a trial or journey before one can seek an audience with a god."

Rachel scowled. "Of course there is."

Halfway up the mountain, the girls paused to rest and eat lunch. Rachel flopped onto a rock and sullenly munched on a piece of cheese. Mid-day sun shining off the snow, plus food in her belly, barely lifted her spirits. She tipped up her face toward the sunlight, and cringed at Arka's especially loud chewing on a dried ambrosia cake.

For a goddess, she is seriously lacking in table manners, thought Rachel. "Can you chew with your mouth closed, please?" she snapped.

"Excuse me?" said Arka, annoyed with Rachel's excessive complaining. The day was only halfway through, and she had complained about everything! The hike, the cold, the encounter with Artemis, the monsters, the quest, her new abilities, her feet, the list was endless! Arka didn't know how much more she could stand. She fixed a stern look on her face, about to give Rachel a piece of her mind, but hesitated when Rachel's eyes grew round with fear.

The cheese Rachel was holding fell from her hands, plopping into the dirty snow at her feet, and she whispered in a strangled voice, "Bear!"

Arka spun around, her braid whipping like a propeller. The sound had been coming from a giant grizzly bear sniffing loudly in their direction. Arka rose from the rock she'd been sitting on and faced the bear, her chest high and arms puffed out to the sides. She reminded Rachel of a gunslinger from the old west about to have a shootout.

The bear rose on its hind legs, meeting Arka's challenge. Arka stretched to her full goddess height to counter it. The bear's ears jerked back, and it snapped its teeth, huffing loudly.

Rachel trembled all over, shakily counting four beats in her head to avoid puking. She was sure the bear was about to charge when Arka spoke in a commanding voice.

"Go away from this place! I command thee!" She jerked an arm toward the trees a short distance from the trail they'd been using, pointing with a force that pushed air and light in that direction. "GO!"

The bear dropped to all fours and swung its heavy head in

the direction Arka pointed. Its giant nose twitched once, then it plodded off as directed, leaving behind giant paw prints in the white powdered snow.

Rachel's mouth hung open.

"Close your mouth, Rachel. I can see your chewed-up food. Honestly, you were scolding me on manners only one minute ago."

Rachel clamped her mouth shut and swallowed. "What was that?! You just told a *bear* what to do, and it listened!"

Arka felt flattered at the admiration, but pretended it didn't faze her. "All gods and goddesses have some influence over creatures and the elements of your world. Artemis isn't the only one who can sway animals."

"Well, it's impressive. I wish I could do that. It was all I could do to not vomit! Or poop my pants!"

"You better not Rachel, so help me!" Arka danced on the balls of her feet, ready to spring away if given even the slightest warning Rachel would explode. "Mortals are so vulgar!"

"Relax," said Rachel, rolling her eyes. "I was just joking." She looked at her wasted cheese on the ground and blew warm breath on her fingers. "Mostly."

"Are all your jokes so awkward?"

"I'm not awkward, you're just stiff." Rachel didn't think it was possible, but Arka's steel rod spine straightened further.

"It's called poise," said Arka, cleaning up their picnic.

Rachel lifted an eyebrow. "I can think of something else it's called, but my mamma wouldn't like it."

"Break is over. Let's go."

"I'm just being honest! What? Now you're telling me your farts don't stink? Friends should be honest, Arka." Arka looked so horrified that Rachel couldn't help but laugh.

105

"Flatulence is not a proper topic of conversation," said Arka, her back stiffer than ever. She headed up the trail, determined to maintain her dignity.

"Wait!" Rachel ran after her, slipping once, but regained her footing by hopping clumsily. "Aren't bears supposed to be hibernating right now?"

"Yes. Obviously, someone is trying to block the path to Harpocrates. It could even be him."

"Oh. Right. *Obviously.* I forgot nothing is normal anymore." Rachel kicked a rock and her icy toes crunched. "Ow," she said, her grumpy attitude settling in again.

Arka gritted her teeth.

The last part of their hike was a scramble up crumbly shards of shale rocks. Arka nimbly climbed the rest of the way and monitored Rachel's progress from her perch atop the mountain.

Rachel lost her footing, spilling grey shards down the mountainside. She cried out in alarm, laying her body flat against the mudstone rocks. "Arka! I can't do this!"

"Yes, you can. Don't give up."

Refusing to look down, Rachel swallowed hard and pressed on. She slipped several more times, bruising her knees, but she finally made it to the top.

"I knew you could do it," said Arka cheerfully, the tip of her nose pink with cold.

Rachel glared at her, her cheeks puffing as she sucked in the thin air and rubbed feeling into her frozen hands.

The girls took in the view for a moment, and it gave Rachel time to catch her breath. The valley was gorgeous. There were no buildings of any kind, only forests and hills, stretching for miles in every direction. The leaves had long since fallen from the trees and their branches stood out like spikes, warding off enemy attacks. Rachel felt small in the middle of the wilderness, but she couldn't help being amazed at the sheer vastness of it all. She supposed Arka was right in not telling her where they were, but she would never admit that to the goddess. She could be so smug, and Rachel wasn't about to give her more to lord over her with.

When the sun was just about to dip below the horizon, and the shadows of the defensive trees stretched long, Arka instructed Rachel to stand next to her in a certain spot and she pulled a piece of soft leather from her capelet pocket. Something was written on it, but she pulled it away when Rachel tried to see.

"I'm just curious. What does it say?" asked Rachel, stifling a yawn, suddenly weary.

"I'm sorry if our quest is boring you."

"It's not! I'm just *tired*, Arka. It's been a long day, and it's not like your sleeping arrangements were the best last night."

Arka took in Rachel's appearance. Wrinkled clothes, with the knees of her jeans torn and covered head to toe with dirt and damp patches from the snow. Her curly hair was a dark ball of frizz with a twig sticking out of it and her round chin had a dark smudge on one side.

Arka scolded herself silently. Exceptions would have to be made while working with a mortal child. Plus, they were friends. She reached up and pulled the little twig from Rachel's hair, relenting a little. "It is an ancient song written by a faun. Legend says the oldest and wisest faun wrote these words on his own body, and it has been passed down in secrecy ever since. The keeper of the song will write the words on themselves and only pass it on if they are about to die. Their identity is unknown, even among the fauns. They are renowned songwriters, you know."

Rachel stared at the piece of leather, aghast. "That's a faun's hide? Gross!" Bile rose in her throat and she fought to keep it down.

Arka almost dropped the poem. "No! I shaved him while he was sleeping and copied the poem on this. Leather keeps better and lasts longer than paper. Good heavens Rachel, how cruel do you think I am?"

"I don't know! You've got me out here hiking in the cold. You really freaked me out for a second," said Rachel, relieved. Then she giggled. "I'm sure the faun wasn't happy about his haircut."

"Oh, no. He was furious when he woke up!" Arka snickered. "Now he always has bodyguards on hand. He did look hilarious though." She snorted at the memory, and they both laughed out loud.

Rachel eyed Arka sideways. "Do you use your weave of hiding to spy on people often?"

"When I have to." Arka sniffed. "Okay, let's do this." Standing tall and holding the song up with ceremony, she quoted the lines in ancient Greek.

Nothing happened.

"You said fauns write songs, Arka. If that's a song, maybe you should sing it."

"Don't make fun of me."

"I wouldn't dream of it," said Rachel with a grin.

Arka sang the lines this time, shyly at the beginning but lifting in the middle, her warm alto voice echoing across the mountaintop. She glanced at Rachel but didn't have time to be embarrassed because a gigantic step sank into the center of the mountain top, blowing up a dusty ice storm all around them.

"Thanks for the suggestion, Rachel!" said Arka excitedly.

"I can't believe that worked!"

They high fived and Arka stopped short, suddenly awkward.

"Did we just high five? I've never done that before."

"Just roll with it. It's a common thing for teammates."

"We really are a team, then?"

"Well, yeah. I'm up here, aren't I? Don't get all mushy on me again. It's getting dark and I don't want to be stuck out here all night."

Arka nodded curtly, clamping down the emotions welling inside her. She had always been excluded from the teamwork her sisters did. Being accepted like this was new territory for Arka, and it felt good.

They both peered over the rim. The lowered step revealed a hole that dropped straight down into the center of the mountain.

"There's only one step, Arka," said Rachel flatly. "I am not about to see if this capelet gives me flying abilities. Nu uh. Nope."

"Come on," said Arka encouragingly, and she stepped down into the darkness.

"Easy for you to say, you're a walking flashlight." Rachel carefully stepped down onto the landing, staying close to Arka.

One at a time, the next step sunk down in front of them as the one behind disappeared into dust. When their heads were below the surface, the top of the mountain sealed up and they stood quietly on a single platform jutting from the side of the cavernous sinkhole. It was pitch black.

Rachel realized Arka wasn't emanating light. "What's wrong, Arka?" she asked, panic rising in her voice.

"No one can help us if we get stuck in here," she whispered. Arka didn't know why she was whispering, but it felt safer to do so. "We are sealed in completely, so no secrets can get out."

"Or people," said Rachel under her breath, and she clutched the back of Arka's capelet, bunching the hem as they crept cautiously down into the musty depth.

They continued like that, forever creeping step by stone step down into the mountain before a soft glow finally appeared from the bottom of the pit. Relieved to be off the perpetual escalator, the girls stepped onto solid bedrock. The last step retracted, leaving them standing like petrified fossils inside the dank tomb.

A soft hum shook the cavern and just as steps had grown from the inside of the mountain, the very rock they stood on rumbled, and a massive monolith stone slab rose in front of them. A solid door hung in a doorframe of cemented rubble, a proud centerpiece, daring them to proceed.

Rachel walked around it once. "There's nothing behind here. Should we knock?"

The stone door scraped open, scattering debris at their feet.

Rachel gasped, jumping back. She hid behind Arka, peering over her shoulder, and both girls braced themselves.

An old man with a white beard stretching to the floor emerged. His robe, embroidered with thorny rose vines dragged along the ground behind him. The girls exhaled at the same time.

Rachel had expected something resplendent, not a feeble grandpa. This guy looked like a harmless street magician. Her lip curled, what was it with these gods and dirt floors?

"I see there is a question on your mind," said Harpocrates.

Rachel started, hearing his deep voice reverberate off the walls. She licked her lips. "Um, I was just wondering why you and Arka like dirt floors," she said honestly. Rachel felt if she made something up, he would know.

"It's what keeps us grounded." It sounded like a joke, but he was completely serious.

Rachel kept a blank face. Did he know about her conversation with Arka? She was suddenly uncomfortable. Harpocrates stared at her with haunting black eyes overhung with fuzzy caterpillar eyebrows.

"What is your name, child?" he asked, never blinking, his black eyes growing larger, bulging out of their sockets until he resembled a giant bug that wanted to gobble her up. Rachel shrank back, pulling her fingers, popping two knuckles, and her eyes darted to Arka, begging for help.

Arka cleared her throat. "Greetings Harpocrates. I am Arka, goddess and fourth Fate of the Tapestry, and this is my quest assistant. We have come to seek your counsel," she said formally.

"Make yourselves comfortable," Harpocrates said, equally formal, granting them entrance with the wave of an arm. He stepped aside so they could see through the doorway. A collection of stone furniture surrounded a stone banquet table set with food inside the dimly lit chamber. A stagnant scent tinged with mildew floated up to Rachel's nose.

Who on earth would want to eat down here trapped with this guy? Rachel couldn't fathom it. Harpocrates snapped his head around and she winced, clamping a hand over her mouth even though she hadn't said anything.

Arka seemed nonplussed by his off-putting scrutiny and waltzed across the threshold, dropping her pack in a heavy chair.

"Thank you," Rachel said too loudly and cringed when her voice bounced off the walls. She skirted around Harpocrates and his creepy eyes, sitting rigidly at the table next to Arka.

The door closed on its own, locking them inside the seamless crypt and Arka got straight to the point. "Harpocrates, we have come to seek your help with finding a powerful artifact."

"I know the thing you seek," said Harpocrates. He chose a high-backed seat across from Arka, spreading the sleeves of his robe over the table and steepling crooked fingers under his chin as he folded into the chair. The chamber acted like a sound booth, completely sealed, dampening all noise. Even though she sat next to the deities, Rachel craned her neck to hear their muffled negotiations.

Harpocrates nonchalantly reached for a large chicken leg on a platter and took an enormous bite, letting the juice dribble down into his beard. "It is hidden. The item you seek is an arm cuff crafted by none other than Hephaestus." He smacked his lips and took another bite. "It is a beautiful accessory, yet also a powerful weapon. If placed on an immortal's arm, they will cease to have power and it will remain there until the one who put it on, removes it."

"That's smart," said Rachel, thinking out loud. "Like insurance, so they won't retaliate and kill you or something."

Arka shot a look at Rachel that said, shut up! Rachel waved her hand in apology and looked down at her lap.

"Would either of you care to eat?" asked Harpocrates, over pieces of chicken falling out of his full mouth.

"No thank you, Harpocrates," declined Arka gracefully. "We already ate. We just need the location of the artifact."

Rachel covered her mouth with a fist, repulsed by Harpocrates' eating. She tried not to think about it, or look at him.

"Indeed." Harpocrates tossed the chicken leg, reduced to a large bone, onto his plate. It clattered loudly in the silence, making Rachel jump in her seat. He reached for a pitcher.

"Perhaps a drink?"

"Thank you, but no."

Harpocrates banged the pitcher down on the table.

Rachel squeaked. His annoyance at their not eating frightened her, and she wanted out of there before he got angry.

Harpocrates' wrinkled face strained. "The Cuff of Capture lies in a basin of acidic saliva taken from the Ladon Dragon."

Arka leaned over to whisper in Rachel's ear. "That's the multiple headed dragon who guarded the golden apples Hercules was supposed to steal."

Rachel nodded, murmuring, "I know the story." She wasn't thrilled about more monster spit though. "How are we supposed to get something out of a pool of acid drool?" The very thought was disgusting, made worse by sloppy old man withers eating dinner in front of them.

Arka rubbed her forehead, embarrassed by Rachel's volume and candidness in the presence of deities. She hoped it wouldn't anger Harpocrates to the point of refusing to help them.

"Anything that touches the liquid will be dissolved. Nothing can reach the cuff, save the Glove of Righteousness," he said. Rachel began to ask another question but Harpocrates held up a crooked finger capped with a dirty fingernail to silence her. He rose and shuffled to a cupboard, unlocking it with a key hanging from his bony wrist, and pulled out a shiny glove.

It looked like a long kitchen glove that had been dipped in silver chrome and sprinkled with glitter. It was rather ridiculous, in Rachel's opinion. It reminded her of dress-up clothes her little sister loved to play with. Rachel's heart twinged painfully at the thought of her sister and she shifted in her seat, bumping the table.

"Get it together!" whispered Arka angrily.

"Take this glove. Go to the Crystal Cave in Bermuda and find the room only a god," he tilted his head toward Arka, "or goddess can enter."

"Like the Bermuda Triangle?" asked Rachel.

Arka made a noise in her throat.

"Yes," said Harpocrates quickly, his eyes flashing.

That was weird, Rachel thought. He'd answered her as if he were up to something. Her eyebrows creased in the middle and she squinted at him. "You can't tell anyone where we're going, right?"

Arka hissed at her through clenched teeth, gripping the arms of her chair with white knuckles. If she ruins this opportunity, I'll cut her life thread myself! She thought, nearly unhinged.

Harpocrates smiled. "Your quest is safe with me. Be well." He waved a hand dismissively and the stone door creaked open in slow motion.

Arka stood, quickly gathering their things, and didn't see his smile turn wicked. Rachel jolted to her feet, knocking over a cup, spilling dingy water on the table. It dripped over the edge, soaking into the ground below. Arka glared at her, furious at her clumsy behavior and lack of manners.

Harpocrates extended his hand to shake Arka's before she crossed back over the threshold and Rachel held her breath. Nothing happened. He gifted her with the glove, she secured it in her bag and walked through the doorway without incident.

Rachel panicked when the door began to inch close. No way was she going to be trapped underground with this guy! She power walked to the door, choosing to bow awkwardly instead of shaking Harpocrates' extended skeletal hand. As she side-stepped past him, Harpocrates caught Rachel's hand in a shot before she could scoot past.

The vision struck her hard, like a title wave. Rachel was floating in salt water, but she wasn't wet. Her eyes stung, as she tried to make out blurry figure in front of her. It was Arka and something was sneaking up behind her. Rachel tried to shout a warning, but ocean water flooded her mouth.

Rachel blinked, and found herself back in the belly of the mountain with the god of secrets staring at her, transfixed. A slow grin crinkled his already weathered skin, showing chipped teeth. Rachel pulled her hand away, backing up several paces and jump-squeezed through the last bit of opening left in the doorway. She glanced over her shoulder at Harpocrates through the crack, and her heart lodged in her throat. He was still grinning at her like a psychopath, his eyes enlarging like a mutant fly, and she swore his canine teeth elongated into fangs before the stone door boomed shut, spewing dust at her.

The mountain steps reappeared, rumbling up the inside wall, a domino staircase to freedom. A sneeze burst from Rachel's lungs, echoing in racketing thunder, propelling her forward. She beelined up the giant steps, pushing past Arka, ignoring her shout, grateful to be out of the bug-eyed god's presence.

Bursting into the frigid night sky brilliant with stars, Rachel sucked in a huge refreshing breath. She'd never been so thankful to smell fresh air in her life! Never mind that the cold air turned her nose hairs into tiny icicles.

Arka stomped up the last remaining steps to join Rachel atop the mountain. "Are you claustrophobic, or just insane?!" she shouted at Rachel, her anger boiling over like a forgotten pot on the stove. The ground trembled, emphasizing her temper, and coughed up more dust, swirling with snow before returning to normal.

"It *was* stifling down there, but Arka, did the god of secrets seem odd to you? Like sinister?" Rachel's heart slowly returned to a normal beat, and the cold seeped in. She pulled her hands inside her capelet, holding them against the soft fur for warmth.

Arka clicked her tongue. "Harpocrates is a very eccentric god. I think being alone for so long has made him a little strange. Sometimes he asks for rare or impossible items in exchange for his help and silence," she sniffed, "in fact, it was odder he asked nothing of us. Especially after you were so offensive!"

"I wasn't trying to be! I'm telling you something isn't right, Arka. I had a vision when he grabbed my hand. Someone is hunting you."

"We already know that."

"Did you see his eyes? Or his crazy teeth?"

"Rachel. I know being near Greek deities is new for you. You must remember that we alter our appearance around mortals. Some of us look like you, others take on strange characteristics."

"Yeah, but . . . "

"Did you get any *useful* information from your vision?"

Rachel stepped back, stung. "I'm sorry. I'll keep that in mind next time."

Arka shrugged. "You're going to have to figure out how to control your ability if it's going to be any good." She brushed past Rachel, making her way to the edge of the mountain top. It was going to be a rough climb down at night.

"I know what your problem is, you don't like that I've been a big sister my whole life and you've been a baby sister. You can't take advice from anyone, can you?"

"How dare you call me a baby, I do not have juvenile tendencies! That's your area of expertise."

"But your sisters treated you like that, Right? Didn't include you, told you what to do, even spurned you? Now you're a control freak. Look, I'm not trying to tell you what to do. I'm not like them, I just think we should look at all the variables okay?"

"Let's go."

Rachel tossed her head. "See, there you go again, shutting down our conversation because you don't like it. It bothers me!"

Arka bared her teeth. "Fine! What do you suggest?"

"Maybe some kind of test for this god of secrets, or for that glove thing. I mean, what are his motives for helping us?"

"Absolutely not."

"But . . ."

"No! You need to learn how to respect those in authority over you. That's what the problem is."

"I have respect, just not reverence for super beings who meddle with people's lives. I think you feel the same when you're not acting so stuck up!"

Arka's eyes narrowed dangerously. "I am in charge and you'll do as I say."

Rachel straightened up defiantly, her eyes shining bright in the dark. "The Creator is in charge, Arka. You even said so, or have you forgotten that?"

"No."

"Then we should ask what He wants," said Rachel, desperate to persuade Arka. She joined her at the edge of the mountain top, feeling dizzy when she looked over the edge into the night shadows below. "Think about it."

"This is my quest, and I'm the one who will see it through. You are a child with a lot to learn about the universe."

"I'm not the one acting like a child."

Arka's hands shook with restraint. It was by sheer will she managed not to slap Rachel. Without saying another word, she took a step over the ledge, sending rock shards tumbling down into darkness.

"I'm not climbing down this mountain Arka. We just hiked up it and climbed a million stairs. It's too dark, my legs are tired, I'm freezing and I'm not about to break my neck for *your* quest." Rachel clenched her teeth to keep them from chattering. "I know you can teleport us."

"It's not teleporting. It's stepping," said Arka, chipping the words like a chisel at an ice block.

"Whatever." Rachel stomped her feet to keep the blood flowing. She couldn't feel her toes and the tips of her ears burned with cold.

"Very well." Arka knelt next to the ledge and started a gateway weave, her braid falling over her shoulder, the tail skimming the snow. "I'll take us somewhere in the woods to sleep."

Rachel shook her head, but she was too cold and exhausted to argue anymore. What did it even matter? She was just the assistant, and it was clear Arka only wanted her around to use her abilities. Apparently, if her visions weren't useful, neither was she.

A bright sphere of light appeared between Arka's hands. She fanned her fingers in a delicate pattern, making the light grow in height and width. Soon an arch tall enough for them to walk through was shining into the night like a lighthouse beacon. "Ready?"

Rachel slumped through the archway and vanished.

"You're welcome!" Arka rose, dusting off her snow-crusted knees. Having a mortal child as a quest companion was taxing! Seer or not, she rankled Arka. This journey was turning out to be harder than she'd originally thought.

Chapter 15: Bermuda

Off season in Bermuda was perfect temperature compared to the freezing forest Rachel had been forced to camp in. The only thing that wasn't pleasant in this paradise was the humidity. Damp air settled in her lungs like thick pudding as Rachel leaned against an outer wall adjacent to the Washington Mall entrance, politely asking passersby for spare change. Unfortunately, the sparse number of tourists ignored her.

Arka had tried making a gateway to the Crystal Caves entrance, but there was a barrier blocking her, and they'd ended up in Hamilton, the capital of Bermuda, a twenty-minute drive away. That had set Arka off in a foul mood. Compounded with Rachel's bruised feelings and winning morning attitude, their travel to a tropical haven was less than ideal. Rachel tried convincing Arka they could ask for cab fare, but she'd stormed off to find breakfast after arguing and refusing to beg for money.

Rachel changed her mind; the humidity was the second worst thing here. She pouted and fanned a fly away from her ear. A flashy couple exited the mall, and Rachel perked up, smiling.

"Can you spare some change please?"

The couple didn't even acknowledge her. They breezed past, floating off on their vacation, arms dripping with shopping bags. Rachel slumped back against the wall. Her shirt clung to her sweat stains, and she was filthy. She'd been so certain begging for money would be a cinch, but it'd been over an hour and she'd only earned one lonely Bermudian dollar and a gum wrapper. Not enough to rent a scooter, or cover bus fare, let alone rent a taxi. Sighing, she pushed frayed curls out of her face and refastened her ponytail. It's just one more thing I can't do right, she thought.

Arka appeared around the corner. "Have you received anything?" She thrust a bottle of orange juice and a poppyseed muffin at Rachel.

"Not enough," said Rachel, begrudgingly, wishing she could wave bus fare in Arka's smug face.

"It's just as I said. Mortals are notoriously selfish, and begging is a waste of time."

Rachel sat on the curb, devouring every last crumb of the muffin and licked the paper wrapper clean, chasing it with the tangy juice. "Yeah. Thanks for your help and great problem-solving skills," said Rachel, swallowing the last gulp of juice and stifling a burp.

Arka sniffed, affronted. "I have provided sustenance and shelter."

"Outstanding job."

"What is your problem?"

Rachel squinted up at Arka. She wasn't disheveled, and the heat hadn't affected *her* appearance in any way. Her braid was perfectly coiffed, she was clean and crisp as usual, with her pleasant aura hovering all around her. "You, Arka. You are my problem," said Rachel, her face pinching. She picked a poppy seed out of a tooth and flicked it away.

Arka puffed up. "What have I done? You're the one who's been difficult!"

"Well, you're the one who gets mad all the time and storms off, leaving me behind! Grow up!" Rachel threw her empty juice bottle at Arka, who caught it easily, her reflexes sharp. The plastic cracked in her grip, her aura blazing.

"How dare you!"

A police officer approached them from the mall's entrance.

"Excuse me, ladies. I have to ask you to move this squabble elsewhere." He pointed to the security cameras, indicating he'd been watching their show. "You're disturbing the customers."

Arka's eyes flashed.

"Yes, sir," said Rachel, "sorry."

The officer tipped his hat. "Family arguments are normal, but we want to be respectful to the business owners and patrons here."

Rachel stood up, her muscles stiff. "She's not my family."

The officer looked between the two girls. "I assumed you were related, cousins or step-sisters or something, the way you were arguing."

"Sisters?" Arka scoffed, "I think not!"

"Well, you two need to clear off."

"We are," said Rachel, and she walked into the parking lot, shaking her head. I'm so done. Arka's the worst! I need to find a way to get home. Rachel looked around, considering her options weaving between the sporadic cars.

"Where do you think you're going?" Arka trotted after her.

"Anywhere that's away from you."

"Why are you acting so ridiculous? We have the Glove of

Righteousness! I admit we've had a setback, and it frustrated me we couldn't step to the caves, but we will find the Cuff of Capture. We're so close!"

"You go find it, Arka. I'm going home." Rachel was through with quests, uptight gods, stepping through gateways, and camping. She could not stomach camping one more day! She wanted a shower and clean clothes. She wanted to go home and be normal again.

"You can't leave! You've agreed to help me and you're a seer!"

"Yeah? Well, being your sidekick sucks!" Rachel spun around, her nostrils flaring. "You don't care about me; you're just using me! You are rude and bossy, and I don't want to be here anymore!" She shoved Arka away from her, but Arka stepped out of reach, and Rachel fell to her knees. She covered her face with her hands, crying loudly into them, cupping the snot and angry tears that ran into her palms.

Arka glanced around awkwardly, checking to see if anyone saw the meltdown. A few people were looking their way, and the cop was making his way toward them again. "Rachel, we have to go."

"No!"

Arka pulled on Rachel's arm. "Come on! There's no time for hysterics."

A shrill cackle split Rachel's eardrum. The laugh echoed through her cells and a seizure shook her entire body. Arka caught her before Rachel fell to the ground completely.

"Rachel!" Arka thumbed her eyelids open, but Rachel's eyes had rolled up into her head and she flopped like a fish on dry land. Arka hooked her arms under Rachel's armpits and dragged her behind the rusted bumper of a nearby car. She rolled Rachel onto her side so she wouldn't choke on her tongue. Fear gripped Arka like she'd never felt before. "Rachel!" She patted her cheek, trying to wake her from the convulsion.

A loud snarl snapped Arka's attention back to the parking lot. A crocotta was sniffing around the front tire of the car. The massive hyena creature followed their scent to the spot where Rachel had melted into a puddle. It licked the pavement, scratching its grey, sandpaper tongue along the ground, tasting its prey. It shuddered and laughed, high and clanky. The laugh was answered by three more of its pack, a cacophony of crazed laughter bouncing off all the cars, setting off their alarms. A piercing headache split Arka's head and Rachel flopped violently.

Arka clamped her hands over Rachel's ears and her eyes fluttered open. She tried to pull away, but the urgent look Arka shot her, stopped Rachel's fighting. Arka willed Rachel to understand that she needed her hands back.

Rachel focused on Arka's face, hovering in front of her own, and slowly covered her hands over Arka's in double sandwiched earmuffs. She knew in her gut she needed to protect her ears.

Arka drew her hands out from under Rachel's, the switch complete, and placed a finger over her lips, cueing Rachel to remain silent. Then she pointed under the car.

Rachel craned her neck back and saw a black nose the size of a softball snuffling around. Terror coursed through her veins, popping them out of her neck and she silently screamed at Arka. "What is that?!" her mouth moved, without sound.

There was no time for Arka to respond. The beast leapt onto the car, the metal roof creaking under its weight, the windows cracking into spiderwebs. With a snarl it pounced onto the spot where the girls hunkered down, jaws open wide to scoop them into its hungry mouth.

Rachel's hands still covered her ears, but her scream was blasting. Arka yanked her by the shoulders and they rolled sideways falling through a gateway Arka'd made a hair above the ground just as the monster's jaws snapped, missing them by a breath.

They fell through the air, onto a white sanded beach, and waves rolled up to greet them, misting Rachel's face. It surprised her so much, her scream cut off.

Arka tugged hard on the threads she'd used, pulling the gateway seam closed just as the beast leapt at it. One of its paws got caught in the fabric of space as it synched closed, squeezing tighter and tighter. The paw separated from the leg with a sickening pop! and fell onto the sand next to Rachel's head. Her screaming started up again.

Arka grabbed the paw, her heart still running a marathon and she flung it, avoiding the claws, like a furry frisbee soaring into the ocean where it splashed, instantly becoming shark food.

Rachel wretched into the sand, a mushy orange juice-muffin concoction stinging her throat and sinuses with blazing force. Her stomach heaved a second time, sending the fiery spray out her nose and mouth once more. She spat the last chunks out and curled in ball, white sand sticking to her lips and chin.

"That's disgusting! I stole that breakfast for you, and now you've regurgitated it all over the beach," Arka complained. "It's disrespectful and revolting. What am I supposed to do with you?"

"Shut up, shut up, shut up!" Rachel shouted over the ocean, her hands still clamped over her ears. "I hate you!"

Arka was so taken aback her aura dimmed faint against the light sand, causing it to turn brown and lifeless under her feet. "I thought we were friends."

"Yeah, well, friends encourage each other and help each other."

"Did I not just save our lives?"

"You say mean things all the time!" Rachel rolled away, still curled in the fetal position.

Arka searched her heart, watching a seagull circling out over the water before diving in for lunch. It was true. She had treated Rachel poorly, the very way her wicked sisters had treated her. Arka vowed silently to do better. She walked around and squatted in front of Rachel. "Sorry."

"What was that thing?!"

Arka glowered at her, rethinking her vow.

Rachel took the hint, and lowered hands, using one to wipe sticky sand off her chin.

"That was a crocotta. It's a dog-like creature that can gulp a man down in one bite."

"I didn't see any teeth."

"It doesn't chew you; it swallows you whole. Prey dissolves in its stomach, boiling alive in the acid." She made a face at the sick spot absorbed in the sand. "It can also mimic a person's voice, and I think its laugh caused a violent reaction in you." Arka did not admit how much it scared her, seeing Rachel's eyes rolled back in her head like a corpse. "Its pack is hunting us."

Rachel threw her arms up. "See! I told you something was hunting you!"

"I'm sorry, okay!" said Arka, her voice rising despite her effort to stay calm. "I'm not used to taking advice or working as a team, or any of those things." She dusted sand off her pants. "My intent isn't to use you, per se, but I do intend to hone your abilities, so that they are an asset. For your sake, as well as mine."

Rachel stood, stone faced and empty. She needed structure and everything was a mess! She looked out over the water. "I don't know if I can do this," she breathed. The ebb and flow of the waves washed the fight within her out to sea with the tide. "I don't really hate you, Arka. This is just so wild and convoluted. I mean, this is more complicated than honors algebra!" She rubbed her elbow, feeling a bruise swelling. "At least with math I can follow a formula and things work out the way they're supposed to. I'm good at it, ya know? But I don't think I'm any good at being a seer."

"Life is indeed more complicated than mathematical equations," said Arka, stepping back from a sweeper wave to avoid her boots getting wet. "We all have things we are not naturally good at. We must work at them to get better, and even then, it may not come easy." She smiled softly. "You didn't always know the formulas. And considering all you've been through; you have grown exponentially in a short time. Give yourself some credit."

"I just want it to work out, to be perfect, but I don't know how to do anything."

"Perfection is impossible, Rachel. Even with plans and formulas. I'd say it's the imperfections in the tapestry that make it so beautiful." Arka started to take a deep breath but thought better of it, breathing through her mouth instead. She followed Rachel's gaze, watching the waves crest. "I cannot swim," she said, offering a bit of vulnerability in a truce.

"Really?"

Arka shrugged and dug in the bag she always wore, handing out a tissue to Rachel. It blew in the breeze, a white flag of surrender. "I commend your willingness to show up and try. I know it can't be easy for you."

"Thanks."

Arka grunted in a 'don't mention it again' way.

Rachel wiped her mouth and hands. "Where are we anyway?"

"As far North on the island as I could get us," Arka said, frustrated she couldn't link a gateway inside the Crystal Cave. Another god had set boundary lines in place, and it was maddening.

"So, we still have to figure out how to get to the caves from here?"

"We will. Together," said Arka.

Rachel smiled. "Together."

Chapter 16: Swim Lesson Fail

Walking on sandy beaches sounds exotic, but it's difficult for long periods of time. Rachel took off her shoes after discovering sand had rubbed raw blisters on her heel. She let the warm sand squish between her toes, trailing her footprints in the water's edge, but they'd walked for over an hour and she wilted in the late morning sun.

Arka rambled on about her plan after they located the Cuff of Capture.

"We don't have the cuff yet," said Rachel, forcing her noodle legs to keep walking.

"A mere formality," retorted Arka, marching on, pressing deep boot prints in the sand.

"Arka."

"What?"

"The way you just blew me off, makes me feel unimportant."

Arka paused, eyes flitting to the clear sky. She'd saved them from a monster attack, apologized, smoothed things over, and still, Rachel found something to complain about! Arka was trying hard to be a team player, sharing her plans and seeking input. She would never admit it, but Rachel's accusations had shaken her. It bothered her to think she was behaving like her sisters. Even if it was only the tiniest bit. "Okay then. What do you suggest?" she asked and told herself she would listen.

"Lunch."

Arka snorted. It was a fabulous suggestion. Maybe listening to Rachel's opinions wasn't so bad after all. She pointed to a cluster of oceanfront bungalows built on the shore several yards ahead.

"We'll find something there."

They crept up to the nearest group of bungalows. Four quaint, one-room rentals were vacant, but the fifth one had its lights on. Arka peeped through the window. There was a bed, mini refrigerator and other furnishings all decked out with tropical flair. "I see suitcases, but there's no one inside."

"Maybe they packed snacks?" Rachel suggested, her tummy hopeful.

"Wait here and I'll sneak 'round."

"Why not just step inside with a gateway?"

Arka looked at the ground. "I don't want to risk making gateways so close to the barriers we've run into." It was hard to admit she couldn't use her power at will, and she suddenly had empathy for Rachel. "It could warp the strands I'm using and send us somewhere random," she said, feeling out of sorts.

"I'll wait for you then," said Rachel, unbothered that Arka couldn't use a gateway and content to sit down a while.

"Why don't you use this room? Shower and change while I forage for food?"

"Steal these people's things? I can't do that!"

"You'd take their snacks but not their belongings?"

"I'm starving, that's different."

Arka chuckled. "Think of it as just borrowing a few things. We can return them after our quest." Arka waggled her eyebrows and disappeared around the bungalow, reappearing inside, flicking the window's latch and lifting the pane. "Come on, it will do you good."

The shower was the most glorious Rachel had ever used in her life. A waterfall shower head rained down a steaming stream of water and Rachel watched dirt and grime swirl away down the drain, leaving her refreshed and renewed. The adorable complimentary shampoo smelled fruity, and the conditioner was coconutty. She left a little on the ends of her damp hair to moisturize and re-shape her neglected curls.

Rummaging in the suitcase felt wrong. Thankfully, there were clothes somewhat her size, but they were all festive vacation outfits. Rachel donned a pair of jeans with a belt and a tacky flower printed shirt with flouncy sleeves.

She pulled her hair up, glad to have it off her neck, and snagged a pen off the end table, poking it through the base of her ponytail. Rachel sighed, feeling somewhat human again. She found a man's duffle bag on the floor packed with practical socks she could use to cover her blisters. She'd shaken out her own socks, but the sand had moved in permanently. Rachel pulled on her shoes but paused double knotting the laces when she heard Arka faintly call her name. She listened hard. There it was again!

"Rachel!"

It sounded desperate. Rachel jumped up, upsetting the suitcase, dumping its contents all over the floor. She stepped over the heap to peer out the bamboo framed window. She saw no one. Rachel opened the front door a crack and peeked out. She heard Arka call her again, louder now, beyond the private pool for bungalow guests.

Rachel yanked a table lamp from the wall and crept outside, trotting to the pool deck, the lamp cord trailing behind her. The iron fence surrounding the swimming pool had its gate standing ajar. All the umbrellas were open, their blue canvas arms spread wide, welcoming the sun and providing relief to the empty reclining chairs surrounding the still water.

Where is everyone? Rachel thought, her breath quickening. This doesn't feel right.

A high-pitched cackle pierced her eardrums, shooting into her brain, making all the hairs on her arms stand on end as if lifted by a super magnet. Rachel fought an internal tremor and wave of nausea that accompanied it, willing herself to not pass out. She slowly turned around, gripping the lamp in both hands.

The devil hyena had tracked her from the mall. It's ears laid back and it lopped slowly toward her on three working legs. The fourth was tucked up under the creature's barrel chest, missing its paw. The stump still oozed, its edges crusted over with dried blood. The beast unhinged its shovel jaws, and its dark tongue rolled out the side. With its mouth opened wide, it tossed its head at her. "Rachel!" called Arka's voice from its throat.

Rachel stepped back, horrified. She was cornered, like a scared rabbit staring down a wolf. She knew running would only make it chase her. The crocotta laughed, taunting her, its maniac voice like nails on a chalkboard. Rachel held the lamp like a banner overhead, and covered one ear with her lifted shoulder. She slapped her free hand over the opposite ear, muffling the sound.

The beast snarled and snapped its vice mouth at her,

charging. Rachel felt her blood drain, but she held her ground. At the last moment, she javelined the lamp into the creature's hungry mouth, jarring its shrill laugh. It shook the obstruction ferociously, hacking and chomping down.

Rachel bolted around the edge of the pool, knocking over a standing umbrella and kicked a poolside chair into the crocotta's path. The creature spat out the mangled lamp, glaring at Rachel, and jumped over the obstacles in one bound, its claws clicking as it landed. It coiled its back legs and leapt at her, knocking Rachel to the hot cement, pinning her down. Rachel struggled under the crushing pressure of the enormous front paw. The crocotta unhinged its jaw, laughing, sending Rachel into a fit of convulsions and scooped her up like a fish on a hook.

"Rachel!" the real Arka shouted, running full throttle through the pool's gate, crashing into the crocotta before it devoured her. Rachel fell out of the thing's mouth, coming to her senses in a blind panic as the crocotta and Arka rolled past in a ball of light and patchy fur, splashing into the pool.

The crocotta yipped twice, pawing futilely at the water with its three working legs as its gaping whale mouth filled with chlorinated water, dragging it under. Bubbles sprayed out of its snout and Arka splashed manically, kicking it away from her. She gulped for air, sucking in a breath before her head also succumbed. She clawed at the water, just beneath its surface, her eyes wild.

"Arka!"

Rachel jumped in after Arka, her big sister instincts kicking in. She looped an arm around Arka's torso and pulled her head above water, paddling them to the side. "I've got you. You're okay."

Arka stopped thrashing when they reached the side.

Sputtering and coughing hard, she gripped the edge of the pool. "One, two, three four! One, two, three, four!"

"Hey-great job calming yourself down," said Rachel shakily.

Arka scowled, still fighting off terror from almost drowning.

"I'm not making fun of you Arka, I'm serious."

Although immortal, the pain of dying and reincarnating scared Arka. She bit her tongue, stubbornly refusing to use Rachel's counting technique again or show her feelings.

Clinging to the side of the pool, completely soaked through, the girls looked at each other and all pretenses fell away. They both laughed, overwhelmed with relief.

"That thing's breath stank so bad!" joked Rachel. She wiped her face, the smile there turning serious. "Thank you for saving me."

"Thank you too. For the rescue, and for teaching me about anxiety control." Arka was calm now, but still had a death grip on the edge of the pool.

"Can you monkey crawl to the ladder?" asked Rachel.

"I can do anything a simple primate can do," Arka replied tersely, secretly horrified a monkey knew how to exit a pool and she didn't. Gritting her teeth, Arka crawled hand over death-gripped hand along the wall to the metallic ladder bent into the disturbed water.

Rachel scissor kicked next to her and helped Arka get her feet on the ladder steps so she could climb out. Arka lifted out of the pool, tepid water pouring from her arms and legs, and looked over her shoulder at Rachel, still treading water. "Rachel, can I ask you something?"

"Sure."

Arka slogged out over the edge and sat down, facing her friend. "What in the world are you wearing?" she asked, taking in the obnoxious top Rachel had on, wicked glee sparkling in her eyes.

Rachel splashed Arka, right in her pixie grinning face.

Chapter 17: The Worst Vacation

Arka stood on a street corner, a scowl drawn on her face. Rachel hovered next to her, abashed. They'd found the hotel's buffet room and stuffed themselves full before Arka stole a taxi, posing as the driver, but they only made it two blocks.

Arka'd never driven a car and Rachel screamed at her the whole way! Admittedly, driving a manual car was more difficult than a motorcycle, but Rachel didn't have a permit. Or any sense in her head, thought Arka sourly, her ears still ringing.

"I'm sorry, Arka," said Rachel, standing uncomfortably on the dusty corner, studying her feet.

"What possessed you to grab me while I was driving?" Arka harrumphed. "Honestly! Choking your driver from the backseat is the fastest way to crash!"

They took stock of the taxi, ploughed over a fire hydrant now flooding the street and wedged under the car's front axle. Distant sirens promised help was on the way.

"We can't stay here," Rachel said, waving on a passing car. "People will ask too many questions."

"I'm sick of walking. I cannot believe you ruined our only mode of transportation!"

"I said I'm sorry! Walking is good for you," said Rachel thinly, fighting the urge to rub the throbbing blisters on her feet. She smiled, pretending the idea of walking didn't make her want to cry.

Arka stomped down the street, passing lush palm trees and hedges sprouting bright pink flowers without a glance, tightening her hands in vexation.

"Hey!" a stranger called, leaning out an upstairs window of the adjacent building, "you can't leave the scene of an accident!"

"I'll get her!" Rachel hollered back and jogged after Arka.

Arka picked up her pace.

Rachel sped up to catch her.

Both girls started sprinting down the street and the stranger shouted after them. His threats to call the police faded when they cut through an alleyway. After a few minutes of dodging through random streets lined with colorful buildings, they paused at the storefront of a cute boutique. Its window display was stuffed with floppy beach hats and sandals.

Winded, Rachel clutched a stitch in her side. "Great, now we're outlaws!" She scrubbed sweat from her forehead, creased with worry. "My parents will kill me if I get arrested!"

The corner of Arka's mouth pointed downwards. Rachel could be so dramatic! She was about to chastise the girl when she suddenly noticed how quiet it was. There were no people on the street. Arka glanced behind them. There wasn't a single tourist or local in sight. Everyone had disappeared. The hair on the back of her neck lifted, and she heard a far-off laugh of a crocotta. The rest of the pack was hunting them! Arka seized Rachel's arm. "Shhhh!" She dug a fresh tissue from her bag and ripped it up, stuffing small wads in her ears, and directed Rachel to do the same.

Shaking like a leaf, Rachel followed Arka up the deserted street with tufts of tissue sticking out of her ears. They communicated in whispers and exaggerated hand signals, darting from shop to shop like mice in a maze, checking every doorknob. They were all locked!

Rachel felt the monsters before she saw them. A heavy vibration buzzed through her limbs and she grabbed Arka's braid, tugging it in warning.

Arka whirled around, ready to punch Rachel. No was permitted to touch her hair, let alone pull it! But she saw the pack of rabid monsters behind them and understood the reason behind such an offense.

Three of the mangy beasts, all with mouths gaping wide, came around the corner following their scent. The closest one sniffed the air and spotted the girls, tilting its head and laughing. The other two joined in causing the air to shake in high, frenzied frequency.

There was no hiding now!

"Run!" Arka commanded, pulling at Rachel, who raced for all she was worth up the middle of the street. Arka was right behind her. "Left!" she shouted at the nearest corner, but Rachel felt compelled to turn right.

"This way!" Rachel shouted back, and she banked right, her arms pumping.

Arka slipped, pivoting mid-stride, cursing at Rachel.

The three crocottas bounded after their prey, heaving and frothing at the mouth. They leapt off parked cars and the sides of buildings, leaving behind raked claw marks in their wake. Two of the beasts veered up a side street to head off the small human herd, while the third chased them into the trap. The single crocotta howled, enraged when the youngling darted the wrong way. It skidded sideways between the two humans, its sharp claws screeching through the pavement.

The monster's gruesome growl chilled Arka to the core. She couldn't let Rachel die in the belly of this thing! The crocotta detangled its claws as Arka tore past it, chasing after Rachel, heading for an empty intersection with blinking lights.

A loud honk sounded and Arka sprung aside to avoid being run over by a small white car barreling straight at her. It missed her, and crashed into the crocotta, sending it flying overhead. It landed in a pile of rubbish with a yelp. The driver of the car flung open the passenger door.

"Get in!" shouted the driver, a dark man, wearing a lime green polo and tan cargo shorts. Arka didn't argue. She dove into the moving car, halfway in the door, scrabbling to pull her legs in. The man rolled up to Rachel, barely slowing down and she piled in over Arka without waiting to be invited.

"Go, go, go!" shouted Rachel, breathless, clambering into the backseat. She stepped on Arka, who grunted at the foot digging into her back.

The man stomped on the gas, tires screeching, and they shot away from the pack of monsters. Rachel sank into the backseat cushions, her body a floppy, wrung out towel. Arka twisted around to sit properly, smoothing her hair back. "Thank you for helping us, sir," she said.

The driver's dark eyes flicked to the review mirror, still racing his car like a professional driver about to win a trophy. "Hey, no problem. Those wild dogs have been all over the news today. No one knows where they came from!" Satisfied they weren't being chased, he slowed down to a manageable speed.

"Several people have gone missing," he said, glancing at Arka sitting like cast-iron next to him. "You guys okay?"

Arka nodded once. "Thanks to you." She spoke into the backseat over her shoulder, quivering with repressed anger. "Rachel, why did you run away from me?"

"I don't know. I had a feeling this guy would be at that intersection."

"The name's Jacob."

"Thanks, Jacob," said Rachel.

"Don't mention it. Where are you headed?"

"The Crystal Cave," Arka said, still annoyed with Rachel.

"Ah, yes. A beautiful tourist destination. I can drop you there, no problem." Jacob offered a kind smile showing all his teeth, a cute gap between the front two made his smile appear wider. It was contagious. Rachel smiled too. Arka was immune.

"Is that where you're going?" asked Arka primly.

"Oh, no. I'm heading to work the other direction on North Shore Road, but I'm happy to help you out."

Rachel hid her giggle at the look of astonishment on Arka's face and pulled the pieces of tissue from her ears. "See Arka? Not all people are as selfish as you think. You should listen to me more often." She leaned back against the covered backseat, gloating that her snap decision had saved them. She clicked her seatbelt into place-just in case Jacob needed to race the car again. "Thanks, Jacob. We really appreciate it."

"Any time friends," he said, flicking the blinker and turning the cracked leather steering wheel.

Arka sat stonily in the passenger seat, looking like she'd just finished eating a basket of sour lemons.

* * *

At the Crystal Cave drop off Rachel and Arka bid Jacob farewell, thanking him again.

"Have a great vacation!" Jacob called out the window as he drove away, late for work.

"Yeah, right," said Rachel under her breath, waving and smiling at him. She stole a glance at Arka, who was refusing to speak to her.

A little gift shop outside the cave's entrance overflowed with colorful trinkets and tourists to match. They hadn't gotten the memo about wild dogs, or they just couldn't be bothered about it. Arka found a map of the cave and poured over it, chewing her lip.

Rachel read a sign at the front counter. "Arka," she said quietly, "there are two caves. The Fantasy Cave tour costs $24.00 per person, and so does the Crystal Cave tour! Which one do we need? And how are we going to pay for it?"

Arka looked over the map testily.

"You'll have to talk to me if you want to finish this quest," said Rachel, irked by Arka's temper.

"Harpocrates said Crystal Cave. We'll join the next group," she said, folding and handing the map to Rachel. "So long as you follow my lead."

Rachel copied Arka in a snarky voice, poking fun at her. "So long as you follow me lead." She tossed a shoulder. "What does that even mean?"

It became clear what Arka meant when she knocked over a shelf in the gift store, creating a diversion and pickpocketed a pair of tickets from a young couple. The girls snuck into the last tour of the day while the poor couple spiraled into an argument over who had misplaced their tickets.

"We're going to get caught!" Rachel squealed, hiding her face behind the map as they neared a guide punching tickets.

"Not if you don't give us away!" hissed Arka. "Act natural." She gave their stolen tickets to the guide dressed head to toe in a khaki uniform, that washed out his pale skin. He smiled cheerfully at them.

"Enjoy the tour! I'll be behind the group while you follow the lead guide. To make sure we don't lose anybody." He winked, handing the punched tickets back to Rachel, who squeaked, staring at him as she inched past. He stared back, the smile on his face unwavering until Arka shoved Rachel forward. Rachel hated sneaking and lying. She felt sure the rear guide knew they were up to something. Her heart stayed in her throat for ten minutes straight as they descended into the cave network. But he left them alone, merely smiling whenever Rachel glanced back at him.

Underground Rachel shivered, admiring the stunning beauty of glittering limestone and white rock walls covered in formations, and she rubbed her arms absentmindedly at the cooler temperature. Standing on a floating bridge, Rachel stared into a breathtaking subterranean lake of crystal-clear water; she could see through to the bottom! The reverence in their group, combined with the prehistoric atmosphere in the cave was so calming, Rachel soon forgot they were fugitive thieves on borrowed time. She jumped when Arka rudely grabbed her arm, pulling her away from the tour.

"Did you hear what the second guide just said?" Arka whispered excitedly.

"Uh, under the boardwalk, there's a large amphitheater filled with water?"

"No! The part where there are two columns and a crack in it."

"That's where the water was during the ice age."

"It's also missing from the map."

Rachel unfolded the paper accordion to check Arka's memory. She took the pen from her hair and traced to where the underground lake was printed in blue ink next to an artistic drawing of a cave. An unassuming empty spot behind it jumped out at her. She circled and tapped it with her pen. "You're right Arka!" Rachel's eyebrows shot up to her hairline. "We have to solve for the missing variable," she said, overlapping Arka who spoke at the same time.

"We have to find the missing tunnel!" Arka grinned. They were on the right track!

Stealthily, the girls climbed over the guardrails, sneaking off the path when the guides weren't looking. As the group moved on, they carefully stepped into a small rowboat for the cave staff left bobbing on the underground lake. Arka rowed them farther away from the tour group until they came to a new section of formations not drawn on the map. She grounded the small boat, and crouching, they tiptoed into a different tunnel.

"I officially detest being underground," Rachel complained, feeling claustrophobic. The memory of Harpocrates mountain nearly suffocating her filled her mind, as sweat trickled down her temple. She hated spelunking.

"I don't enjoy it either. I spent fifty years in a pit," Arka said, deftly squeezing between two formations. "My sisters thought it was funny."

"What? That's awful!" Rachel took a breath and wiped the sweat away with her flimsy, borrowed shirt. I'm not trapped, I'm just nervous. Everything will be okay, she told herself, hoping fervently that it was true and squished through the formations, snagging the shirt.

They got lost twice and Rachel had a panic attack before Arka suggested Rachel touch a stalagmite. Rachel argued that the oil from her fingers would kill it.

"Everything in the universe will die if we don't find this artifact!" Arka retorted, losing patience. "The least you could do is try using that Seer intuition again. Or does it only work when monsters are chasing you?"

Rachel's lips pinched and she jabbed her finger at a cluster of stalagmites jutting up from the ground like elongated candles. The one she touched was cool and slightly damp. Rachel focused on their need to find something and to her astonishment, it worked! She sensed which direction to go and stepped past Arka. "This way."

Acting as their new guide, gently and sparingly touching formations, Rachel led them deeper into the cave system. She sensed a heartbeat in the earth that strengthened as she followed it. Arka marked each turn in the tunnels by carving notches in the limestone with her pocketknife. The last turn opened up before them into a grand, spacious amphitheater with two columns on either side of the entrance. Arka's soft aura was the only light in the large room, but it was enough to see how magnificent it was. "This is the room Harpocrates spoke of!" said Arka.

"I certainly hope so. I'm exhausted." Rachel's body was tired, and her mind drained. It took more energy out of her than she'd expected to concentrate on the earth's directions.

Arka handed her a water bottle from her pack. "Stay here at the entrance and I'll check it out. Remember, only a god can enter here." Arka crept cautiously through the columns, making her way to the center of the huge cavern and jumped out of her skin when Rachel whispered in her ear to veer left.

"What are you doing? I told you to wait!"

"I didn't want to sit in the dark by myself! There are probably vampire bats down here."

"First the pool, then the car, and now *here*? When I tell you to do something, you need to listen to me!" Arka said, livid, her voice carrying through the cave. "I don't know why you just didn't spontaneously combust crossing that threshold, but if you ignore my instructions again, I will tie you up! Vampire bats or not!"

Rachel took a sip of water. "You'd have to catch me first."

Arka snatched the water bottle from Rachel's hand and stuffed it back in her pack. "This is serious! You're lucky you're the seer," she ranted, "or I'd teach you a lesson about," she paused. "That's probably why you crossed the threshold unscathed."

"Whatever. Can we get on with this?" Rachel didn't sense any danger and wanted to finish their scavenger hunt so she could rest. Dealing with Arka's pompous attitude was better than napping alone in a dark cave.

"Fine." Arka allowed Rachel to direct her. She wouldn't have *found* the room without her after all. Still, it grated on Arka's nerves how Rachel was using her abilities for the quest. She wasn't used to being reliant on anyone but herself. She was so disturbed, she failed to notice how drained Rachel was.

Rachel guided them through the empty cavern to a wall lined with identical tunnels. Each one led out of the great room to a perilous trap, but one led to the Cuff of Capture. Rachel pointed, unable to keep her hand from shaking, to a shadowed entrance three tunnels down on their left. "It's in there."

Chapter 18: The Artifact

"How fortuitous," said Rachel, rolling her eyes sarcastically, standing over a massive bowl of foggy liquid. "If we touch it, our skin will disintegrate off our bones." A bubble popped in reply.

They'd found the wide basin perched chest high on a marble column atop a stepped dais in the last alcove of the tunnel. A single torch burning with Hephaestus' ever-flame had been placed in a sconce on the stone wall to light the small space. Rachel pulled it free, lifting it high to see better.

Their mirrored faces stared back at them from the drab pool. Arka patted Rachel on the back. "Don't fret! Hephaestus, the god of fire, made the Cuff of Capture and he fashioned the Glove of Righteousness to retrieve it. He's a magnificent craft smith." She held up the gauntlet, her green eyes shining brightly.

"Hope it works."

"Did I not just say . . . never mind." Arka squeezed her eyes shut. It wouldn't help anything getting dragged into another quarrel with Rachel. It was likely her fear talking, or teenage hormones. Not worth the distraction when they were so close to securing the artifact!

Rachel shifted her feet. "Something doesn't feel right."

"You're nervous. It's normal."

"I am nervous." The torch fizzed, and Rachel's arm sagged. "Alright, let's do this. It's why we came here, right?"

"Right." Arka pulled the glove on, wiggling her fingers, cinching it in place at her elbow. She drove her arm into the thick pool, acidic bubbles hissing the second her hand breached the surface.

"Eww, gross!" Rachel gagged, tipping the torch.

"Don't you dare get sick!" said Arka, moving her arm slowly through the cloudy liquid. "If a single droplet touches this, it will cause an explosion."

Rachel clamped her free hand over her mouth, making her nose respire loudly.

Arka took her time, careful not to splash. If the Ladon Dragon's saliva touched anywhere but the basin, it would burn away everything in its path, returning to Tartarus and the monster it was stolen from.

The shiny glove turned rusty brown and smoking. It was burning, albeit slowly. Rachel gasped. "Arka! The glove!" She hopped up and down, pointing at it. "Hurry!"

"I'm trying," growled Arka, "stop jumping around, you might bump something!" Her arm stretched as far as she could reach into the pool without the fatal saliva spilling over the top of the glove.

Rachel anxiously examined the pool, lowering the torch, searching for a glimmer of something floating in it. Only their distorted reflections could be seen, hers becoming frantic and Arka's more determined.

"I can't feel anything!" Arka huffed, blowing loose strands

of hair out of her face.

"Maybe it's not in the center, check around the sides!"

Arka followed the suggestion of her seer. She dragged her fingers in a claw shape along the edge, walking carefully around the basin. A tingling sensation crept through the glove and sweat sprung to her brow.

Three quarters around, Arka shouted in triumph. "Ha!" She pulled up a beautifully scrolled platinum arm cuff, but the action was too quick. The curve of the cuff retained some liquid, and it sloshed out at her. Arka jumped back, avoiding the deadly saliva, and it splattered onto the dais. The girls gaped at each other in a beat of panic.

"Out!" shouted Arka, jumping down and shooting past Rachel like a glowing fireball. Rachel scrambled after her, following the streak of light.

Behind them, acid ate away at the marble stone, sizzling and popping. The pillar toppled. The crash of the basin followed by a rush of acid contacting the earth was deafening. The force shot a gust of wind through the tunnel, blasting into the cave, knocking Rachel over and she dropped the torch, scraping her knees painfully on jagged rocks as she fell.

The beautiful stalactites hanging above them shook violently and several crashed to the ground, in giant skewers. Rachel gasped, rolling aside. She jumped up, leaving the burning torch behind and saw Arka darting through the rain of stones, following their marked trail, trying frantically to pull the melting glove off her arm. Arka managed to peel the thing off and threw it to the ground. It slapped a rock and as Rachel sprinted past, she could see that parts of the fingers were almost see-through.

Arka blew on her stinging fingertips, never slowing down. She knew the saliva hadn't touched her skin, or else she would be on her way past the Underworld to meet the dragon.

An earthquake ruptured the earth, sending Arka and Rachel crashing to the ground. Recovering quickly, Arka wedged the cuff under her chin, feverishly starting a gateway for them to escape through. There wasn't enough time to get back to the entrance before the entire cave collapsed around them. She didn't care that the strands were warped, or where the gateway sent them, so long as it was out of there! She bellowed loudly over the noise of crashing stone. "Rachel, grab the cuff! I have to concentrate!" A roaring sound, like a huge landslide drowned out Arka's voice and the ground shook beneath their feet in a second quake.

The famously serene lake in the Crystal Cave splashed and swirled from the unseen commotion. The lead tour guide watched the ground split along the bottom of the lake and panic-struck, abandoned his tour, running up steps two at a time to save himself before a cave in. The other tour guide dove into the lake, swimming like a madman. Tourists screamed, stampeding madly toward the exit in utter chaos. Their pandemonium echoed deep into the caverns where Rachel picked herself up unsteadily, calling out over the clamor. "What's happening?!"

"The acid is burning its way through the ground, returning to where it belongs and pulling down everything around it too!" Arka stuck out her tongue in concentration. The strands weren't cooperating, and she had to modify the pattern, twisting them together in a rushed design.

"Like a whirlpool of death? How big will it be?" Rachel opened her mouth to ask another pestering question.

"Quiet!" snapped Arka, and the cuff fell from under her chin, rolling on the ground.

"I got it!" Rachel snatched up the cuff as another earthquake shook them and she fell, landing ungracefully on her backside. She checked if Arka had seen, but the goddess was too busy to notice. She was glowing brightly, bending the air apart and forming a small gateway. Rachel's heart hiccupped with hope. They were going to make it! She twisted the cuff onto her forearm for safekeeping.

"You go through first and I'll follow!" barked Arka.

The gateway was only three feet high, but that was enough. The ground surged as Rachel body crawled toward the low arch. The arm cuff grew inexplicitly warm and Rachel cried out, horrified to see it changing shape into a scaly snake. She tried pulling it off, but the cuff melted together, shackling her to the snake. The serpent grew into a giant monster with the torso and face of a woman. It had viper eyes with vertical pupils that flexed against a yellow gleam. From the waist up its sickly grey skin, speckled with dark blotches, unfolded in front of Rachel's eyes.

Clasped to the snake woman's voluptuous arm was a matching sealed cuff, connected by a linked chain to Rachel's. The thing hissed and slid on its belly, scales glinting in Arka's light, through the gateway, yanking Rachel's arm and dragging her behind it.

Rachel screamed, clawing at the ground, ripping her fingernails, leaving a trail of blood. Arka dove for her, grabbing Rachel's legs but in doing so released the gateway threads.

The creature was too fast! It pulled Rachel through the gateway, snarling back at Arka, speaking directly into her mind.

"Your sisters will be furious you gave the cuff to a mortal!" it hissed. "They blackmailed Hephaestus into making this decoy to capture you and I've waited so patiently." It bared its fangs. "May you rot in the Underworld for stealing my reward!" It slithered away, dragging a struggling Rachel as the weave unraveled.

"No!" cried Arka, but it was too late. The trap had been sprung.

Venom dripped from the snake woman's fangs when she caught the scent of the terrified girl's blood. Perhaps the Fates would let her eat the girl. She laughed, flicking her tongue to savor the scent again. The snake didn't care about the turnout of the Fate's plan, only that they fed it. She'd been promised an endless supply of delectable meats in exchange for her service.

Rachel heard the creature's guttural, hissing laugh and the last thing she saw through the closing gateway was Arka's face, twisted in despair as she was sucked away into the void behind her.

Chapter 19: Falling Upward

Hurricane winds rushed in Arka's ears. Helpless against the pull of the vortex, the last glowing strands of her gateway fizzled from view as it sucked her backward. Arka flew through the tunnel, scrabbling at rock formations, fighting against the gale force wind. She grabbed ahold of a large stalactite hanging from the ceiling, and clung tight as debris flew past her. Why hadn't she listened to Rachel's concerns? How could she be so foolish? She'd walked right into this trap, and now Rachel was gone! The initial shock of watching Rachel being dragged through the gateway turned into fury.

Harpocrates had tricked her! That wasn't his nature, Arka thought. Perhaps it was Dolos, the god of trickery or Apate, the goddess of deception who'd appeared to be Harpocrates to send her searching for the false cuff. That meant the real Harpocrates was most likely being held against his will somewhere.

A cold ball of fear dropped into Arka's gut. If her sisters set the trap, they placed the barriers. That meant Arka's gateway would end up near their lair. The trap was meant for her. It was mere chance Rachel had put the cuff on her forearm before Arka tested it herself.

Arka feared returning to the lair, but even more frightening was thinking about what her sisters would do to her friend. Arka shuddered involuntarily and prayed they wouldn't take their anger out on Rachel. The wrath of a Fate was something no being ever wanted to face. Arka set her jaw. Well, I have my *own* wrath to unleash, she thought grimly. The stalactite cracked and Arka let go, twisting away to face the growing vacuum behind her. Diving gracefully with strands of hair whipping her face, Arka nimbly planted her boots on a nearby boulder flying alongside her. She bent her knees and pushed off, shooting like an arrow toward the opening in the ground where the basin had been. She sped toward the edge, plunging over headfirst into the abyss.

Crystal Cave lake water flew about, stinging Arka's skin. Her aura helped her make out pieces of the cave walls flying around the vortex. She used them to steer herself, skydiving with purpose through the bowels of the earth. Plummeting to Tartarus would take a considerable amount of time, but she needed that time to focus. Although the sensation of falling was disconcerting, Arka knew if she could avoid colliding with the surrounding debris, she might have a chance to form another gateway once she was far enough away from the barriers.

The moment of opportunity came when a boulder the size of a pickup-truck edged into view. It was gaining on her own descent, inching closer to her feet. When the boulder kissed her toes, she turned herself like an aerial ballet performer, spinning to the side, then flattened herself out again, gripping at the boulder for a handhold.

Just as her fingers locked into a crevasse, the boulder

smashed into a smaller formation, sending its particles flying past her. One sizeable chunk struck her cheek, the pain ricocheting through her skull. Arka ducked her head to avoid further pummeling, and the boulder shielded her from further assault. "Oh!" She gasped in surprise when the wind was suddenly knocked out of her- like someone kicked her in the ribs. She felt another blow and heard a rib crack. Struggling for breath, she fought for purchase, lost in fear of what lurked in the dark.

What creatures would love to devour her when buried in the Underworld?

Arka shook her head. The Underworld couldn't hold her!

She could be trapped in Tartarus, though, for eternity.

"No!" Arka yelled, stopping the intrusive thoughts. Hades appeared next to her, clinging to the boulder. His abnormal frame was covered in ashen skin, and hollow eyes shone from inside his helm of darkness. Large horns sprouted from the top, pointing at her.

"Dropping in for a visit, Arka?"

Arka's spirit filled with dread, drowning her in a sea of hopelessness.

Hades smirked, his face twisting, and he disappeared. A new beast manifested in his place. A chimera with three lion heads snarled at her, clawing at the boulder, breaking off hunking pieces that flew into the chasm. It blasted her with fire so hot, Arka was forced to let go of the boulder, crossing her arms to shield her face. The chimera's heads attacked one another, and Arka watched it blink through several monsters. Each time she thought of a monster, it appeared like it. The thing changed again, into a copy of her.

"Very good Arka. You do remember me," said the clone.

"You! You tried to kill Rachel in the bathroom!"

Arka watched her copy distort, bones grotesquely popping until Harpocrates clung to the boulder instead, his long beard blowing in the wind like a runaway kite as they continued their descent. "I nearly had you! You've ruined everything and you're going to pay for it!" he shouted at her.

This is the god Dolos, a master of deception and ill intent, Arka realized, free falling and holding her side, the broken rib stabbing with each breath. Suddenly everything made sense. He manifested as fear and poisoned hope, wearing his victims down to capture them. He'd posed as the god of secrets, sent them on this fool's errand, and was probably responsible for releasing the crocotta hounds. Rachel had been right, Arka thought, doubling over in pain.

"How dense are you?" Dolos blinked into the pasty faced Crystal Cave tour guide in his khaki uniform. "I even gave you the final clue to find the cuff! I've had to follow you all over creation since you left your post. I've been working with your sisters to repair your negligent damage of the tapestry!" The tour guide shook a fist at her, flickering in and out as Dolos screamed in rage. "Now look what you've done! You weren't supposed to spill the dragon's saliva! What will become of us when we pass through the Underworld and land in Tartarus?!" The tour guide faded into a dense blackness so dark, it extinguished Arka's light.

A tremor passed through Arka at the horror of it. The one thing she feared more than her sisters was eternal darkness in Tartarus. What if she couldn't escape? What if Rachel died because of her? It doesn't matter, she thought. I don't matter. I cannot make a difference, anyway. What is the point? If I'm gone, no one will miss me, and the universe is doomed anyhow.

Emptiness weighed down Arka's heart. She felt ashamed she'd abandoned the tapestry, her duty, and her calling. Everything was her fault, and the situation was hopeless. Arka pinched herself. "This is not real!" she said aloud and pushed against the shameful guilt blanket, wrapping her emotions tightly around her like a straitjacket.

I make new threads for the tapestry! If the patterns in the weave are fading, it's my sisters' fault! Dolos is feeding me these lies, making me afraid and hopeless. Wait! Arka thought, struck with an idea, that's his weakness!

She straightened up, her face grim with determination. "*You* sent us here to retrieve the false arm cuff!" she shouted, twisting with a painful grunt to avoid large rocks. "You are to blame, Dolos! What will Hades think of you impersonating him? Who will *you* face in Tartarus?" Arka squeezed her arms to her sides, rocketing downward, and reached out blindly in the dark, feeling for the giant boulder.

The weight of the other god smashed into her, and they grappled in mid-air. Dolos punched her and Arka's head snapped back, her nose crunching. She tasted tangy ichor gush down her face and returned fire. Her fists landing in his abdomen before his hands latched on her throat, strangling her.

Arka's lips turned blue. She threw her arms up between his, breaking his grip and head-butted him, giving herself a second to weave threads of binding. They were working! She must be below her sister's barriers! Arka wound the threads around Dolos, pinning his arms down, and the thick velvet blackness faded, his power contained. She could see again by her aura and almost dropped the weave when she saw Rachel bound in the threads, glaring at her.

"No Dolos," said Arka coldly. "You don't get to have her, or me, or this quest." She punched him, her knuckles blasting across his cheekbone for good measure.

Dolos flickered through several monsters, straining against the threads. "You're going to pay for this Fate!" he shrieked, undone and laughed hysterically. "You'll pay!"

Arka drop-kicked the wicked shapeshifter further into the abyss with all her might. "Not today, Dolos!" Arka wedged her fingers in a crevice of the giant boulder, her split knuckles stinging and pulled herself close, her arms shaking from exertion, and fought through the throbbing pain in her ribcage, to hold on tight.

For several minutes she clung to the boulder, her feet trailing behind her like the tail of a comet blazing through space. Summoning her strength, Arka pulled in her left leg, locating a foothold with her toes, followed by her right. She wiped ichor away from her nose and chin, gathering her thoughts. Her preferred way to manipulate the strands of fate was in the air, but she would have to use elements of this rock within the gateway weave because she was falling. Using solid compounds in a gateway was complicated, but it would be strong. It could end up being too strong, Arka mused, remaining permanent. That would be a problem if the boulder landed whole in Tartarus. Any number of horrible gods or monsters could use it to escape.

Arka hesitated. Could she risk that for the sake of a mortal? Rachel isn't a simple mortal, Arka argued with herself, she's a seer and my friend. She's probably about to be made into mortal stew and the chances of the gateway remaining open are marginal. Rather than worrying about what if, Arka focused on facts. Her sisters wouldn't hesitate to end the life of a mortal they deemed unnecessary or troublesome. It would unleash havoc on the world if they discovered Rachel was a seer and abused her abilities. The universe was at stake, and a few extra monsters wouldn't make a difference if the tapestry continued to disintegrate.

With fresh resolve, Arka let warmth grow in her hands and reached into the boulder with her light. Illumination spread from her fingertips inside the stone, binding with the minerals. The essence of the rock became one with her senses. A dank, earthy smell filled her nostrils, and she tasted it on the back of her tongue. Her skin felt cold and solid, like the boulder, making her shiver. As Arka let the elements of earth into herself, she gently molded them, changing their pattern. A solid form was more difficult to manipulate than air. This gateway could use the stability though, she thought, careening towards the center of the earth.

Arka closed her eyes in concentration. It would be the strongest gateway she'd ever built. Roots of soft, gold light curled from her fingertips into the base, intertwining with the boulder as they wove and circled in a complicated pattern. The gateway stretched taller, a floating lighthouse in the spinning debris. Its center shimmered as bits of dirt spun up along the sides in a solid rope, enveloped with light. Arka directed all her energy into the gateway, and it grew into a radiant beacon in the chasm of darkness. When it was tall enough, she cast off the threads and kicked off the boulder with both feet in an intense, graceful backflip through space. Driving her legs up over her head, with toes pointed towards the gateway, Arka let the momentum carry her, boots first, through the brilliant arch.

Arka lurched over her legs with tremendous speed and caught herself in a low lunge on soldi ground. Wincing and holding her side, she quickly surveyed the new landscape. Mount Olympus!

Before someone noticed her or the gateway, Arka crouched down, breathing through her teeth, digging her hands into the grass where the base of the gateway sprouted. She willed the light and energy to return to her, draining it from the stone on the other side, pulling the strands back together. She drew from internal strength, praying nothing would be left on the boulder. Abruptly, a force struck inside her chest, knocking her backwards. Sprawling in the fresh grass, her braid half undone, Arka gulped thirstily for air like a dying fish and her broken rib screamed insults. The boulder must have struck the bottom of the Underworld, Arka thought, coughing painfully, spitting up pieces of dirt. She sat up, eyes darting, to see if any creatures had followed her through, but the gateway was no longer visible. Arka collapsed back in the grass.

Mount Olympus was a tricky place to be. There were those here who would help her, but also those who would oppose her. Arka rolled over, moaning quietly, and worked to make a weave of hiding. She drew it over herself like a blanket. I must tread carefully and unnoticed, she thought. But before anything could be accomplished, she needed to regain strength. Confident she couldn't be seen, Arka closed her eyes, soaking in the power of Olympus, preparing for battle.

Chapter 20: Mother of Monsters

Every inch of Rachel's body displayed angry scratches from being dragged across the ground. The moment the gateway disappeared, she lost all energy. Rachel hadn't realized how much Arka's power sustained her. She was shaky and had a raging headache. When was the last time she slept or ate?

Rachel glanced up at the thing dragging her along and her heart stopped. It had black claws extending from gnarly hands covered in oily slime gripping the chain connecting them. Rachel weakly jerked her cuffed arm, but her struggling didn't faze the snake woman.

Stubbornly, Rachel used her free hand to grab at anything she could to slow its progress, whimpering at the pain shooting up her torn fingernails as she pulled up bushes and twigs. She even pressed her heels into the soil, catching them on a protruding root. The creature hissed, shaking its shackled arm, flinging Rachel around like a worm. It tossed her over its meaty shoulder like a sack of dog food, snarled and slithered onward through low scraggy grass on an unkempt path. The gateway had opened into a wasteland of dying trees and brambles near the three Fates' lair. The monster knew her masters well and wasted no time on her journey there.

Rachel remembered her mom telling her that if ever kidnapped, you weren't supposed to let the abductor take you to a second location. She looked around at the sickly vegetation that bent in unnatural shapes. Well, it was too late for that. She had no idea where she was, but perhaps there was someone around who could help her. Rachel screamed as loud as she could for help, directly in the creature's ear hole. That got its attention. It flung her to the ground and snapped its jaws at her, its ear holes pinching shut against its scaly head.

Its face would have been beautiful if it weren't for the snake-of-death part, Rachel thought. What was this thing? It wasn't a Gorgon, that would be Medusa, who was long dead. This thing didn't have snakes on its head either, it *was* a snake. Black and ocher scales covered its head, running down its back blending into a huge, coiled tail. It stared at her with unblinking reptilian eyes for several seconds, as if deciding whether or not to eat her. Rachel shuddered. The thing flicked its black forked tongue, tasting the air, and its thin, black lips peeled back in a smile, showing serrated fangs.

It likes when I exhibit fear, Rachel thought. She set her jaw and screamed for help again, right in its ugly face. Hissing, the thing clamped an icy hand around Rachel's throat, choking off her scream, and slammed her against a scraggly tree. The creature's touch permeated evil, and the lack of oxygen made Rachel's vision swirl with little white dots. With its free hand, it clawed rotten moss off the tree and tried stuffing the wad into Rachel's mouth. Rachel resisted, clenching her teeth shut.

The thing apparently didn't want to strangle her to death

because it gave one of its gurgling laughs and let go of her throat. Somehow Rachel had the presence of mind to not open her mouth and gasp for air, but instead sucked a breath through her nose, sending it trampling painfully down her bruised windpipe. This act of defiance enraged the beast, and it slapped Rachel so hard she fell to the ground thinking her eyes would pop out of her skull. Blood trickled from a fresh split in Rachel's lip, but still, she refused to open her mouth.

Glaring at the thing in abhorrence, Rachel saw in her mind a vision of an ornate picture book. The pages flew open, stopping on a matching photo of what she was looking at and the image overlayed her sight like a popup screen. A name etched over the live picture in ancient Greek runes: Drakaina, Rachel deciphered, a she-dragon named Echidna. Ice ran through Rachel's veins. This thing is the mother of monsters! She blinked and the book vanished, leaving her staring into Echidna's eyes. Before Rachel could flinch or scream, Echidna raised a finger, slime dripping off her knuckle, and pressed a single claw to Rachel's forehead, indenting the skin. Rachel's eyes rolled back, and she slumped forward, incapacitated.

Grunting with satisfaction, Echidna easily hoisted Rachel back onto her shoulder, letting the girl's head loll from side to side and slithered on her way unencumbered.

Chapter 21: Mount Olympus

Night settled over the realm of the gods and Arka's eyes shot open. It didn't take long for her power to be restored and she was stronger here than in the mortal world. She felt invincible!

Careful not to outstretch her disguise, Arka felt for her broken rib. The rib had mended and was sore, but no longer stabbing her. Gingerly, Arka touched the bridge of her nose. There was a bump, but no pain. "That's good enough for me," she said under her breath, sitting up and fixing her braid. Velvet soft grass cushioned her, and she tasted nectar on the evening breeze. The weather was always pleasant at Mount Olympus. Arka smiled. It had been a long time since she'd visited here. The last time was to meet with one of her informants. She nodded to herself, that's exactly what she'd do right now.

Melting into the evening shadows, Arka made her way to the scholar district. She could care less about the glitzy architectural wonders housing the many gods living there, or the throne Zeus kept at the top of the highest peak. She sought someone with less fanfare.

Tucked in a cobblestone alley, a little hut resembling a child's playhouse waved warmly glowing windows at Arka, as if inviting her in. Without knocking, she pushed open the arched wooden door, ducked her head and stepped inside, jangling a little bell that hung over the doorjamb. It smelled like crisp parchment, with stacks of books and scrolls strewn about in organized chaos atop a maze of tables that stood only to Arka's knee.

"Hello?" called a thin voice from the back. "Who is it?"

A friendly faced satyr with a little white beard and wisps of white in his dark hair, that tufted out around mini horns, poked his head up from behind a large stack of aged books. He saw that the door was standing open, and narrowed his furry eyebrows.

Arka slammed the door shut.

"What in the name of Olympus?!" cried the satyr, jumping three feet in the air, knocking a pile of papers to the floor.

Arka laughed out loud as she unraveled the weave of hiding, and the poor satyr's eyes grew in alarm as she appeared in front of him. His cry of surprise cut short when he recognized her. "What are you *doing* here?!" he demanded, pushing himself up, his hoofs slipping on several papers before he stood up in a huff, straightening his dark red vest and half-moon spectacles.

"I have come for your help, Christodoulopoulos," said Arka bluntly, making her way into the shop. She bent over to avoid hitting her head on a low ceiling beam and approached him as one would a scared puppy.

"I have already helped you!" said Christodoulopoulos, scooting backward, jostling his giant stack of books. He caught them before they toppled over and whispered loudly, "There is still an ongoing investigation over the missing ambrosia!"

"I am grateful to you for shouldering that burden," said Arka honestly, straightening a few titles that had shifted in the disturbance. "I have a new quest, however, that needs immediate attention." She leaned close, eyes pleading. "A mortal girl is in great peril."

"That's just too bad," Christodoulopoulos snapped. "Finish your first quest." His ruff stood on edge and he wouldn't look Arka in the eye as he rearranged the books she'd just straightened.

Arka knelt, getting down to his level. "I'm sorry I scared you. I had to stay hidden, and that was just a bit of fun. The girl I'm talking about says I need to have more fun." She hid a smile when he scowled. "I'm serious. Chris, she's more than just some girl." Arka glanced at the floor. "She is my friend."

The satyr's mouth fell open. He was quite taken aback. "You have a friend? The great Arka, who only works alone, has a *mortal* friend?" He clopped around a table, tossing his hands up in exasperation. "Well then, go ahead and throw away everything we've worked for. Arka, I have been living in constant panic since your last visit! You ask too much of me!"

"She's a seer, Chris!" Arka shouted over his ranting.

An extended moment of silence fell between them, broken by the popping of a melting candle burning at his desk. Keeping his back to her, Chris cocked an ear in Arka's direction. "Surely you jest."

"I tell you the truth," Arka swore, placing a fist over her heart.

Chris turned sharply and stared into her eyes, reading her like a lie detector test, then squealed with delight. "Really?!" He pranced from hoof to hoof then darted to an overloaded bookshelf, rummaging for something. "Do you think she'll be my friend too? Oh, I do hope so!"

"Listen, Chris. Christodoulopoulos!" Arka used his full name and clapped her hands, to get his attention. "My sisters hid Echidna in a false cuff to capture me, but caught Rachel instead!"

Chris gasped, clutching a parchment to his chest. Shaking his head sadly he said, "Well, there goes any chance I had to meet her." He handed the parchment to Arka glumly.

She glanced at the discolored paper scrawled with information about the last known seer. Tiresias was a renowned soothsayer for the gods. He was blind but had the ability to understand birds. His shade had long since traveled to the underworld. Arka smiled sadly, remembering how Artemis has scared Rachel with his story. Arka crumpled up the paper. It was amazing Chris could find anything in the jumble of documents he kept, but she didn't need a history lesson, she needed to rescue Rachel. "I know it's been a long time since the last seer graced our realm, Chris, but Rachel's not dead. Not yet. I would feel it if she were."

"Really? How so?" he asked, speculating. Ever the scholar, he pulled a small pad of paper and whittled pencil from his pocket ready to take notes.

"Never mind. The point is, I'm going to rescue her, with your help."

Chris' eyes bulged. "My help? You are quite mistaken, my dear." He snorted, the nostrils of his little nose quivering and tossed the notepad on a crowded table. "I only give information and advice. For a fee, if you do recall." He looked over his half-moon spectacles her. "My opinion is free of course, take it or leave it."

Arka sighed in exasperation. Why was it always like swimming upstream to get help? She rummaged in her pack and

165

pulled out the song for the god of secrets. Even if the god wasn't there, the song still worked to gain entrance to his mountain. "Would this make it worth your while, Chris?" she asked, holding it just out of his reach.

Chris pushed the center of his frames up with a finger, inspecting the bit of hide. He sucked in a startled breath. "Where did you get that?"

"It's none of your business where I got it. But if you help me, it's yours."

Chris reached out a mesmerized hand to touch the piece of hide but caught himself. "I'm not stepping hoof in the Fates' lair! You can't bribe me, or force me, or persuade me, or . . ."

"I get it!" Arka cut him off, her anger rising. "Don't tempt my patience, Chris. I too am a Fate." Chris balked, and she softened her tone. "You only have to help me get to the entrance. You have my word."

He scratched his head, thinking. "With that song, I can get Old Goat McGee to give me a proper place at the table of elders. He'd do anything to have that a secret again!" Not to mention the price everyone would pay for a copy of it. Ambition lit his eyes, and he tugged his short beard. "I will help you travel to the Fates' lair for payment of that song. Do you agree to these terms, Arka?"

"I do. You'll be paid when the job is done."

"Then let's get to work."

"Can you steer a boat?"

"Of course!" Chris' chest puffed up, the polished gold buttons on his vest straining.

"Great!"

"Well, er," the buttons drooped back into place, "I'm sure I have a book on it somewhere."

Arka surveyed the disheveled, colorful library he lived in. "Pack it. I'll wait."

After a few minutes, Chris emerged from the back of his bookshop home wearing a freshly pressed adventure vest. He'd never had an occasion to wear it before and took care to smooth the velvet front. It looked much like the other one he'd just changed out of, only without ink stains and more pockets. He held up a small leather briefcase, patting the front. "All set."

"You're bringing luggage?"

"One briefcase is hardly luggage. It's half the size of a small suitcase. Besides, I need it to carry my essentials."

"You mean books?"

He swung the briefcase handle. "Maybe."

Chapter 22: No Escape

Rachel awoke still slung over the monster's shoulder, her head throbbing. She didn't know how much time had passed, but found she'd been blindfolded with a filthy ribbon strip torn from her stained vacation shirt. Echidna had also ripped off the shirt's ridiculous sleeves and used them to tie Rachel's arms behind her back. It was extremely uncomfortable. Rachel thought about screaming again but decided it wouldn't get her anything but a concussion. She tried loosening the knots at her wrists, but it was no use. She was at the monster's mercy.

After hours of holding her bladder, Rachel finally spoke up. "Hey, I need to use the restroom."

Echidna ignored her and slithered on.

Rachel tried again. "Seriously, if you don't want me to pee on you, I suggest you let me step into the woods." That did the trick.

Echidna roughly put Rachel down and removed her bonds. Echidna shook the tethered cuff, signaling for Rachel to pull it off her arm. The device had been made to capture Arka, and

Echidna didn't need it to manage a mortal. She snarled though, when Rachel reached for the blindfold.

"Okay, okay," Rachel said, rubbing her sore wrists. I guess I'm a blind seer after all. The snake woman shoved Rachel toward the bushes, hissing maliciously. Taking the hint, Rachel held her hands out in front of her, feeling for branches. She did the best she could under the circumstances. Although she couldn't see, Rachel knew this was her best chance to escape. Without the cuff, she was free to run! It didn't matter where, so long as it was away from the drakaina. She stealthily pulled the pen from her sagging ponytail, praying her idea would work.

Rachel stumbled out from behind a dead tree, holding her hands up in fists as if to let Echidna tie her up again. When she sensed the snake woman was near, Rachel jabbed upward with the pen concealed in her hands. She felt the point drive home and sprinted away, yanking her blindfold down.

Echidna screamed in pain, hissing, spitting and thrashing her tail, knocking over brittle tree stumps in the dead forest.

Rachel crashed through the woods, her heart beating wildly, shoving branches out of her way. They cracked and snapped off, falling to the ground where she jumped over them, desperate for escape. She heard the viper monster roaring behind her, chasing her through the trees.

Keeping her eyelids half closed against stabbing branches, Rachel ran without watching where she was going. Brambles and twigs whipped her face and arms, leaving red stripes in her skin. She stepped on a rotten log, twisting her ankle, and smacked into a tree trunk, sending chunks of bark flying. Catching hold of the grey split wood to regain her balance, Rachel turned course. Tears stung her eyes when she put weight on her foot. Her ankle wasn't broken, but the sprain was enough to stop her sprint.

Choking back a sob, she pressed on, limping fast. She wasn't fast enough; the serpent was on her in a flash.

Echidna wound her tail around Rachel's body in a crushing hold, lifting her like a doll, with brute strength.

Overwhelming cold swept up from Rachel's toes. She didn't know if it was from blood restriction or if she was about to have another vision. Held up face to face with the snake lady and fighting to get air into her compressed lungs, Rachel saw the pen had punctured one of Echidna's eyes!

Rachel watched in horror as the monster pulled it out with a squelch, blood gushing from the socket, and threw the speared eyeball to the ground. Rachel would have puked, but the squeezing snake tail trapped the bile.

Echidna had two pit organ holes above her cheekbones that allowed her to see with infrared, so losing an eye hadn't slowed her down at all, just pissed her off. She hissed curses in Rachel's face, her repugnant breath blowing back Rachel's disheveled hair.

That's when everything went dark.

Rachel stood in a vast room divided by a heavy curtain. It was thick, like several walls glued together. Her hands shook as she tugged an ornate rope attached to a pulley system to open it. Painstakingly, the curtain folded back, revealing part of the Tapestry of Life. Several blackened holes punched straight through it, dripping a dark, oily substance on the floor. She watched it trickle, then pool and stream to the center of the room where it poured in a thick waterfall over the edge of a large chasm. Rachel ran to the edge, dropping to her hands and knees and looked over.

In the torrent of melted tapestry tar, Rachel saw Echidna writhing and twisting against the current. She swept down to the

Underworld and was attacked by her monstrous children. Her mauled corpse sank into the dark pool, and the mob of gruesome monsters began crawling up the well, straight for Rachel.

Rachel scrambled away, slipping in the black tar. Desperate to stem the flow of darkness, she threw herself at the tapestry, pressing her hands into the growing hole. Her arms pressed in, followed by her body, squelching through the soggy threads like mud. Darkness devoured her, leaving behind the impression of her silhouette, flooding with tar.

Rachel's eyes flew open. Black spots swirled her vision, but she focused on Echidna's empty eye socket, forcing out words with her last breath. "I am a seer," she whispered, her voice scarcely audible.

Echidna partially released her tail's constricting death grip, and her forked tongue flicked the air.

Sucking in a reviving breath, Rachel whispered with more vigor, "Believe it or not, I've just had a vision and you were in it, lizard lady."

Echidna's working eye watched Rachel's fixedly, the thin sliver of its black pupil expanding in sickly yellow, and she bobbed her head.

"If you're trying to speak into my mind, it's not working," said Rachel. It probably had to do with her abilities as a seer, but she had more sense than to say it out loud.

Echidna shook Rachel with her thick scaly tail, rattling Rachel's teeth, nearly snapping her neck. She threw Rachel to the ground, circling her, gesturing with deformed, clawed hands.

Rachel braced the fall, catching several splinters in her palms. Quavering, she pushed herself up, knees pressing into the underbrush, and tried making sense of the horrid monster's rant. "You want to know what I saw?"

The scaly head lowered in acquiescence. There was a reverence Rachel hadn't expected. She took a moment to pull out a particularly large splinter. It hurt, but so did everywhere else. "Well, you overgrown zoo animal, I saw you die." She glared up at Echidna's stricken face and mustering a prophetic voice she said, "If you eat me, your journey to the Underworld will involve a family reunion with your awful children. They await your return." Rachel flicked away the piece of somber wood she'd pulled from her palm, weak with exhaustion. "Your survival is tied to my survival," she lied, hoping it might save her from being eaten alive.

Echidna raged, clawing at herself, hissing and showing her serrated fangs. It was like watching a Jurassic anaconda throw a teenage hissy fit. Sidewinding in her fury, Echidna made a gap in the circle near the tip of her tail.

Rachel wasted no time in crawling for it. Her arms shook but she had to try. A twig snapped under her weight and sensing the snake was going to strike, she curled into a ball, protecting her vital organs. Echidna coiled and struck! Toxic fangs bit deep into Rachel's shoulder, lodging a scream in her throat as paralyzing venom flooded her nervous system.

Tearing her jagged fangs free without mercy, Echidna warred with herself, snapping at the mortal several times, tasting her blood. It was intoxicating. She didn't have to eat the whole girl. Maybe just a small part? The Fates had starved her half to death, trapping her as an inanimate object for so long, and now this delicious morsel turned out to be a seer! She knew a seer was special and could win her favor, perhaps even excuse the fact that she hadn't captured the fourth. Still, she was so hungry, and now her beautiful eye was lost forever! This mission was turning out to be more than she'd bargained for. Echidna circled

Rachel and scratched at her scales, flaking them onto the dead forest floor. It would be time to shed soon.

Finally, Echidna decided to take the seer to the Fates' lair as instructed. She wanted to avoid a trip to the Underworld. Replacing the mortal's blindfold, she dragged the girl out of the woods unceremoniously.

Rachel remained conscious, unable to move, with her eyes stuck open under the blindfold. Although her body was frozen, she felt through aching muscles the change in terrain from wooded, to grass, to smooth ground. Occasionally, Echidna would pick her up and carry her like a plank of wood. Rachel was thankful for a break from feeling like a battered piñata. Slowly, the venom wore off, and she painfully wiggled a few fingers and worked stiff joints. When she could move her legs, she was forced to walk. It was like walking through quicksand. When Rachel trudged too slowly, Echidna pushed her from behind, pressing on the puncture holes in her back until she wailed, deliberately torturing her.

The ground became solid through Rachel's sneakers and she could smell the ocean. She couldn't hear any waves, so she was uncertain how close they were to the coast. When the breeze on her arms disappeared, Rachel deduced they were entering some sort of cave. Oh, great, she thought sarcastically, my favorite!

The weary journey came to an end when Echidna jerked Rachel to a stop. Rachel strained to feel or hear any clues as to where they could be and jumped when she heard a female voice speak in front of them.

"Hello, Echidna. Whatever happened to your eye?" The voice paused, then spoke again after what Rachel assumed was a mental conversation. "I see, an accident with the prisoner."

Rachel's skin tingled as she sensed the owner of the voice

draw close to her. The voice spoke, warm on her cheek. "I suppose you want to eat this girl?"

The answering jaw snaps made Rachel's skin crawl, and she nearly buckled at the knees.

"You FOOL!" roared the voice, blasting Rachel's eardrum and echoing through the cave. "You bring me mortal garbage and think you deserve my favor? You're nothing but a scaley dragon, born to slither on your belly! You were to bring us Arkaeivahina, and instead you brought yourself dinner? This is your reward."

Not that Rachel had any love for Echidna, but she didn't care for her whimpering during the tirade and the horrible hissing shriek she made at the end of it.

A gagging stench filled Rachel's nostrils and she plugged her nose, stifling the bile rising in her throat. The voice spoke again, calmer now, but cold. Rachel kept still. If the mother of monsters was afraid of this woman, then Rachel was knocking at death's door.

"I suppose I'll have to find out why my sister has been spending so much time with you before we dispose of you. Consider yourself lucky."

For sure, this was a Fate. Which one, Rachel hadn't a clue. Although terrified, she was grateful Echidna hadn't had time to reveal she was a seer. She was even more grateful to still be alive.

Chapter 23: Bandits

"This is humiliating! Why are we going by sea anyway?" said Chris, frowning so deeply at his loss of dignity that his short beard touched his chest. He and Arka were hiding under a heavy tarp in the back of a pickup truck parked near the water at WHOI, the Woods Hole Oceanographic Institution. The wharf bustled with energy in the midday sun, full of people in colorful winter gear going about their business, running errands, and Arka dove for the first cover she found. Her weave of hiding didn't conceal Chris, and if he walked around with his goat legs visible, there would be questions.

"Echidna took Rachel through my gateway to the wood beyond the cliffs, near the cave entrance to my sisters' lair. They know it's easier to weave a gateway a second time in the same place. They'll set a trap there," said Arka, reminding him as one would a small child. "You know I can't make a gateway inside any dwelling for a god. One must enter without use of powers, humbly, and seeking."

Chris snorted and smacked the tarp away from his face for

the hundredth time, uncaring that it was the only thing keeping them from freezing. "How is the pool under their lair reserved for sea beings seeking an audience, *if* they dare, better than the ground entrance? Your plan is ludicrous!"

Arka stiffened at the insult, her voice going dry. "They don't expect me to use the underwater entrance because . . . it's difficult to reach."

Chris harrumphed, his glasses sliding down his nose. "What will the seer say when she learns you stole her mother's ID badge?"

"Her name is Rachel," said Arka, lifting a shoulder, "and her mother would want us to use any means necessary to save her."

"You didn't answer the question."

"Look, I'm sorry we have to hide. Would you prefer we run in now?"

"Run in? Arka, if a security guard shoots me, I'm gone. If *you* die, you get to wake up in the Underworld with a chance at getting back here." He crossed his arms. "No thank you."

"So, we must wait until nightfall when the port is minimally staffed before we sneak aboard the ship." She shifted uncomfortably, pushing tangled ropes out from under her back. "I don't enjoy waiting either."

"Just have your weave of hiding ready so you can conceal yourself the moment it's clear." He gave her a resolute look. "I will disguise myself with the clothes you found for me. Only to get aboard the vessel, mind you, I will not wear them for the duration of the trip!"

Arka bit her tongue to keep from laughing at the absurd image in her mind of a satyr dressed in a child's ski suit. Chris stared her down, reading her thoughts until she turned away chortling. "Why don't we go over the plan again?" she suggested. She knew he enjoyed being a know-it-all and listening to him hash out their plan kept him from complaining.

"Once you administer the dream weave on the night crew, just a short one mind you, we don't want them all in comas," he cautioned, pointing a finger at her. Then he ticked tasks off his remaining fingers. "I will get to the primary controls, use the mother's security card to log into the system, direct us to open water, cross the barrier between worlds in the Atlantic, then steer the submersible to the underwater entrance of your old home." Chris nodded to himself, reassured by his list, tinking a hoof against the wheel well of the truck bed.

"Stealing a U.S. Navy owned ship sounds easy the way you describe it. Don't forget the three-tier security system!" She turned her head to the side, looking him in the eye. "Theoretically the people on board won't have any issue crossing the barrier because we are acting as guides. Right?" she asked, seriously.

"That is correct," said Chris. "Of course, there's is a risk that when the ship hits the barrier it will explode. Honestly, I cannot recall another instance someone drove a vessel of that size loaded with mortals into the realm of the gods, let alone attempted to get them all out again." He shivered. Their muffled hiding place suddenly more confining and cold. The jerky movement bumped his briefcase, and the latches sprang open, popping the lid like a can of biscuits. Colorful handkerchiefs exploded in tiny parachutes, filling their cocoon. Arka caught one, grabbing it before it fluttered onto her face.

"What-why do you have these? You said you were packing for the quest."

"You gave me time, so I packed extra hankies!" Chris snatched the vibrant argyle square out of Arka's hand, smoothing the wrinkles she'd made balling it up. "It's my first adventure, Arka. How am I supposed to know what I'll need?" He placed the now folded handkerchief carefully next to its siblings, storing it neatly. Chris loved order and arranging the briefcase gave him a sense of alignment. His parchments at home never seemed organized, but he knew where everything was. Deities and creatures always came in needing information and re-arranging his things. With a small case like this, he knew where each item belonged, and could keep it that way. Satisfied it was just so, he clicked the latches shut, punctuating his statement.

"I thought you'd pack maps and books; not accessories!"

"I did!" said Chris, defending himself. "Who are you to judge, anyway? I'm not questioning your packing decisions." He gestured at her stuffed bag, wedged between them.

"I brought necessities."

"While we're on the subject . . . did you happen to bring any food?" asked Chris, still gazing at her bag, trying to guess what kind of treats it contained. He wished for a fresh apple but looked away, embarrassed. "I forgot to pack some."

"I did," Arka said, rolling her eyes at his skewed priorities. "Would you care for a snack?"

Chris swiveled his head back, nodding eagerly, his eyes hopeful.

Arka rummaged around and pulled ambrosia wafers from her pack, handing Chris a few. "You should put on your, um, disguise," she said, taking a bite of her own copper colored wafter, "for warmth."

Chris accepted the wafers graciously. And although they weren't as delicious as a crisp, crunchy apple, he ate them with impeccable manners, not dropping a single crumb. One didn't want to be wasteful, even when snacking in the back of a truck bed. Also, the longer he munched his snack, the less time he'd have to spend wearing the abominable outfit Arka called a disguise.

Chapter 24: Yacht Club

Under the camouflage of night, Arka and Chris crept out from under the tarp, climbing quietly out of the truck. Silence covered the wharf like a blanket, ruffled only by the soft rolling of the tide.

Arka draped a weave of hiding over herself and popped her spine softly as she stood to her full height.

Chris stood next to her, a puffed-up marshmallow in a blue ski suit with silver reflective tape sewn in a V down the front. His arms stuck out at the sides, too round to put down. Child size mittens dangled lifelessly from the armholes, attached by yarn strung through the inside. A pair of fluffy pink earmuffs completed his look of shame, the band effectively hiding his horns but the poufs widening his head circumference substantially. He looked like a grumpy, bearded miniature snowman.

"Would you like a pocket square hanky pinned to the front?" teased Arka in a hushed whisper. The weave of hiding didn't conceal her snorting, and Chris glared harder, which only made him look more hilarious. Arka covered her mouth to stave off a burst of laughter.

"If you please," Chris whispered back through his teeth, "let's get on with it!"

They edged closer to the docks, the poufy legs of the one-piece snowsuit swishing noisily with every step.

"Hush!" Arka hissed, tossing her braid off her shoulder and glancing around to check if anyone was nearby. They'd almost reached their targeted guard shack, and she worried someone would hear and stop them.

Irritated, Chris flapped his scarecrow arms, indicating he had no control over the squeaking noise.

The port security guard on shift poked his head out the shack door upon hearing a strange sound. He saw a small figure heading his way and stepped outside the shack's entrance, pulling his hat down tight over his ears to investigate.

"Hey there, little fella, are you lost?" he called, taking a few steps forward. A crease formed between the guard's full eyebrows when the lost child he'd spotted turned out to be a tiny businessman, clutching an adorable briefcase, all bundled up for a winter storm. The guard frowned in confusion when he got a good look at Chris's bearded face, pink furry earmuffs, and fogged up spectacles. "What the?" The guard brought his walkie talkie to his lips just as Arka placed a weave of dreaming over him.

"That's cutting it rather close, Arka," said Chris, swishing over to help her drag the guard, now a life size mannequin asleep with his eyes open, back into the guard shack.

"Sorry," Arka said. "My fingers are cold. I'll be as quick as I can with the others." She lifted a plastic cover attached to the wall inside the wooded shack and pressed the large red button inside, releasing the exterior gate lock. Darting through the gate like an invisible ninja, she snuck down the dock placing a weave over each mortal still there. The people stayed in whatever position they'd been in, but their minds fell into a deep dream state that Arka made sure was pleasant. Unlike what had happened to Rachel, this dream manipulation was gentle, coaxing their minds into dreaming they were superheroes, mighty champions, and whatever else their hearts desired.

In Arka's wake, Chris clopped as quietly as he could manage, pretending the air whistling between the rasping waterproof fabric around his legs was an audience cheering him on with every step. Swish, *Go Chris,* swish, *go Chris,* swish, *go Chris!* He was on a mission, and the thrill of it filled him. Nervous excitement welled in his stomach as he approached the research ship that sat hulking in the water, the side of its dark hull proudly displaying her name–ATLANTIS in white block letters. The behemoth ship weighed over 3,000 gross tons, stretched 274 feet, and had two hydraulic cranes built into the rear deck. The submersible vessel *Alvin* had been loaded on the back of the ship, ready for underwater exploration.

Chris avoided the still-life scientists and crew members Arka'd put to sleep on the ship. They creeped him out. He climbed a steep graded staircase to an upper level and, glancing around, ducked through a door to the ship's bridge where he wouldn't have to worry about them.

He slid toward the numerous panels full of controls and glowing lights arranged in a semi-circle, enjoying the soft hum of electronics; and bleated loudly in surprise when he noticed a man standing stock still, staring at him.

Chris shook his head, scolding himself for being foolish. Of course a captain would be here! He'd read that in his Sailing for

Novices book. Chris relaxed, it was a good thing Arka'd been so thorough.

"What the devil do you think you're doing in here?" demanded the ship's captain. His hat had decorative gold leaves embroidered on the dark bill, shadowing his sharp features.

"Gah!" Chris sputtered a response, trying to remember the proper title. "Well, Sea Captain Commander Sir, I um, was sent here to ah . . ."

The officer stepped up to Chris, who snapped to attention, his ski suit squeaking out air as if someone had stepped on a dog's chew toy. He grimaced, struggling to think of what to do. Chris tried to salute but the blasted contraption he wore stopped his elbow from bending properly! He ended up managing a half arm bend, with a mitten tick-tocking back and forth like a tiny pendulum at his wrist.

"Children are not authorized on the bridge," the officer said sternly, jutting his pointed chin at Chris. He opened his mouth and giggled.

Chris looked at him confusedly. "Erm?"

"At ease," said Arka as the air shimmered and she appeared next to the captain, her eyes dancing with amusement and her aura lighting up the officer's frozen face of condemnation.

"Arka, I just don't know about you sometimes! Your idea of fun is completely abnormal." Chris yanked down on the ski suit's zipper and stepped out of the fluffy pile, kicking it to the side.

"Aww, you were so darling," said Arka. She made a cutesy face like she was admiring a baby.

Chris stuck his tongue out at her.

Arka laughed. "It took me longer to reach the bridge than I initially thought. My apologies."

Chris tilted his head sideways, deciding whether or not to believe her. Arka'd always been extremely serious. He didn't care for the fun seeking version of her. "Right," he said, still doubtful she hadn't scared him on purpose. Regardless, he was thankful to be rid of his mortifying costume and onto more important matters. He shifted his attention to the ship's complicated control systems, folding his hands together, cracking his knuckles. Operating a man-made ship would not be easy; especially with Arka playing practical jokes on him.

Chapter 25: Meet Your Fate

Rachel heard water dripping as the Fate led her deeper inside the lair, blindfold intact, twisting through an oppressive labyrinth, making it impossible for her to get any bearings. They paused in an open space; the air laden with a powerful weightiness that gave her goosebumps. Rachel sensed the presence of two more goddesses. Her skin tingled as one of them circled her several times before speaking. An unfamiliar voice gently crooned in her ear.

"Tell me child, where is Arkaeivahina?"

It was the most beautiful voice Rachel had ever heard, full of her fondest memories wrapped in sunshine, and she wanted to answer, even after being called a child, but she hesitated. This isn't right!

The voice sweetly coaxed again. "You may know her as Arka. Tell me child, where is Arka?"

The voice compelled her to answer. No matter how much the tiny part of her brain told her to keep quiet or lie, she had to speak truth to the sweet voice. After all, there was no harm in it.

Was there? "Arka has fallen to Tartarus," said Rachel, glad she knew the answer to the question and could please the voice. She turned her head toward excited murmurs, but the delicate voice lured her back.

"How is it you know her child?"

"I'm helping her mend the tapestry and fight her sisters."

The voice laughed, chiming little bells, accompanied by two other laughing voices that brought Rachel partially out of the hypnosis. One of them hollered at her, charred and ragged.

"You? Help fight three powerful goddesses even Zeus himself doesn't meddle with?!" The burnt voice cackled. "Tell us how you plan on doing that!"

Rachel frowned. This voice mocked her, and she didn't like it.

"Tell her to answer me!"

"I ask, Atropos. Something you could learn to do," retorted the honeyed voice. "I simply *ask* people for information, and they naturally want to please me."

"Shut up and ask then, Lachesis!" barked Atropos.

Lachesis leaned close to Rachel, purring in her ear. "My dear, can you share your plans to defeat the three Fates?"

Rachel nodded, pulled back into the hypnotic questioning like a downhill rollercoaster, thrilled to answer. "We visited the god of secrets and he sent us on a quest for a special artifact powerful enough to weaken them," she added whispering, "to even steal their powers."

The other Fate who'd been listening this whole time laughed with superiority. "You never met the god of secrets because he is here with us! That artifact was a ploy, and you fell for it, stupid mortal." She sniffed. "Lachesis, have her tell us who else is working with Arka."

Rachel did not like that voice. It was bossy and rude. It was the first voice she'd heard when Echidna delivered her here. It must be Clotho. A gentle touch on her cheek and the smell of vanilla brought Rachel's mind back to Lachesis.

"Would you mind telling me who else is working with Arka? Who is helping her?"

Suddenly a bright light shone through Rachel's blindfold. The charming voice disappeared, and her head filled with a different one. It was distinctly male, full of purity and power; not manipulating at all. I'm having a vision, Rachel thought, reaching to remove the blindfold.

"Do not remove the blindfold, dear one," the voice warned her gently. "If you look upon me, you will perish. Keep it fast, for your protection."

The voice filled Rachel with peace. She lowered her hands.

"Listen closely, and I will tell you how to resist Lachesis."

"I'm listening," she said. The moment Rachel accepted instruction, miraculously, the pain in her body vanished. Her scratches, bruises, and splinters all disappeared!

"Tell Lachesis the Creator is helping Arka, and He has been protecting you. Can you do that?"

"Yes."

"Good. The only destiny the Moirai cannot see is their own. Therefore, they are afraid of it. I bring judgment and extinction to them and am the only being they fear. You can use this fear against them. Tell them these three names as well: Chris, Poseidon, and Hephaestus."

Rachel nodded, closing her eyes behind the blindfold at the brilliance shining through. "Will saying those names put anyone in danger?" she asked tentatively.

There was a soft chuckle. "There is always danger, my dear.

187

It is the choices made that influence the outcome. Chris is with Arka as we speak. Poseidon ignores the machinations of these wicked ones. Hephaestus was forced to create the false cuff, but he left the torch for you to see by. He forged the real Cuff of Capture to inhibit the power of a deity. These three know it could be their undoing, and still search for it."

Rachel smiled, relieved Arka was okay. "Thank you."

"You are most welcome child."

Rachel didn't feel patronized when he said the word child. It felt comforting, like she was *his* child.

"I have bestowed a gift upon you. In your pocket, there is a metal plate with a piece of used thunderbolt embedded in it. It will have to be powered, but once unfolded, anyone who stands upon the plate will be substantially electrocuted if you touch them."

"If I touch them?"

"You are the spark, Rachel. The ignitor of light. You can see things the gods cannot and that makes you useful to them; but remember, it is up to you to share your knowledge or not."

For the first time, Rachel was grateful for her abilities as a seer. "I will do the best I can."

"I knew you would child, that's why I chose you. Wait for the best moment to use the Plate of Power. You'll know when." The light faded behind the blindfold. "Fear not Rachel, I will always be here when you have need of me."

"Wait, how can I resist Lachesis' voice?"

"You just did."

The light disappeared, but her wounds remained healed. Rachel shivered, the chilly cave pressing in on her once more. She marveled at the additional weight in her pocket, and the metal plate secretly tucked away there.

Lachesis spoke loudly, barging into her thoughts. "Who is helping her?"

Without missing a beat or changing demeanor, Rachel answered. "The Creator is helping Arka and protecting us."

There were several gasps at this revelation. Standing still, with eyes closed behind the blindfold, Rachel recited the other names from memory. "Chris, Poseidon and Hephaestus are also involved."

A heavy, stunned silence filled the air, like frozen custard filling a cone. Then all three sisters scrambled around, calling to one another.

"We must use the eye!"

"Locate the motorbike!"

"Search for these gods!"

"They dare challenge us?"

"What about the girl?!"

The flurry of activity halted. Rachel awaited her fate, but she wasn't afraid anymore. She knew the Creator was with her.

"Let her meet the real god of secrets. Harpocrates could use a little company, I think," rasped Atropos.

"Yes. We will keep her alive to question further after we have investigated her claims and nullified these threats," agreed Clotho, making the final decision.

Still pretending to be under Lachesis' spell, Rachell followed her blindly, deeper into the lair, where the air smelled rotten. Lachesis called out in singsong.

"Brought you some company Harpo!" She laughed, her high-pitched chiming giggle stabbing at Rachel's eardrums now that the charm had dissolved.

Atropos joined in and roughly grabbed Rachel's arm. Rachel felt herself falling and crashed to the ground, crying out in pain.

The two Fates laughed from far away, their voices dissipating.

So much for not having any injuries, Rachel thought. She'd landed on her side, knocking her shoulder out of joint. It throbbed fiercely and she tried not to cry from the pain, breathing through her mouth to lessen the stink in her nose. After a few breaths, she shoved it back into place. Nauseated, she reached up to remove the tattered blindfold, her shoulder burning with the movement. When no one stopped her, she pulled it free, relieved to have it off.

Unfortunately, it was too dark to see anything but shadows. Rachel looked up and rubbed her eyes. Far above her, a dim hole teased the only exit. She'd been tossed into a deep pit. A garbage pit by the smell of it, she thought. I bet this is the same one Arka was stuck in. Maybe I can climb out. She massaged her shoulder thoughtfully and scooted through damp dirt, feeling for the wall. She froze mid reach when someone spoke in the darkness.

"I wouldn't do that if I were you. The stones in the walls are electrified, they will shock you."

Rachel drew back, surveying the darkness. "Thanks for the warning," she squeaked. She couldn't see anyone, and the hairs on the back of her neck lifted. "Are you the god of secrets?"

Silence.

He wouldn't be very good at keeping secrets if he gave away his identity anytime someone asked, Rachel reasoned. She tried again, willing her voice to cooperate. "How long have you been down here, sir?"

Silence.

Rachel kept still, listening hard, and eventually heard a soft sigh.

"I think by human standards of time, over a year. Closer to a year and a half, I think." The deep, quiet response was half swallowed by the shadows.

"What?!" exclaimed Rachel, splitting the darkness with her surprise. "They set up that trap a year and a half ago?" The revelation slowly sunk in. She pulled her knees up, slumping over them, dismayed.

Hopelessness squeezed Rachel's heart. Biting her lip to keep from crying, she tried thinking about the Creator and his peace. It was hard after realizing her entire journey had been a trap from the beginning. "It's pointless," she whispered, lamenting, and a tear slipped down her cheek. She didn't bother wiping it away.

* * *

Rachel lost track of how many days she wallowed in the pit. Every so often a pile of rubbish was thrown down, and she scrounged through, desperate for something to eat. How she longed for one of her dad's charcoal burgers! Instead, she learned to suck marrow out of leftover bones.

Harpocrates waited for her to scavenge first, and when she'd finished, he would pick through whatever was left.

Water that seeped through the wall's stones was enticing. Rachel couldn't touch the wall without being shocked, so she waited for the water to condense and trickle to the ground. She scooped the wet dirt into her hands and squeezed out meager drips onto her dry cracking lips.

I can't go on like this, she thought, sitting in the silent darkness. What would Arka do in this situation? Probably scold me. Rachel's shoulders bounced with a halfhearted chuckle.

Moving always helped her think, but she was weak with hunger. Angrily, she pushed herself to her feet, burying her feelings of defeat. Her friend wouldn't give up, and neither would she!

Carefully taking a couple steps one way, making sure not to walk into the wall, she turned back, following the steps in the other direction. In this pattern she paced, racking her brain for a plan. Arka would surely come for her. When she did, Rachel needed to be ready.

"Think!" said Rachel out loud, accidentally overstepping her designated path. She felt her cell phone buzz and reached to answer it. Wait, I don't have a cell phone! Pulling the metal plate from her pocket, it vibrated again, a faint shimmer appearing on the smooth surface, then quickly fading. The pieces of Zeus' bolt needed re-charged like a cell phone!

Rachel laughed. The Fates had literally dropped her in a life-sized charging station. Cautiously, she put the palm length metal plate on the ground and unfolded it. It looked like a tiny metallic book held together in the center with a delicate hinge. Pulling her shoe off, Rachel slid her hand into it, and using the rubber sole to protect herself from the electric current, nudged the open plate closer to the wall. The Plate of Power shivered. Another nudge, and it stayed illuminated longer before going blank again. It was working! Rachel pushed the plate closer, and it pulsed, a soft lighthouse beacon eclipsing in the night. Her eyes were sensitive to the gentle lumens, but her excitement kept them open, completely rapt.

Rachel heard the god of secrets shamble closer and she tensed, wary of his presence. What if he tried to steal the plate and used it as a means for his own escape?

Harpocrates rumbled softly, bemused. "Are you charging parts of an old Zeus bolt with the very walls of our prison?"

Rachel sensed he didn't pose a threat, but she needed to be sure. The last god of secrets had gotten her captured by a snake woman who nearly killed her! The glowing metal plate helped her make out a lump of shadow. "I sure am. I'm going to charge this puppy with enough juice to electrocute those crones senseless. And since you wouldn't even tell me your name, I'm hoping you won't tell them about this."

"Of course not," Harpocrates assured her in his deep bass. "I wouldn't want to ruin the surprise."

Rachel smiled. They sat quietly in amiable silence, hope kindling inside the dark pit as the plate absorbed its power.

Chapter 26: First Boat Race

"I can't see a thing!" shouted Chris, searching frantically for a switch to defrost the wide window glass surrounding the bridge.

Arka found it for him, flicking it up with a click. The frost melted back, retreating to the window's corners, revealing personal yachts and boats scattered like pale confetti in the starlit harbor, anchored obstacles in their way. She cringed when the bow of their mega ship nosed a small fishing boat, sideswiping the smaller vessel, leaving its side hull dented in half.

"Careful, Chris!"

"Balderdash!"

They crash-pushed three more boats out of their path while turning out to sea, one of which tipped over, sinking into the dark water, its toothpick mast bobbing once before disappearing completely into the sleepy depths below. They cruised over its watery grave without apology, striving for distance.

Alarms sounded all around the harbor, swarming with Coast Guard law enforcement like a disturbed beehive, spitting out angry bees, stingers at the ready. Several cutter patrol boats were

THE FOURTH FATE

already pursuing the stolen ship as Chris maneuvered them
further out to sea. "They won't fire on their own ship," he said
confidently.

Arka leaned over a blinking radar screen, spotting five
objects heading straight for them. One was moving incredibly
fast! She tapped the screen. "Are you sure about that?!"

BOOM!

The walls of the research ship rattled like a tin can, tossing
Arka off balance. She gripped the control counter, barely
catching herself before toppling over.

"Apparently, I was wrong!" hollered Chris defensively,
flying over the controls in a frenzy, managing all the operations.

BOOM!

Chris bleated loudly. "It's not torpedoes!" he hollered,
"What are they shooting?"

"Maybe cannons?"

Chris screwed up his panicked eyes at Arka, in the middle of
a fight-or-flight response. His tendency was flight.

Arka tried steadying him with an even tone. "Maybe they're
rubber cannonballs. It doesn't matter, we can't leave the ship;
you have to steer us to the border, Chris." His eyes had bulged so
much that all the whites showed, like protruding ping pong balls
glued in his head. "Chris!" Arka yelled, trying a different tactic,
and he jumped. "They can't cross into the realm of the gods with
us! Go!" she commanded.

Chris nodded vigorously, his glasses bouncing, and whipped
back to the central command station. "Hold on!" he said,
slamming the rudder and thruster leavers. The ship pitched,
sending several items crashing to the floor.

Arka lunged sideways and caught the falling officer before
his head hit the arm of a command chair. There were three seats

on the bridge, a pair up front and one in the rear. Chris scurried around all of them, focused on their getaway. Arka laid the man carefully on the floor. His right arm stuck out, still pointing angrily at Chris. "Careful!" Arka admonished him. "We don't want crew members getting hurt while they're sleeping."

"My apologies goddess!" he bit back, raking a hand through his hair. It poked out wildly around his mini horns, adding to his crazed look. "It's not like I've ever done this before, you know!"

Arka pressed her lips together to stop her retort, something she wouldn't have done before befriending Rachel. Time with the girl had grown her tolerance. Arka smiled sadly. She missed arguing with her young friend.

Another explosion shook the ship, but it wasn't as powerful. "We're gaining distance," said Chris, mostly to himself, concentrating on his work. He poured over one of his precious books he'd brought along. It was propped up on the control station, next to a perfectly creased map, unfolded neatly for him to plot their course on. He checked and rechecked their position, tweaking levers and knobs as needed.

"Good. I'll check on the other mortals to see if anyone got injured during your, maneuvers," said Arka, biting back annoyance. She'd rather be of use anyway, and her presence made Chris nervous. He didn't need her hovering, stealing his concentration.

Arka quickly inspected four of the seven decks she'd found mortals on earlier. She discovered two crew members who'd toppled over. One had fallen backward onto a bunk in the sleeping quarters. The woman's hair was in disarray, but she was otherwise unscathed. The other had, unfortunately, hit his forehead in the galley and was growing a nasty bruise. Arka applied some ice she found in the freezer, so he wouldn't wake up with too bad a headache. She lowered anyone she found still standing to the floor and surrounded them with nearby items to prevent them from rolling around.

Arka hurried back to the bridge, where Chris was busy with sonar headphones. He twisted dials, listening intently, directing signals from the spinning radar attached to their ship's tall mast.

"Arka, push that lever to port!"

"What's port mean?"

"LEFT!" he screamed at her. Arka shoved the lever, and the ship lurched dangerously. Chris dashed from the radar systems to the navigation charts, to the controls, his hands working fast. "One more to outrun!" *Crack!* A window splintered into a spiderweb of glass.

They both dove for cover, landing on either side of the grounded captain, still frowning at them. It felt like a harsh judgment to Chris, considering the circumstances. He crawled to the window, peering out with a pair of high intensity marine binoculars. They looked absurdly large in his hands.

A bright light pointed at them from a coastguard cutter, revealing their line of pursuit over the dark, rocking waves. A sharpshooter, with elbows braced against the deck held a rifle steady, aiming the barrel straight at Chris.

"Gah!" Chris ducked just as the glass split into deeper cracks, fanning in a million directions. A large bullet lodged in the window where he'd been standing. The bow windows were bulletproof, an anti-piracy measure, but they wouldn't stay intact forever. "They're trying to shoot *us* now!" Chris announced, chagrined. He patted his chest, checking for wounds, his fear shifting into outrage. "How dare they!" He didn't want to return fire on the mortals, exactly, but a firm lesson couldn't hurt. He depressed a button by squashing it with his thumb, engaging water pumps all around the ship. They hosed any vessel that got too close with the pressure of a fire hydrant. He peeked over the windowsill with the large binoculars again.

"Well?" asked Arka, still on the floor with a protective arm around the captain, in case the glass blew.

"Quiet! I need to concentrate!" Chris hopped up, the thrill of battle consuming him, and sent all power to the thrusters. Their ship ploughed through the ocean, charted for the realm of the gods, forcing the coastguard cutter to veer sideways, avoiding another hosing and the dangerous rogue wave Chris created with their wake. "Ha!" Chris shouted triumphantly, throwing a fist in the air. He was master and commander now, full of confidence. "Deal with that!"

As the research ship raced toward the invisible veil between worlds, Arka felt vibrations all around her. Normally she stepped through realms at will. It had been eons since she'd passed through a border and she fretted about the wellbeing of the unsuspecting crew members.

"They'll never catch us now!" Chris pulled a cord blasting a foghorn and let out a battle cry, blaring with the horn, his adrenaline pumping. "Brace for impact!" With thrusters at full speed and the popping rifle chasing them, Chris steered the massive ship head on into the barrier. They crashed through the veil between worlds and *Atlantis* shuddered violently, the metal groaning and popping. The humans aboard convulsed sharply and Arka's skin tingled, filling with energy when they broke through to the other side. Thankfully, there were no explosions.

Within seconds, the mortals' spasms dwindled into minor twitching. They continued dreaming away, otherwise unaffected by the crossing.

Chris blew out a breath puffing his beard, and proudly spun

around to find Arka. His exhilaration winked out when he saw her wearing the same expression as the captain, ablaze with anger on the floor of the bridge.

* * *

An hour passed in silence before Chris glanced at Arka, shifting uncomfortably in his command chair. His bottom lip protruded as he twisted to face her. "I am so sorry," he said. "Please don't ruin my life thread, Arka. I didn't mean to yell at you! I was stressed and the, er, excitement, got to me," he finished meekly, his face scrunched with remorse.

Arka sat straight backed in the second leather command chair, a stern reprimand on her tongue. Chris flinched when she turned to face him. She chose to extend him grace instead, seeing as it was his first experience with battle. "I wouldn't tamper with your life thread, Chris. That's what I'm trying to prevent my sisters from doing, remember?" Arka reached over and squeezed him reassuringly on the shoulder. Chris slumped in the chair, relieved.

Something pinged and Chris leaned forward, his hooves dangling over the seat, to check new dots on the sonar screen. He listened intently with large, attached headphones. The coastguard ships had blinked off the green monitor the moment they crossed the barrier, but he watched and listened for unusual underwater activity, still jumpy from their escape. Everything read normal. The dots were a nymph family. Chris pulled off the headphones and tossed them on the panel.

Now that they were out of danger and he knew Arka wasn't going to skewer him, he returned to his normal, proper self, all business and planning. He changed out the map he'd been using with a new one from his briefcase. It had curved purple lines segmenting blotches of territories with unique markings jotted on them. "How will you get Rachel out of your sisters' lair without them knowing? Will she walk through and pay the toll on the way out?"

Arka had forgotten about the toll. As a Fate herself, she wasn't required to pay one. Mortals never walked in or out of the Fates' lair without payment, or scars. Getting Rachel out of her sisters' clutches was going to be difficult. Arka scrubbed a hand over her face. She eyed Chris, and he lifted a bushy eyebrow into a question mark. It was probably time to fill him in on her plan. After all, he was the linchpin.

Chapter 27: Homebound Reckoning

The ocean in the godly realm teemed with creatures. Everything lived to the highest potential, a richness of abundance felt even in the tiniest of beings. The majesty was lost on Arka. For her, time dragged and the further they sailed into the godly realm, the more a cumbersome feeling settled over her, weighing her down like a cement blanket.

Three days later, morning sun stretched awake in a clear sky, its rays reaching into the distance, waking up the entire ocean in a glittery cacophony of light. It set Arka's teeth on edge.

They approached a severe coastline where ocean life abruptly faded. Arka flexed her fingers, her apprehension mounting as Chris slowly brought their vessel towards rocky obsidian cliffs towering ahead of them. The cliffs jutted out of the waves, a castle-like wall of terror forcing anyone to think twice before seeking an audience with destiny.

The cliff's shadow swallowed the ship, drowning the morning sun and darkening the bridge. "We're here," Chris announced, a tremor shaking his voice, as if it wasn't evident they'd reached their final destination.

"I owe you payment." Arka reached into her jacket and withdrew the piece of printed leather scrawled with the coveted satyr song. Chris' eyes lit up when he saw it. He reverently extended his hands and Arka dropped the soft hide into them. "As promised," she said. "I hope it serves you well."

"I know it will." Chris tenderly folded away the hide, tucking it into one of the many pockets adorning his adventure vest. He smiled to himself, feeling accomplished at earning his first accolade.

They both stared out the wide bay windows, examining the jagged black rocks that piled into the sky, stabbing out the sun. Arka's aura dampened considerably. Chris felt her fade and shivered. If Arka was nervous, he was petrified. "I hope this girl is worth it."

"She is," said Arka after a moment, tearing her eyes away from the window.

"Are you sure about this?" asked Chris, bringing the ship's thrusters to a full stop.

Arka looked at him grimly, her green eyes dark. "No."

* * *

At the stern of *Atlantis*, the three-person submersible *Alvin* dangled above the ocean, attached to specialized winches. Chris had manipulated them to drop the sub when the hydraulic cranes lowered close to the water. They'd gotten stuck halfway, and he consulted an operation manual, pouring over scribbled notes as they swayed in the air.

Shoulder to shoulder with Chris inside the packed sphere at the head of the mini-sub, Arka stared out a ruler sized porthole at bleak scenery. Without warning, Chris pulled a leaver, and the *Alvin* detached from the jammed crane, plummeting straight down, excited to marry gravity. Arka's stomach somersaulted, and she hollered the entire freefall, lifting off her seat in weightlessness. Her braid floated up by her face and she yanked it down as *Alvin* splashed violently into the ocean, breaking off one of its robotic arms. Arka's skin was pale green inside the white steel cork bobbing madly in the water. "Never mention that to another soul."

Chris made a noncoherent sound of agreement.

Arka blew out a breath, her aura flickering. She had so much empathy for Rachel's weak stomach now. Nausea was awful! A wave rolled them sideways, and she counted out loud in quick repetition. "One, two, three, four . . ." why did she plan this? She hated water! She could have planned something else. Anything else! Arka fought to calm her nerves. She had to do this. For Rachel.

Chris looked sideways at Arka, but he didn't say a word. He knew better than to make her angry again, especially when she was this stressed out. He fumbled with different controls, getting a feel for the sub when the single propeller spun to life, sending them shooting toward the shining, black obsidian cliffside, jerking their necks back. They hammered through the saltwater and Arka shot her arms out instinctively as if she could stop them skipping over the wave tops. "Chris!" she shouted, slamming a foot on the dash full of blinking buttons, pressing back into her seat. "If you push one more button without telling me, you'll regret being born!"

"Sorry," mumbled Chris, "the controls are finicky. I'm going to take us under now."

Arka looked like she'd swallowed a pair of dirty socks, but she managed a small nod of encouragement. Chris pressed ballast tank buttons, and the tanks flooded with water, simultaneously venting out air, submerging them. He manipulated the stern's hydroplanes, controlling their dive angle.

Arka concentrated on not hyperventilating as water rose over the porthole, fizzing with bubbles. This little man-made sub could handle this trip, she thought. It was built for deep aquatic scientific research. It found a lost hydrogen bomb once and had even explored historical wreckage from the Titanic- where all those mortals perished in the water. She pictured bloated purple bodies dragging them to the ocean floor and squirmed in her seat. She reached out and squeezed Chris' hand, seeking reassurance. He squeezed back.

Fear was a beast Arka seldomly fought, and it was attempting to consume her on multiple levels. She concentrated on breathing through the panic, letting it rise, trusting that it would wane if she could just keep her head. Chris' hand was warm in hers and lent a slight comfort. At least she wasn't alone. She allowed the panic to drain away slowly with her breath, as they sank further into the deep.

Two miles below the ocean's surface, an opening appeared in the underwater cliff wall. Chris pried his hand out of Arka's vice grip to control the sub's remaining robotic arm, clamping a steel claw on debris covering part of the opening and moving it aside. The debris floated away in slow motion, leaving the entrance gaping. It was not inviting. There was no light, and Arka's aura was of no use, so Chris used the sub's headlight and a computer screen to navigate them through the gash in the wall

and down the dark, watery hall that followed. Not a single fish or
piece of coral could be seen. Chris swallowed dryly.

Inside a still cavern beneath the Fates' lair, an eerie pool
streaked with green algae gurgled, disturbed by lapping ripples
as the *Alvin* breached its surface. The sub's red top hat shaped
hatch pushed open, and Arka thrust her head out anxious to be
out of the claustrophobic space and suffocating water. She drew
in a shaky breath. Damp mildew filled her lungs, and she gagged.
It's better than drowning, she thought, covering a cough with the
inside of her elbow. Through watering eyes, she stared at the
lair's raked entrance tunnel just past the stagnant pond. It
beckoned her. Murky water toying around its dark rocks,
laughing at her agitation.

Arka looked down at Chris, huddled in the small pilot's seat,
eyes wide and beard drooping. "Wait for her, Chris. I forbid you
to leave until Rachel is aboard. She will need a ride back through
the barrier." She took a slow, deliberate breath, and dropped her
arm. She reached down and patted his shoulder. "Don't forget,
the weave of dreams evaporates twenty-four hours after the
people cross back into the mortal world. Promise me you'll see
to their return, once Rachel is safe."

Chris bit his lower lip to keep it from trembling. "Alright."

Arka appreciated his attempt at bravery. "Steady Chris," she
said, smiling gently. "Thank you for your help."

He nodded, swallowing a lump in his throat as he watched
Arka's boots pull up through the ceiling hatch.

Obsidian columns engraved with threats stood on either side
of the entrance, their final curse arched over a foreboding
pathway ascending into the earth. Murky water danced around
the grooved columns, laughing at her agitation. A burning
sensation ran up Arka's spine. She swore she'd never return to

205

this place and yet here she was, because a mortal girl had befriended her. She was already trapped and hating the feeling. Better get used to it, she thought, her shoulders tightening. Once inside, she wouldn't be able to make a gateway out. Arka clenched her jaw so tight, the corner creaked. Praying for strength, she held her head high and walked up the path.

Clotho's head snapped up at the sound of someone approaching outside the oceanic entrance. She expected a mermaid or some other creature had come to seek their fate. A slow, cruel smile stretched her pale lips when she saw Arka in the ornate archway.

"Welcome home, little sister. My, how we've missed you."

Chapter 28: The Bargain

Rachel huddled in a ball, attempting to conserve body heat, the metal plate long since tucked away in her back pocket. She saw a flicker of light above her. There was no mistaking it. It was too dark not to notice even the smallest amount of light. She lifted her head. There it was again! The light became a pinpointed glow in mid-air and grew wider in a circle. She knew that glow! It was Arka! Rachel's heart soared.

Arka wove a gateway in the air, chest height, taking care not to make it too wide, less it touch the electrified walls inside the pit. She knew the size well since her time spent as a prisoner there.

Rachel saw an arm appear through the light. Without hesitation she reached up and clasped it. It pulled her upward and in an odd twist, gravity was suddenly next to her rather than under her and she fell forward. Arka caught her.

"Arka! The Creator told me you were alive, and I wanted to believe so badly, but I was scared to hope." She babbled loudly, grinning from ear to ear, her dimple an exclamation point to her joy. "I knew you'd come! I knew it!"

"Shhhh!" reprimanded Arka, but she smiled too and hugged her friend. "I'm glad to see you as well." It had been less than a week, but Arka could feel Rachel's ribs. Her sisters had been starving her! Rage boiled inside Arka and she clenched her fists so tight, her nails pierced her palms.

Just then a head popped out of the gateway, floating in the air in front of them as if through an invisible wall. Rachel was astonished to see it was the head of a little boy. His dark hair flopped down over his eyes and he pushed it out of the way, reaching his arms out.

"Pardon me, but may I join the party?"

"Harpocrates?" asked Rachel, "You're a child?"

"I am a god. You are the child," he said in his deep manly voice. It sounded bizarre coming from his cherub mouth. It was the same voice she'd spoken with in the pit, but she couldn't get over the fact that he looked like he was seven years old, with cute freckles sprinkled over his nose and large teeth that showed when he talked.

"But, you were an old man before," said Rachel doubtfully, afraid to trust another god again.

"That was Dolos. He appears like your thoughts," corrected Arka.

"A little help please," rumbled Harpocrates, wiggling his fingers.

Arka jolted forward. "Of course. I'll take your arms and if you jump up, the momentum will carry you through."

Even with her support, Harpocrates ended up in a heap on the ground. He hopped up nimbly, shading his eyes in a small salute against her aura.

"Here, let me help you two," said Arka, noticing her

companions were light sensitive. She spun a small weave of shade and placed it over their eyes. The invisible fibers clung delicately to the sides of their temples, dulling the intrusive light from their surroundings, including Arka's. "It's not quite sunglasses," she said, "but it should help a little."

"It helps a lot," said Harpocrates. "Thank you."

Now that her eyes were adjusted, Rachel saw that Harpocrates wore a short tunic trimmed with gold. She assumed it had once been white, but it had long since turned brown with stains. A small purple cape draped bedraggled over one shoulder, an amulet hung from a leather cord around his neck and a gold band encircled his head, obscured by his unruly hair. He looked like a kid just in from recess who needed a good soak in a tub. For once, Rachel made no comment. She probably looked the same, if not worse. Instead, she glanced around, happy to be free, and her jaw went slack in disbelief.

They were standing in a beautiful fairytale courtyard! There were exotic trees, flowers of every color and size, rows of impressive marble columns, and stunningly carved statues all around them. Inviting benches lined the walls of their secret garden, and steppingstones dotted the thick carpet of luscious grass they stood upon. Next to them a precious wishing well with a shingled roof overgrown with sweet smelling wisteria vines, dripping with purple flowers, stood pleasantly awaiting wishes. Charmed, Rachel leaned over the edge and glanced in. Her stomach lurched. It wasn't a wishing well. It was the pit.

"Careful," said Arka, pulling Rachel's elbow, guiding her away from the well. "It will lure you over."

"We're still in the Fates' lair?" asked Rachel, bewildered. "It's so pretty."

Arka glanced around unimpressed. "What did you expect?

Three goddesses live here. It's pretty, but it's also practical."

"I thought it was underground."

"Some parts dip below ground, others below sea-level, but the living spaces are above. You can't see this from outside though, thanks to yours truly." Arka took a mock bow.

It was overwhelmingly beautiful, and Rachel was so glad to be out of her dark prison, she wrapped Arka in a big bear hug. "Thank you," she said. Harpocrates forgot himself, joining the hug as well.

"You are welcome." Arka remained wooden until they broke apart awkwardly. Harpocrates cleared his throat.

"My apologies. I give you my thanks as well, Arkaeivahina. I am indebted to you."

Arka's nose wrinkled at the use of her full name, but she nodded thanks. "I will have need of it Harpocrates."

"Are you going to create another gateway for us to escape this horrid place, or must we walk out?" he asked matter-of-factly, sitting on the cushiony grass in a shady spot under a tree.

Rachel's heart filled with fear. "Do we have to battle something?" She wobbled, turning in a circle, looking for danger.

"About that," said Arka, glancing at Rachel and flinching at her sunken cheekbones. "Sit down and I'll explain." Digging in her pack she handed them both an ambrosia wafer. "I cannot create a gateway inside the gynaikon." She tried explaining so Rachel could understand. "That's the primary room the goddesses use for working. Its position in this lair is like the underground hole of a doughnut surrounded by an invisible barrier, and the only exits are through it. I had permission to make this one gateway, on the outskirts, but the interior barrier will not permit more."

Rachel packed a bite of food in her cheek like a chipmunk. "Like at the caves in Bermuda?" She finished chewing. "We're basically stuck at the farthest point from the exit."

"Correct." Arka and Harpocrates said at the same time.

"I am allowed here, as a Fate, but you cannot stay." Arka looked back and forth between the two prisoners, grungy and starved, and bit her lip.

Harpocrates finished his snack, wiping his hands on his caplet. "Must we pay the toll to be granted exit unharmed?" He knew how these things operated and was very practical.

"I can grant you entrance from here, which is the back door, so to speak, and cover your payment but," Arka trailed her words, spreading her hands.

"But they'll kill all of us before we get out the front door," finished Harpocrates.

Arka gestured between herself and Harpocrates. "We'd wake up in the Underworld, but Rachel . . ." Arka shook her head and stuck her hands in her pockets. "A small submarine is waiting for you both at the water's entrance. It's just a matter of getting to it."

Rachel looked up sharply. "Did you say submarine?"

Arka stared at the ground.

"Arka, did you steal my mom's work project?" asked Rachel, aghast.

"I used resources I had access to. It's a long story." Arka hid a smirk. Rachel was about to press her, but Harpocrates interrupted.

"So, there is no way around your sisters knowing we have entered their protected domain." He stood, invigorated after a couple bites of ambrosia, stretching to his full height, which was still shorter than Rachel. "It's a dilemma."

"Yes."

Rachel groaned. "How will we get away then?" She leaned back against a rough tree trunk for support, exhausted but chewing her food thoroughly, enjoying the flavor.

Arka shrugged. "I struck a bargain with them."

Rachel dropped her wafer. "Are you nuts?! There is no way those crazy witches will bargain with you, and even if they did, there's no way they'd keep their word!"

Arka narrowed her eyebrows at Rachel. As ever, the mortal girl could get under her skin.

Both girls realized they'd fallen into their pattern of exchanging barbs before solving a problem. They both cracked up laughing. Rachel slid down the tree hiccupping, and landed with her legs splayed out next to Harpocrates.

Harpocrates couldn't believe a goddess, a Fate no less, allowed a mortal child to speak to her in such a way, and laughed about it. His head swung back and forth between them, his youthful face screwed up in confusion. Arka saw his bewildered face and another fit of laughter shook her to the core, doubling her at the waist. It felt good to laugh!

"It's alright, Rachel is my friend. We understand each other."

"Yeah, she's always trying to boss me around," joked Rachel, rubbing a stitch in her side.

"And she never listens," Arka said, straightening up with a smile.

"This is highly irregular," said Harpocrates, still baffled.

"We know," said Rachel, tucking a free-spirited curl behind her ear. "I am sorry though Arka, I shouldn't snap at you like that. I think I'm a little overwhelmed."

"I should think so." Arka snorted at Rachel and held out a

hand to help her up.

Rachel took Arka's hand, and the world spun away. She looked down dizzily at her feet, through the ground into a large chamber. Four high-backed marble chairs sat in a circle around a large black chasm. Rachel had seen that before. She knew the monsters down there wanted to climb out. Arka was restrained in one of the stone thrones, solemn faced and laden with chains. Rachel stomped madly at the ground. She had to jump down and free Arka! Her feet couldn't break through the ceiling and she saw something crawling up the hole. It cast a long shadow over Arka. She jerked against the chains as the shadow grew. Rachel fell to the ground, punching and tearing at the dirt ceiling but was yanked upright. She stood on shaky feet looking the real Arka straight in the face, with worried eyes shining as green as the surrounding foliage.

"Rachel! You collapsed, are you alright?"

Rachel swayed, leaning close to Arka, who had ahold of both her arms. Not wanting Harpocrates to hear, she whispered, "Arka, I just saw you bound with chains in a demented throne room!"

Arka bowed her head. "Then it's time to go." She embraced Rachel tightly. "It was good to see you. Be well, my friend," she said and pushed Rachel toward Harpocrates. "Get her out."

Harpocrates nodded in understanding.

"What?!" Rachel stumbled, and Harpocrates was by her side in an instant, lending his support to keep her upright.

"I told you, I already struck the bargain." Arka turned away and strode through the courtyard, trailing fingertips over a bushel of flowers that lit up at her touch. She passed under the ornate archway that led to the inner dwelling of her sisters without looking back. Truthfully, she couldn't. Tears streamed down her cheeks, and she didn't want Rachel to see.

Chapter 29: Left Behind

Against her wishes, Harpocrates hauled Rachel out of the Fates' lair over his shoulder. "She can't do this! We have to leave together! Put me DOWN!" She weakly pummeled her fists on his back, barely registering that they passed through the lair, and into a dark tunnel without seeing another soul.

Harpocrates was unphased by Rachel's tantrum. He had the strength of a god and hurried down the path leading to the ocean, eager to be out of Fates' clutches. He knew the bargain Arka struck with her sisters. She'd agreed to stay with them in exchange for his and Rachel's freedom. It was the only price they'd accept. He didn't want to hang around to see if they kept their word after Arka surrendered herself.

At the sea entrance, he found a boxy metal craft floating in the ocean pool just as Arka promised. A satyr poked his head out the top hatch, waving at Harpocrates to hurry aboard.

Harpocrates nimbly carried a sobbing Rachel down the rocks and dumped her unceremoniously down the hatch. The satyr helped load her into the small rear seat. She'd exhausted herself and was too weak to protest.

"Greetings, I am Harpocrates, the god of secrets," said Harpocrates, sitting at eye level next to Chris.

"Greetings. I am Chris. Um, satyr, scholar, and captain of mortal ships." Chris flipped several switches and quickly navigated the small sub, diving beneath the water once more. He steered them out of the underwater cliff wall without incident and propelled them back to the *Atlantis*.

Just like that, Rachel found herself aboard her mother's work ship, headed back to the mortal realm, the quest abandoned. How could Arka willingly stay with her wicked sisters? She was supposed to stop them, not allow them to win! Hot tears stung Rachel's eyes.

Harpocrates delivered her to a small room on the ship where she collapsed onto a narrow cot, furious with him and Arka. He mumbled condolences before closing the door, but Rachel couldn't hear him through the waves of emotions she was drowning in. Whatever horrors awaiting Arka was her fault; she didn't want to be the reason her friend was tortured! Heavy guilt crushed her. She curled into a ball feeling like an utter failure and cried herself to sleep.

Startling awake sometime later, it took Rachel a moment to remember she was aboard a ship and not in the bottom of a pit. Her upper lip had crusted over with snot and she scratched at it, letting her eyes adjust and surveyed the small room. One a chair, a tiny table, and a narrow door she assumed was a bathroom all squeezed into the sardine-can room. It must be officer quarters to house a single bed, she thought, sitting up slowly. Her body ached, but it was better since the ambrosia. The memory of her rescue and Arka walking into hell alone made Rachel shake, profusely leaking tears again.

Maybe Arka could think of a way to escape, she'd done it before. Or maybe she could fix the tapestry while held as a prisoner. Rachel's hopes weren't probable. She needed to help Arka somehow. She was a seer after all, wasn't she? Rachel sniffed and dashed her tears away. She stood up, still dizzy from dehydration, and crossed to the thick oval door. She tried turning the large wheel to open it, but it wouldn't budge. She tried again, grinding her teeth. It was stuck fast.

Did Harpocrates lock her in these quarters? Rachel peered out the circular window into the passageway on the other side. She cupped her hands to see better, but there was no one in sight. Surely there were a few scientists aboard? The glass fogged up and Rachel banged on the door. "Hello! Anybody?" Frustration at her circumstances rose like steam, and Rachel was whistling hot. She pounded on the steel door, ignoring the throbbing in her hands. "Harpocrates! You better unlock this door if you want to live!"

Harpocrates appeared in the passageway, the top of his head barely reaching the bottom of the window. He looked up at her, determining whether to let her out.

"NOW!"

The wheel squeaked, metal rasping over metal and Rachel watched it turn from inside her temporary cell.

"Did you sleep well?" asked Harpocrates innocently when the door swung open.

Rachel glared down at him, fuming and crossed her arms.

"I didn't want you trying something foolish," he said, his deep voice quiet.

Rachel snorted, setting her jaw, refusing to speak to him. It was passive aggressive, but better than starting a fist fight with a god while on a ship in the middle of the ocean.

"Follow me," said Harpocrates, unperturbed that she was looking daggers at him.

Stooping through the doorway, Rachel followed Harpocrates down a long corridor in silence. She didn't remember walking this far before, she thought. I must have really been out of it when he brought me aboard. They climbed a steep angled flight of alternating tread stairs, and Rachel had to pause and rest, pressing against the cool, whitewashed steel walls for support. Harpocrates offered a shoulder, but she lifted her chin in rebuke. Two decks up on the ship's bridge, Rachel swallowed a strangled gulp when she saw a distinguished half-goat man seated in one of the captain's chairs.

Chris hopped out of the leather seat, excited to properly meet the fabled seer. He stopped short, looking her over, his chin tucked disapprovingly, like he'd just eaten a spoiled egg. "You are the mortal girl Arka sacrificed herself to save?" He took in her ratty appearance and red rimmed eyes. "Through with the crying fit, are we?"

"My name is Rachel. Who are you?"

"I am the satyr called Christodoulopoulos. You may call me Chris. I piloted the sub that brought you here and I am the acting captain of this ship."

He looked like a tiny librarian, not like someone who should be controlling a maritime ship. Rachel rubbed her forehead. My mother is going to kill me! If I ever get home. Rachel glanced around. She'd never been on the research vessel, since her mom mainly worked in a lab at the port. Once, Rachel had touched a piece of robotics for the sub *Alvin* in the ship's lab, but only for a second when her mom wasn't looking. Just then Rachel gasped. She was thinking about her mother because her face smiled from an ID badge clipped to a lanyard around Chris' neck.

"You used my mom's ID to steal the ship?!"

"It was Arka's idea."

Rachel shook her head. "Oh no, no-no. She'll have a fit when she finds out I was gallivanting across the ocean aboard *Atlantis* with elementary sized thieves!" Rachel saw a pair of shiny shoes behind Chris. "Good LORD! I suppose that's the actual captain?" she asked, pointing at the frozen man lying on the floor under a series of consoles.

"Never mind him," said Chris, tucking the lanyard inside his collar. Perhaps hiding the evidence would preserve his authority. "I am in charge now and I was told to take you home."

"About that." Rachel wiped her nose with the back of her wrist and eyed Chris. He seemed like a knowledgeable fellow, even if he was part goat, and prone to theft. She didn't know if he'd help her rescue Arka, but it was worth asking. She wouldn't ask Harpocrates. She wasn't on speaking terms with him yet. "Chris," she said tentatively, "I've been thinking, and I'd like to find the Cuff of Capture to save Arka."

"No. Arka gave orders to take you, and the crew home safely," Chris said sternly. He gestured at her, a disheveled grimy mess. "What could you possibly hope to achieve?" He turned toward the captain's chair shaking his head. "No. I'm taking everyone home, where we'll be safe."

A fierce stillness came over Rachel and she squared her shoulders. "You're a coward," she said quietly.

Harpocrates inhaled sharply. This girl was too candid!

Chris flinched, stung. "I am a collector of knowledge, not laurels."

"I'm not after a trophy here, people's lives are at stake!"

"We will be safer if . . ."

"Safety will be a moot point if the universe unravels! I

realize we've just met, and you don't know me, but I have to try." Rachel raised her voice. "Are you going to follow Arka's orders, or are *you* the captain?"

Chris looked over his shoulder, studying her, and his lip twitched. "I am."

"Then help me."

Chris' eyes darted to Harpocrates, who shrugged. Chris faced Rachel and adjusted his glasses. "What do you have in mind, Rachel?"

Rachel stooped and pulled off the frozen captain's hat, handing it to Chris. "You're the captain now, and I'm the commander." She felt ridiculous saying it out loud, but she had to. "I want to locate the Cuff of Capture and I want to finish Arka's quest." She interlaced her fingers together to stop them from trembling.

Chris' eyes widened in surprise. For a young girl, Rachel had a warrior's spirit within her. The bravado impressed him. He took the hat from her, accepting the gift and title. "Is that so?" he asked, a smile playing at the corner of his mouth. He tugged the captain's hat on, covering his horns, feeling stately under the bill. "Well, I happen to be searching for just that. It's recorded under different names, so it's been hard to research." He clopped over to an unobtrusive chart room the size of a broom closet tucked away at a rear corner of the bridge, beckoning her and Harpocrates to follow.

* * *

"Armlet, armband, it's even called an arm ring if you're talking about a male wearing it," Chris said, excited to share his knowledge as he rolled out a large map on a high table, studying it intensely. Harpocrates stood next to him and together they looked like little boys gushing over a pirate's treasure map.

"You think you found it?" asked Rachel, surprised he'd already been searching for it. He seemed like such a timid creature.

"It doesn't sit well with me, leaving Arka like we did. Mind you, I hate adventure and I'm no hero, but once I located the hiding place, I was going to ask if maybe you could be." He peered over the top of his crescent shaped spectacles at her, his face pinched in consternation.

Harpocrates looked at Chris, thinking satyrs were poor judges of character.

"I'm not a hero either, but there wasn't anything wrong with our original plan. Plus, I think the Fates won't expect a mortal girl to follow through with the quest of a goddess." Rachel was sure even Fates fell into the trap of hubris. Prideful unbalance was a weakness she could use against them. "I'm not going to sit around while Arka gets all the glory being a martyr." She smiled at Chris, her dimple showing genuine trust.

Chris returned the smile. "That's good enough for me." He tapped a spot on the map. "I've been searching these nautical maps for a section of Atlantic Ocean not too far from here, and," he clapped his hands with glee, "I finally found it!"

"Found what?" Rachel squeezed in closer to the navigation table, clicking on an overhead light to see better. Chris hadn't done it because he couldn't reach it. The map was a creamy beige, frayed at the edges with Greek writing crammed in the margins. It didn't look like any map she'd ever seen. It was missing half the continents.

"Doily Island." Chris leaned over the map. "Satyr legend says it's where the cuff is hidden!"

"Isn't a doily a crocheted lace circle for old lady couches?"

"Yes," said Chris, straightening up, tugging on his vest. "But it's also an island."

Harpocrates checked over the map, silent but curious. He'd only heard about the artifact from legend, never of anyone finding it.

Rachel inched away from him, still upset he'd carried her out of the Fates' lair like a baby and locked her up. Thinking about it made her resentful and imagining Arka in the pit churned her stomach. "Alright, tell me about it," she said to Chris, feeling nervous to attempt Arka's quest again. It didn't turn out the best last time, but it was the only way to save Arka from her horrible sisters.

"Arka was right about you. A loyal friend is a treasure indeed," said Chris.

"Well, like I said, I'm no hero." Rachel waved a hand in the air, dismissing his praise.

"Sometimes just trying is heroic, my dear."

Rachel's cheeks flushed at the compliment.

Chris pretended not to notice. "Here are the island's coordinates." He pointed to a section on the map where latitude and longitude lines intersected. "Getting there is the simple part."

"Don't tell me, there are booby traps or invisible force fields and deadly monsters guarding it."

"Er, well, the island is mystical. Think of it as being made of sugar. At high tide, it melts away. It only appears again at low tide under the light of our moon."

"So, it's in the realm of the gods?"

"Yes and no. It is part of the spiritual realm, you see. Depending on the tide, it shifts between the mortal and godly veils and we need both moons to shine brightly for the island to solidify completely. We'll have to wait for a clear night to be able walk on it, and find the cuff before the tide changes."

"Or it dissolves?"

"Correct."

"Holy bananas. We'll have to move quickly."

"You'll have to move quickly. I can get you there, but you have to do the dirty work." He waited a moment to see if Rachel would back down. She pressed her lips together but made no comment, so he went on. "Mystical wolf creatures inhabit the island. They are from the spirit realm, neither good nor evil, but simply guardians of the isle."

"Oh, great. I just have to hop on a melting island and battle a bunch of ghost wolves before everything dissolves into the ocean?" Rachel rubbed her temples and looked at Chris with bloodshot eyes. "Why is everything so difficult?"

"Nothing worth fighting for is ever easy, my dear," he said, rolling up the map.

"But it is worth it," said Harpocrates in his rumbling baritone. Rachel pretended not to hear him. She knew silent treatment was childish, and hated it when Arka did it to her, but she was still mad at him.

"Now here's the bad news."

"There's more?" Rachel's head slumped forward.

"Because the island is part of three realms, once we cross the veil, the mortals aboard this ship will awaken after twenty-four hours. We won't be able to bring the cuff back through to the realm of gods when all of them are awake, unwilling travelers."

Rachel forgot other people were aboard. She eyed the
scowling mannequin-man awkwardly lying on the bridge deck,
waiting to take over his ship again. "If we can even get back on
the ship without them attacking us for stealing it!"

"The *Alvin* doesn't have enough fuel to get us back to the
lair," Chris said, before she could suggest it.

Dismayed, Rachel pulled her ponytail out and vigorously
scratched her scalp before bundling up her hair and twisting the
band around again. "We're still in the realm of the gods now,
right?"

Chris and Harpocrates both nodded.

"Can we ask Poseidon to help us out? Maybe he'll give us a
ride back to the lair."

Chris grabbed his beard, taken aback. "I can't just demand
favors from a prominent god! Neither can you, even if you *are* a
seer."

Harpocrates' head snapped up, his hair flopping to the side.
Suddenly it made sense why a goddess would exchange herself
to protect a mortal. He had suspected something was important
about Rachel, but not that she was a seer. There hadn't been a
seer in millenniums!

It made Rachel nervous the way Harpocrates was studying
her. She glared at both of them. "It would be on Arka's behalf,
not my own. On behalf of all our worlds!" she argued. After
recently surviving the three Fates and a snake monster, she
wasn't too worried about the wrath of other gods.

"I take your point. Poseidon may grant you favor, but," he
pawed a hoof sheepishly, "I don't know how to contact him
directly."

Harpocrates spoke up, his deep baritone filling the small
room. "I can help with that. I am a messenger for the gods, you

know. They trust me with their secrets, and I often deliver those secrets personally." He looked pointedly at Rachel and clasped his hands behind his back. "I am also a protector of children. Rachel, although your quest is a serious one and you are a seer, you are still a child. I offer my services to you if you're finished being upset with me."

He looked like a child himself, but Rachel conceded, knowing she needed his help. "Um, yes. I will take you up on that." She tried sounding official. "Please take a message to Poseidon asking for passage from Doily Island to the Fates' lair. All realms depend on me getting back there, rescuing Arka, and repairing the tapestry before it disintegrates."

Harpocrates' boyish eyebrows lifted at the last part. He wasn't aware the tapestry was so damaged. Everyone suspected it, but no one knew for sure. Now there was a seer? It was proof the situation had become dire. Knowing the full weight of Rachel's quest gave him a sense of urgency. "I will go now, Rachel. May the Creator watch over you."

"He is. He told me so. He's the reason I want to ask Poseidon for help." Rachel spoke confidently, but her palms were sweaty. She wiped them on her pants.

Harpocrates exchanged a stunned look with Chris, who spread his hands. No one knew the extent of a seer's power. Harpocrates turned on his heel like a little soldier, and marched out of the chart room, taking leave of the bridge.

Chris darted out to the control panels, flipping a few switches and pressing buttons.

"What are you doing?" asked Rachel, making herself comfortable in one of the command chairs, basking in the ocean view displayed through the panorama windows.

"I'm lowering cranes off the ship's stern to drop the sub into

the ocean. I hope Harpocrates can deliver your message in time."
Rachel watched, fascinated, as Chris manned the controls. She
could see the sub *Alvin* her mother worked on lowering into the
water in a small monitor. It jerked sideways, swinging heavily.

"Be careful! I'll be grounded for life if anything happens to
that thing."

"It already lost an arm."

"What!" Rachel pitched forward, glancing at the steering
controls, itching to take over.

"Don't touch anything," warned Chris without looking at
her.

"I wasn't going to." She crossed her arms and flopped back
into the chair.

He reached over and adjusted a knob in front of her with one
hand, keeping his other hand on one in front of him, his pink
tongue stuck out in concentration. "Onward to Doily Island," he
said when the *Alvin* detached and sped away behind the ship.
"We have no time to waste."

"We really don't. They've already started draining Arka of
her essence." Rachel looked up, surprised by her own words. She
didn't know how she knew that information, but she did.

Chris' face paled. "Right," he cleared his throat. "High tide
is at 10:09 this evening. That gives us plenty of time to reach the
coordinates I've plotted. We'll wait until low tide at 2:27
tomorrow morning for you to visit the island."

"A quicksand island of misty wolves, just the vacation I
always hoped for," said Rachel sarcastically, so over the idea of
visiting any more islands, ever. "Man, I'd rather eat candy off a
witch's house."

"What?" Chris shot her a startled look.

"Never mind. I'm going to find a cot to sleep on."

"Good idea. You may want to change out of your, er, rags too," he suggested, wrinkling his nose.

Rachel took stock of her clothing. The stolen pants and shirt were in tatters, painted with several stains, some of them bloodstains. Delicately, she sniffed an armpit. "Blech! I reek!"

"I know."

Rachel scurried out of the control room. She found a shower the size of an outhouse and cleaned herself up. She searched the sleeping quarters, lifting a few bunk beds to access the storage underneath, and borrowed a set of civilian clothes. Rachel sidestepped a few people laying on the floor, with their limbs stuck out in odd positions. One was staring straight at her with unseeing eyes.

"That's disturbing," said Rachel. "Is this your bed? Mind if I borrow it for a few hours? Oh, don't look at me like that, I'll fix the covers when I get up." Rachel covered the lady's eyes with a sock so she wouldn't have to look at her vacant face. Nestling under the snug sheet, keeping the top blanket tucked, she sighed heavily and fell asleep before her head touched the pillow.

Chapter 30: The Dissolvable Island

Rachel fell out of bed when Chris blasted her name over the ship's intercom system. She vented about it, making the bed as promised. "Can you believe that joker? I haven't slept well in forever and he's waking me up like that?" She stuffed a blanket corner under the mattress. "Rude."

Her frown eased when she noticed a cross-body bag made of sturdy brown leather stashed beneath the cot with the woman's personal items. It was beautiful, and would probably come in handy. Arka always carried a bag. "Hey, I'm going to borrow this," Rachel said, sliding the satchel out, admiring its quality. Pretty flowers were beveled into the outer leather flap and it had a gold clasp. "It's for an important quest. You wouldn't believe me, even if you could hear what I was saying." She looked down at the lady's sock covered face. "I'll find a way to return it to you, I swear."

"Who are you talking to?"

"Aaaaaggggrrrgg!" Rachel, spun around, clutching the bag to her chest. "Don't do that!"

"My apologies. I called your name over the intercom and when you didn't report to me, I came to find you." Chris stood outside the door and held out a bleached napkin with provisions bundled inside. "Here's some food I foraged from the galley, and a bottle of water. I don't want you passing out."

"I'm more likely to pass out from being repeatedly scared to death," said Rachel flatly.

"You were just startled at being caught in the act of stealing."

"I am not stealing!" Rachel puffed. "I am *borrowing* this bag with every intention of returning it." She snatched the cloth napkin lumped with food and stuffed it into the haversack, proving it was necessary. "The same goes for this outfit." Rachel waved a hand dramatically over herself and the clothes she'd found. Simple jeans, a plain white T-shirt and a navy zip-up hoodie made the ensemble. She didn't love the clothes, but it was all she'd found remotely her size.

"All I'm saying is, you can't be upset with me for stealing this ship when you are stealing the personal effects of the crew." Chris turned and trotted down the narrow passageway, the echo from his hooves stretching before them. He listed off their to-do checklist and mentioned that he hadn't heard anything from Harpocrates.

"I hope a monster didn't get him, that'd be a shame."

Chris gasped, his mental list blown apart. "Did you have a vision?"

"Relax, I was just joking."

"You and your joking will be the death of *me*. First Arka, now you!"

"Well, it's not my fault, you're the one who made me grumpy!"

"I do not control your emotions," said Chris, his voice rising. They'd stopped in the tight passageway, crowding it further, and Chris thumped his briefcase down on the deck. "Are you really concerned for Harpocrates' safety or just concerned we won't have a ride back to the realm of the gods after this?" He took off the captain's hat, turning it in his hands.

Rachel's head tilted to the side, avoiding long pipes extending down the bulkhead. "A little of both," she said honestly. "When I was in the pit, scared out of my mind, he never once tried to talk with me. It was very lonely. Then he hauled me out of the lair without Arka. I guess I still have a grudge about it and," she yawned, her jaw popping, "it's like two in the morning."

"Chatting with people isn't his way, Rachel. He is secretive by nature, and loyal. He saved you, as Arka wished it. Now he's out in the ocean someplace delivering your message, you should be grateful. As a seer its especially important to guard your tongue. Words have power." Chris pointed an accusing finger at her. "Don't let your anxiousness about the quest boil over on him, or me for that matter. And I didn't sleep at all, so consider yourself lucky."

"Fine. Sorry," Rachel apologized, stifling another yawn. "I hope his Uber system for the gods works."

"I don't know what an Uber is, but I assure you he won't let us down, have some faith." Chris nodded to himself, his short hair bouncing over his horns. Feeling like a proud professor who'd taught a core lesson, he pulled his captain's hat on and took up his briefcase, satisfied they could embark on the next stage of their journey.

On the outer deck, crisp night air wafted around them and waves splashed against the hull. The rhythmic sound was drowned out by the remarkable sight before them. Rachel's breath hitched, her brown eyes deep pools of wonder. "Wow," she whispered, her hushed voice drifting away on the cool breeze. Doily Island glimmered moonlight white beneath a clear, starlit sky. The pearlescent beach, trees, and mountains further inland married midnight blue with beautiful scrollwork made from a billion crystals.

"I took the liberty of inflating one of the rescue boats for us," said Chris, ruining the magic. Rachel peered down at an orange raft dimly bobbing next to the large bow of the ship. Her heart skipped a beat, and her eyes crossed at the distance. Chris heaved a disembarking rope ladder over the ship's side rail. "All set."

"A rope ladder? Get serious goat man."

Chris growled, an uncommon noise for a satyr to make. "The island doesn't have a dock, Rachel." With an air of importance, he explained further. "We have to row ashore. I'll go first if you're scared. I read how to do it in my manual." Chris looped a thumb through his briefcase handle, where the manual was tucked tidily away. He climbed over the rail of the ship, feigning confidence, clinging to the side ropes, determined to show Rachel the proper textbook way to disembark a ship using an escape ladder. Stepping down the ladder proved difficult, however. It hadn't been manufactured with satyrs in mind. His legs were too short and halfway down, one of his hooves slipped off a rung. Chris lost his grip and down he went, falling unceremoniously the rest of the way!

Bleating loudly spectacles and hat flying, Chris curled around his briefcase, protecting his treasure, and dropped like a rock, landing in the sturdy raft. The captain's hat landed in the ocean, floating a second before capsizing. Chris yelped in a blind, panicked fit trying to right himself, flailing his arms and legs bouncing the raft wildly against the ship.

"Stop rocking the boat!" shouted Rachel, scrambling down after him. Descending quickly, she leapt off the ladder's last few rungs into the raft, nearly trampolining Chris overboard. She pulled him up by his vest lapels, checking him over, making sure he was alright. Seeing only his pride was wounded, she let go, smoothing them down for him.

Rachel sank back relieved and felt a crunch. Twinging, she lifted his spectacles from under her back. Miraculously, they weren't destroyed, only severely bent. "Sorry," she said, handing them over to Chris and he shakily righted them, looking pitiful.

Serves him right for waking me up the way he did, scaring the daylights out of me on purpose and lecturing me to death, thought Rachel. He'd just scared her again, and she couldn't handle any more stress. "So, we're leaving the ship here?" asked Rachel, avoiding talking about his tumble, impatient to get on with their quest.

Chris sniffed, holding back tears of embarrassment, glad to avoid discussing his failed ladder tutorial. "Yes. Can't you feel the conjunction of veils between worlds? The energy here is unique and very powerful."

Rachel took in the cold, salty air and a stillness settled over her soul. "It feels magical." There was no other way to describe it. Something within her connected with their location.

"You didn't notice when we were crossing over?"

Rachel shook her head.

"Hm. Well, the mortals on board noticed. They went all twitchy again. Arka's weave will wear off and they'll signal for rescue with their transponder radar. They don't have access to the other realms, so they won't see the island. Its vector is part of three realms, remember?" he eyed her seriously. "I hope you'll be able to navigate it."

Rachel hoped the people woke up okay. She was disappointed she hadn't noticed when they passed through the invisible veil between worlds. Another side effect of being a seer, she supposed.

"Take an oar, we have to paddle the raft," ordered Chris.

"But there's an engine."

"It is too noisy."

Rachel made a face at Chris. "Seriously?"

"We mustn't disturb the guardians, Rachel." He unhooked a paddle attached to the raft's side and dipped it in the twilight water.

Rachel puckered her lips disapprovingly and took up the other paddle. After some frustration at their inability to pull in sync, Rachel took over completely. She gritted her teeth at the strain, refusing to show how hard it was. It was frustrating that after everything she'd been through, now she had to paddle a goat through the freaking ocean in the middle of the night! As they drew near the beach, Rachel saw the delicate patterns weren't *on* the sand and trees, but rather, they were *made* of them. Everything was hollow, structured with intricate crystallized designs. It was the most curious thing she'd ever seen, and she'd seen a lot of weird stuff lately. But this, this was breathtaking. She paused and took in the beauty, her cheeks and ears stinging with damp cold.

"We can't waste time sightseeing Rachel," said Chris, his hands stuffed in his pockets for warmth.

Rachel gave him a death glare and jerked the oars back in the water.

Chris was too distracted with his new lecture to notice her

irritation. "When you set foot on the island, you must state your intentions and wait to see if the guardians allow passage. It's rather like the Fates' lair."

"I didn't ask permission to enter when I was there," said Rachel. "I was pulled inside by the bossy one. Clotho, I think."

Chris whistled and drew out his hands to clean ocean spray off his spectacles. He used a colorful pocket square he untucked in his ever-dapper vest. "You were lucky she had ahold of you. If you walk in there without an invitation and payment, you burst into dust."

"That's what Arka was worried about at the Crystal Caves. I was fine though."

"Hm." Chris made a mental note. It was fascinating learning about a modern seer's abilities. "Well, that threshold may have been less obstructive seeing as how that location was a trap. Typically, you have to give a formal request and pay a toll." He pulled two silver coins from the same pocket he was stuffing the cloth back into. "Here are a couple drachma in case these creatures require payment, its better to be prepared. Payment for assistance is common in my world." He looked pointedly at her.

Rachel quirked a dark eyebrow. "Yeah? You going to pay me for rowing this boat?"

"Call us even," Chris said shrewdly.

Rachel snorted.

Chris explained at length how a request for passage should unfold while Rachel paddled toward the shore. Her shoulders screamed at each pull of the oars, the strain making her feel like she was rowing them through cement. She bit her tongue to avoid asking for a break.

Chris remained oblivious. He had her go over requesting passage several times before he was satisfied she wouldn't bungle it up too badly. "Speak with authority when you recite the request," he said. Checking his little pocket watch an inch from his face to see in the moonlight, Chris clicked his tongue. "I'll stay in the raft, but you should drag us ashore quickly. Hopefully, you make it back here before the island melts at sunrise. You have three and a half hours. I thought you'd have four, but rowing to the island took longer than expected."

Rachel wiped sweat from her brow. "Sounds great, you stay dry and comfy while I'll do the heavy lifting."

"I've heard the creatures here eat satyrs, and I'd rather not set hoof on the island. Just in case," he said, glancing down the dark beach nervously. Brilliant starlight refracted off the island's crystals, bending it into a halo around the ocean water rimming the island. There was nothing untoward to be seen.

The raft ran aground and Rachel pulled in the oars, relieved to rest her burning arms and rub her blistered hands. She took off her shoes, tying the laces together, and draped them over her shoulders. She stuffed her socks in the borrowed bag, laying its thick strap across her chest and clipped the latch shut. Then she rolled up her pant legs to the knee. She didn't want to sneak around with soggy pants and squelchy shoes. Hopping over the side of the raft, Rachel gasped, the frigid water numbing her feet instantly. She shivered and pulled the raft up shore as far as she could. A large blister popped below her thumb and Rachel hissed at the pain. To his credit, Chris helped push the raft onto dry land with an oar.

Intricate latticework made of salt crystals scratched at the bottoms of Rachel's feet. She took a few cautious steps, worried it would crumble, but it held her weight. "Any idea where I should start looking?"

"Sorry, no. Legends are vague about this place. Maybe ask

one of the creatures?" suggested Chris, already crouching down in the raft, the top of his head barely visible. The island inched into the spirit realm with the tide and his spine tingled. Rachel didn't show any signs she noticed a change. He took another mental note. It was proof to Chris she was a true seer. She belonged in every realm. Once back in his warm bookshop, he was going to chronicle his adventure and write about everything! That didn't mean he wanted to prolong the quest, though. "Hurry up!" he said, shooing her with his hands.

"Okay!" Rachel trudged up the beach, exasperated. It felt like walking on Legos. Morgan loved building with Legos. The sudden memory of her sister playing on the living room floor made her stop. She missed her family tremendously. "Lord, I pray they're alright." I'm doing this for them, she reminded herself. For their safety and Arka's freedom.

Rachel sat down, hurriedly drying her feet and rubbing feeling back into her toes before lacing up her shoes. She studied the ground while tying double knots. It was fascinating to think about how the crystals formed. She was geeking out and yearned to break off a piece to keep as a souvenir. She glanced back toward the raft, but couldn't see Chris in the dark. He'd have a conniption, she thought with a smile, imagining his face. I better leave the crystals be.

"Here goes nothing," Rachel said, climbing to her feet and zipping her hoodie to her throat. She cupped her hands, calling out into the stillness. "My name is Rachel Soarenson and I am here to find the Cuff of Capture!"

The only sound was rolling surf on the solidified salt beach, crackling at the edges when water fanned over it. Rachel had the sensation someone, or something, was watching her. Her eyes darted around, but she was alone. Cautiously, she hiked further inland. Each step made a soft crunching sound. The ground had swirling designs and Rachel swallowed hard when she looked through the cracks and saw the swelling ocean several feet below the crystalized ground.

This place is freaky, even if it *is* pretty, she mused. It's like the starched lace snowflakes I made for my mom to decorate the Christmas tree. Rachel's heart grew heavy with the memory. She squashed down sentimental feelings about her family, but they popped up again. She missed them terribly and felt so alone. Rachel started bawling. "What is wrong with me?" she sniveled. Maybe the island was making her homesick somehow, to keep her away? Rachel clamped her mouth into a hard line and wiped her sleeve over her eyes. Well, I have a mission to accomplish. She pressed on through the overwhelming sadness, deeper inland, allowing the intrusive thoughts to surface and then float away. She saw a clear path cut through the salt hardened vegetation and she headed for it with focused purpose, ignoring the crunching of her sneakers. She didn't have time to think about her family right now, and she couldn't let the torrent of memories stop her progress.

The moment Rachel reached the path, her sadness faded, and a thick mist swirled around her. It grew thicker, spreading across the path, and billowed into a giant wolf, blocking her way. The incorporeal wolf's paws were the size of her head, and its shoulder stood as tall as she did. It was unnervingly fluid-like, rolling silently as it lowered its massive head, sniffing at her.

Rachel squeaked in alarm. This gave the term spirit animal a whole new meaning! The creature swirled and dissipated, only to refigure a few paces down the path. It was allowing her to walk on! Tensely, Rachel followed the wolf creature. They progressed that way, creeping up the path until it dead ended. The hound dissolved through the lace patterned ground, washing away in the black ocean under the floating island.

Rachel stood at the base of a hollow mountain made of the most beautiful scrollwork she'd ever seen, like a giant, delicate Fabergé egg. She peered through the intricate designs where the mountain's interior lay dark and mysterious. The sound of heavy breathing lifted her neck hairs. Alarmed, Rachel held her breath and realized the heavy breathing had been her own. She exhaled roughly, snorting at herself.

I hate ghost stories! Yet here I am, literally sneaking around in the spirit world, scaring myself. Rachel hunched her shoulders and glanced around, spooked by the stillness. She was alone in the early morning dark, with nothing threatening her. "Get it together, Rach," she said, stretching her neck side to side to relieve tension and made herself stand up straight with her shoulders back.

Tentatively, Rachel placed a hand on the mountainside. It was cold and rough, but she could just work her fingertips through delicate openings in the design. A few parts crumbled at the pressure and suddenly the wall gave way, her hand busting completely through! A waterfall of thick mist poured down the mountainside, covering the hole and her arm that was extended through it. "Oh!" cried Rachel, as freezing mist engulfed her arm. She yanked it back, quickly backing up several paces, cradling her arm.

The mist poured after her, puddling at her, circling her in a thick white lasso that blew out into a great fog behind her. Petrified where she stood, Rachel faced the mountainside in eerie silence, scarcely breathing. A small whisper of mist touched her shoulder, and she nearly jumped out of her skin.

Slowly, Rachel turned around to face the mist, her eyes

stretching wide. Three massive wolf creatures blocked the path before her. A fourth one billowed, forming in front of the pack. It was much larger, clearly the alpha, with its hackles raised. It opened enormous jaws, letting a tongue of mist fall out and disappear.

Unsure of what to do, Rachel spoke for the second time since stepping foot on the mystical island. Her voice sounded obscenely loud in their quiet presence. "H-hello. I'm Rachel," she croaked, her throat suddenly dry. "I'm looking for a, um, magical arm bracelet. It's called the Cuff of Capture."

The alpha wolf bared its teeth at her, and the other three followed suit.

Rachel rushed on, "Hephaestus made it to steal the power of a god."

The pack of wolves stopped swirling in and out of focus and solidified, all stepping forward in unison, ears pressing back. Their hind legs stiffened, and their tails bristled, ready to attack.

Rachel retreated backwards, bumping against the mountainside. She was trapped! She held shaking hands out in surrender. "I don't want to steal anything, and I'm sorry I broke the, er, mountain?" her voice rose shrilly. "But I need to save a goddess to repair a damaged tapestry and hopefully save the world. Please, can you help me?"

The alpha wolf lowered its head level with Rachel's face, its snout wrinkled in a silent snarl. She squeezed her eyes shut behind raised hands, swallowing a whimper, and tucked her chin into a shoulder dreading another animal bite. Rachel held her breath. There was no gnashing. They didn't chomp her head off! She peaked through her fingers.

The alpha wolf sat back on its haunches, once again a swirling mist. Its ears pricked forward, and Rachel sagged when its hackles lowered. It fixed empty eyes on her, lowering itself to the ground, tail swishing ghostlike behind it and the other three dissipated altogether, melting into the cut-out trees.

"Should I pet you?" asked Rachel, feeling its sign of acceptance was a big deal. The wolf inched forward on its belly and tossed its massive head. How she was supposed to pet a spirit animal made of water droplets Rachel didn't know, but she reached out a nervous hand and gently scratched behind the wolf's ear. The fog tingled, rolling through her fingers.

Chapter 31: Flying

Ice crystals in condensed water vapor brushed Rachel's fingertips. They were so cold, her fingers stung. She fought the urge to ask, "Who's a good boy?" before floating into a vision.

Soaring above the island, the fog spoke to Rachel, its voice like running water. "It has been many moons since the last traveler asked to walk our island. He did not fare well. You must forgive us, we have never smelled a seer. Welcome, Rachel Soarenson. The pack is at your service."

Astonished she understood the waterfall voice in her mind, Rachel tried to answer, but her response was drowned out. It was like trying to talk with her head in a sink, and a mouth full of popping bubbles. She growled in frustration and sensed the mist found it comical.

"Think of what you wish to say," the mist instructed, speaking into her mind again.

It was intrusive, the way the fog's suggestions and feelings bulldozed her thoughts. Echidna couldn't do it, so why could this spirit creature?

"Echidna was evil. We are here to serve."

Rachel thought about a term she learned in science. "Like a symbiotic partnership?"

Patience exuded from the spirit. "Your presence is acceptable here because you carry the scent of the true Alpha. His anointment makes you worthy. Thus, we are honored to serve you. There is nothing you can do for us."

"Oh. Sorry. Um, thanks."

"Now, think about the object you seek, before the moons fade."

Good thing I've seen a fake one before, thought Rachel. She pictured the cuff, and they drifted downward. She saw herself standing on the island's path and panicked. How could she see herself from the outside?

"Do not be afraid. Only your mind is one with us in the spirit realm, your body is whole. The thing you seek is here, but if you break our crystals to take it, you will perish. Only one with pure intentions and permission may take something from our island. You, Seer, have a spirit of power and love, a sound mind, and a heart for service. You are granted passage."

"Thank you," thought Rachel, humbled by the sincere praise.

The gigantic wolf appeared in front of her body, terrifying and mesmerizing. It bounded over her head, blowing apart through the mountainside, reforming on the other side.

"Bit of a showoff, aren't you?" thought Rachel, floating past her solid form right through the latticework of the mountain. She swirled, joyfully eluding gravity "This is so surreal!"

Inside the mountain's hull, Rachel trailed along, one with the fog. They flew around a slender podium and upon it a mini treasure chest encrusted with jewels rested. There was no lock.

"There is no need to lock it," said the wolf, rushing through her mind, both tickling and uncomfortable. "We guard it."

The rumble of water in her thoughts growled so loud, Rachel felt herself starting to rattle apart. She gasped, stunned by the ferociousness, scared she'd fade away into the spirit realm. Abruptly the example of prowess ceased, and her mind went quiet again. Rachel was glad the wolves had accepted her. She didn't want to imagine what they'd do to a thief on their island. Thank goodness she'd chosen not to take a souvenir!

The wolf loped up to the chest and touched its nose to the latch. Springing open, the chest revealed the real Cuff of Capture resting on a soft cushion of blue velvet.

Rachel thought the intricate design on the cuff looked a lot like the island itself. It was fancier than the fake one she'd encountered before. Graceful swirls bent through tough silvery-white platinum, curving into a crescent shape. The desire to try it on was so intense Rachel was thankful her body waited outside. She didn't want to experience the cuff's power firsthand, especially after her last experience.

The wolf took the cuff gently in its jaws and carried it back to the wall. He dropped it there, and they floated out onto the path. "You must bring the collar through the wall. I have delivered it thus far, gifting you time to escape the island." They swirled around her solid figure. "My pack received word from Poseidon. He sends assistance for your travel to the Den of Destiny."

"The Den of Destiny?" thought Rachel. "You must mean the Fates' lair."

"Wolves have dens, Seer. Do they not?"

"Sorry," Rachel thought apologetically and felt the wolf's forgiveness. "How do I get back to myself from here?" she asked.

"Think of the thing you seek." The wolf's presence faded from her conscience. "May the wind be at your back, Seer."

Grateful, Rachel pictured herself whole and her mind floated back, fully present again. Her eyes fluttered open and water droplets evaporated off her skin, making her shiver. Rachel glanced at the wolf, who nodded in approval. She kicked a hole through the intricate salt crystal mountainside, scattering chunks to the ground and into the ocean below. She used the napkin Chris had given her to snatch the cuff off the ground, fold it up, and stuff it into her cross-body bag. No way was she about to put it on her arm to carry it. "Thanks for your help," she said aloud to the spirit wolf. It leaped into the air, trailing liquid smoke, and Rachel let out a dimpled laugh.

Suddenly, the wolf crouched down, ears laid back and whooshed around Rachel, before speeding down the path toward the beach. Rachel saw the wolf look back at her, but it never stopped running. She knew it wanted her to follow it. A tremendous roar shook the island, rattling the hole Rachel had kicked into the mountainside. It began to crumble, shaking the entire structure of the island in a massive avalanche. Rachel tore down the path after the wolf.

The brink of dawn met Rachel as she sprinted down the path to the beach, arms pumping, and her shins burning. The ground heaved, and she tripped, almost falling, but the pack of spirit wolves appeared, surrounding and catching her in a gust. The pack ran alongside Rachel, guiding and pushing her toward the beach. The water's edge was noticeably closer. Another quake shook through the island and it sunk lower into the ocean, simultaneously sinking and imploding.

"Chris!" yelled Rachel, as loud as she could through her

panting, scanning the beach for the raft. She tried pausing to see which way to go, but the wolves wouldn't let her.

The tide is shifting, I have to get back to the raft, now! Then she saw it, bobbing like a toasted marshmallow in a cup of frothy milk. Chris was standing up, waving the oars above his head like maritime signal flags to get her attention. Rachel veered toward Chris at a dead run, her breath chugging like a train engine, and he in turn paddled toward her with all his might. His arms were too short and he turned the raft in circles.

The island grew smaller by the second and Rachel's feet broke through the ground with every other step, frigid water seeping up, soaking her shoes. As she got closer, Chris shouted in horror at the pack of massive wolf creatures fading in and out of a billowing fog, running after Rachel, heading straight for him! In a boiling rush of ocean water, the island dissolved and Rachel made a mad leap for the raft. The last wolf lifted her feet with a gust of its head and Chris wildly swung an oar at it, dissipating the mist. "Get back! Rabid beast!" he screamed, swinging the oar again, narrowly missing Rachel's head. "Try to bite her and I'll knock your block off!"

"No, no, Chris!" Rachel shot a hand up and caught the oar mid swing. "They're helping me!"

"Helping?" Chris shuddered fearfully at the swirling mist. "I thought they were chasing you!" He and Rachel watched the fog reform into the wolf and its head tilted up in a silent howl as it melted into the waves.

Rachel and Chris collapsed back into the raft, spinning it about. Pressing a fist into the burning stitch in her side, Rachel peered over the edge. Sure enough, the entire island was gone. She and Chris were floating in the middle of the ocean under a blazing golden sunrise.

"Well?" asked Chris, staring at her intently, his little eyes magnified behind his spectacles. He didn't know if the mission had been successful or not.

Rachel grinned, rummaging in her bag, and produced the bundled treasure. She folded back a corner of the napkin to show him part of the cuff. "I got it, Chris. It was so amazing! Scary as all get out, but mostly amazing."

"Yes!" Chris shouted, pumping an arm in the air before he collected himself, straightening his vest. Then he bleated a cry of alarm and pointed the oar at something over Rachel's shoulder.

Twisting to look behind her, Rachel's grin widened at the giant wolf head of swirling mist hovering there. She laughed when it licked her face in greeting, leaving damp sea spray on her cheek. "It's okay, Chris," said Rachel, giggling, "the spirit wolf is saying goodbye and reminding me to wait for our guide to the Den of Destiny."

Chris blinked several times as Rachel blew away the foggy face trying to lick her again. He did not like wolves; they were notorious for always hunting innocent goats. "Den of Destiny? Is that what these beasts call it?" he said, keeping his distance.

"Don't worry, Chris. The wolves obey Poseidon, they are spirit creatures of the sea after all. They won't eat you."

"How would you know that?" Chris demanded, still spooked by the wolf head nuzzling Rachel.

Rachel shrugged. She didn't want to reveal her ability to travel in the spiritual realm just yet. She knew Chris was taking notes about her. "I can sense it, that's all," she said.

Chris harrumphed, dubious. He knew of no one who could communicate with these creatures, and if Rachel could, she was special indeed. As special as Arka had insisted. "Well, we'll see if they follow through."

Rachel spoke to the wolf, "We're ready when you are." The wolf's head dove into the sea, its fog blanketing the water until it was under the raft and began rolling the waves, calling to the deep.

"What's it doing?" cried Chris.

A figure rose to the surface that made Rachel speechless. It looked like Aquaman himself swimming up to the raft. He was a proud centaur with forelegs pawing the water, except his back half wasn't part horse, it was a fish tail. His long navy hair slicked back from the water, and he was totally chill, unlike his centaur cousins.

"Greetings, Seer," he said in a relaxed tenor, dipping his chin to his pale blue chest, where a string of colorful shells hung from a length of cord.

Rachel beamed. He was magnificent, and she was stunned. "Hi," she said. It was all she could say. She'd forgotten all other words.

"I have volunteered to transport you to the Fates' lair. My half-brother, Poseidon, sends his greetings."

"Uh, hu."

Chris came to her rescue, regaining his composure. "Our most humble thanks to you, Bythos, and to Poseidon. We appreciate the Ichthyocentaurs' assistance."

"Yes, thank you," said Rachel, coming to her senses. She felt her cheeks burning and smiled weakly, fixing her ponytail. I'm such an idiot! Could this be any more awkward?

The ichthyocentaur's ocean-blue eyes swiveled back to her. "It is my honor," he said, hooking an arm over the raft, the waves dipping below his chest.

Rachel's ears went pink and she studied his hand inside the raft, intently observing the blue tinted skin and webbing between his fingers. His twin, whom Rachel hadn't even noticed, took hold of the other side. His hand was webbed as well, but his skin tone had the hue of fresh seaweed. He bent his brow toward her, in greeting.

"Hello, Seer. I am Aphros. I too have volunteered to aid you on this journey."

Rachel mustered a surprised, "Hello."

The ichthyocentaur brothers glided through the water, easily towing the raft between them. They were the most gallant creatures Rachel had ever seen. Chris leaned over to her, whispering loudly, "Wipe your face, it's covered in fog spit."

Dying from embarrassment, Rachel scrubbed her face with the inside of an elbow, but several strands of loose curls stuck to the spots she'd missed. Rachel pulled up her knees, tucking in her head and arms to block the wind, and to hide. So much for feeling accomplished. How could she be so fazed after everything she'd been through? I should be able to hold a simple conversation! What if I can't speak when I'm supposed to request entrance to the Fates' lair? Her head popped up, the fleeting drama of youth replaced with concern. "Chris," she said worriedly, speaking loudly to be heard over the wind, "how will we get into the lair?"

"I've been thinking about that," Chris said, yelling in her ear. He was a decorated sea captain now, but this was his first experience sailing over open water and he was extremely nervous. Naturally, he jumped at the chance to hide it with a lecture. "You are not a common mortal! You survived Doily Island, and as a seer, you have leeway, I think. Crossing through realms doesn't seem to affect you. Plus, we are lucky."

"Lucky?" asked Rachel, puzzled. She pushed hair out of her face, but let a hand hover over her ear, protecting the rattled eardrum.

"Today happens to be Leap Day, Rachel!" Chris' eyes glinted with superior knowledge. "Every four years there is an extra day in February."

"I know that. So what?"

"Well," he said somewhat crestfallen, "it's the only day all creatures are permitted to enter the lair; if they are audacious enough, that is."

"Wow. That is lucky." Rachel's eyes met his. "It feels like fate."

"One's destiny reveals itself in many ways. If we are but still, we will notice," said Bythos. His jaw was firm and serious.

Rachel stared at him.

"Of course, you still have to pay their toll," said Chris, grabbing her attention again.

"But you just said . . ."

"What I mean is, they cannot *reject* your request today." Chris wound a finger around his beard. "Plenty of creatures have asked to gain entrance, only to be told to return in fifty years, or a century!"

Rachel hadn't thought of that. Her face fell. She'd assumed if she paid the entrance fee, they had to let her in. It never occurred to her they could say no. A ball of nervous energy stirred in her gut and she nibbled a fingernail. She hoped Chris was right about the date and her being special. She didn't feel special at all, and the enormity of completing Arka's daunting quest weighed her down.

"It is also considered lucky to be charioted through the ocean by the Ichthyocentaurs," said the other centaurine sea-god. Aphros winked a green eyelid trimmed with thick lashes at her. Rachel's cheeks flushed bright in the morning sun.

249

Chris chuckled at their chauffeur. "I'm just glad you aren't wolves," he said cheerily and leaned back into the raft, attempting to enjoy the ride. Rachel fidgeted with the zipper of her jacket, wishing fervently she could dissolve like the island had.

Chapter 32: Level Up Buttercup

Unable to dive below the ocean to the Fates' lair, the sturdy orange escape raft bobbed in shallow water on a narrow, rocky beach while Chris consulted a manual on knot tying, trying four times to tether its rope securely to a large, mossy rock. Still, he was having a better time than Rachel. She clung to the craggy cliff face eight yards above him, ruefully thinking over her life choices.

"Oh goody! Another rock climb!" she said facetiously, inching upward. Rachel thought back to the last time she scrambled up loose shale with Arka in the lead. There was no one to lead her now. She had to do this on her own. I've done it once, and I can do it again. How much harder can scaling this lava glass be?

It was a lot harder. The deep black rocks were slick with ocean spray, covered in live mollusks and moss. Sunlight reflected against the obsidian, bringing out midnight green undertones, and Rachel thought it was almost pretty. She reached up, feeling for a dry spot to hold and her hand touching something slimy. It squished between her fingers. "Ewww!" Rachel lost her grip, her arm swinging in a windmill, and her bag swayed dangerously, pulling her balance with it.

Rachel overcorrected and slammed against the rock wall, her head spinning with vertigo. Gulping, she looked down to get her bearings- big mistake. Her stomach churned in a wave of dizziness and her palms started sweating. Rachel closed her eyes and gave herself a pep talk. "Don't let go, Rach. Don't look down, just keep going. You've got this." Her nose flared and Rachel clutched the next handhold, digging her fingertips into the fissure without caring what lived on the glassy rock. She jabbed her foot into a crevice and using strong leg muscles, rose another crag level, grunting with effort. "Nearly there! Take your time. Take the fear and use it, put it into the task at hand."

At an agonizing snail pace, Rachel slowly pressed her way up the slippery rock wall. A broken, curved piece of razor-sharp obsidian sliced at her fingers, but still, she climbed. Finally, gripping the jagged ledge, Rachel swung a knee over and rolled onto the landing, gasping. "Yes! I did it!" she breathed, the words too tired to travel past her own ears. Her chest heaved. Arka better appreciate this, she thought, laying on the cold stone, exhausted and exuberant. She knows how I feel about rock climbing.

Rachel flopped her head to the side, sucking on her cut up fingers and stared at the ground entrance to the lair. A severe stone archway made to unnerve the fainthearted was carved into the dark cave mouth, ready to devour the next willing victim. Dread seeped into every fiber of Rachel's being. The thought of venturing into the Fates' lair again scared her to the core. Falling off the cliff would give her a fairly good excuse not to, but her friend needed her. Her family needed her. She had to try. Rachel sat up with a moan, adjusting the shoulder strap of her haversack, and leaned over the ledge, giving a halfhearted thumbs up to Chris.

Chris had worriedly watched Rachel from below, gasping and covering his eyes the whole time she climbed up the cliff face. He waved back encouragingly and sat on a wide rock, comfortable to wait and see how the fate of the universe turned out.

Like he can't climb up here with those nimble goat legs, Rachel judged, watching Chris fidget. He's scared, she realized. Just like me. I guess that means we're smart. It bolstered her courage knowing she wasn't completely alone. Rachel inhaled deeply and prepared herself, tucking the Cuff of Capture inside her jacket for safekeeping, zipping it up all the way. "I'll clasp it onto a Fate's arm and use her power to free Arka somehow," she planned, keying herself up. "If anything, I can use it as a bargaining tool."

Rachel crept near the archway and hid her bag in a stone cleft next to the entrance. A familiar rancid scent filled her nostrils, and she sniffed the air, immediately sorry she did. It smelled awful. The stench wafted from a scorch mark on the ground where Echidna had been torched! No animals had dared to scavenge the bits of remains rotting on the ground, and it had turned putrid.

It's a perfect welcome mat, thought Rachel sarcastically, pinching her nose. She stepped over the scene, the repugnant odor making her stomach lurch, and passed beneath the arch, sealing her fate. Deep inside the cave, a faint glow pulsated with her heartbeat. This was it. All she had to do was follow the path. So many people had worked together for this moment. This wasn't about making the easy choice; it was about making the right choice. Do or die, now or never. Rachel summoned her courage, and boldly marched forward, ready to face destiny's deities.

Chapter 33: Meaning

The three Fates nonchalantly hung about. None of them ever expected a mortal girl to waltz into their lair, let alone one who managed to escape only a few days prior. It took Clotho a full minute to realize Rachel was standing just outside the entrance to the main chamber. When she finally noticed Rachel, Clotho leapt up from her lounging, sputtering in surprise.

"YOU!" she screeched, pointing a long finger tipped with a pointed white nail at Rachel. The other two Fates spun around, shock contorting their features, to see who their sister was pointing at. Lachesis' eyes, thickly traced with eyeliner, bulged and Atropos dropped an enormous hedge trimmer she was sharpening. It clanged on the stone floor, echoing loudly in their stunned silence. The trio glared at Rachel, wicked intent replacing their shock.

Rachel remembered her instructions from Chris and kept eye contact with Clotho, since she was the first to speak to her. Rachel spoke clearly, formally stating her case, the way anyone who wished to know their destiny would. "I, Rachel Soarenson have come to seek wisdom from the Moirai known as Arkaeivahina."

The three sisters hissed at the use of Arka's full name and the start of a binding contract. The mortal girl knew what she was doing!

Rachel tossed a solid silver drachma coin through the doorway. It rolled along the stone floor a ways, spinning in a little circle before coming to rest at Clotho's feet. Clotho wore impressive sandals that wove up her calves, tying under her knee. A dark plumb chiton gown held in place with gold ropes allowed her arms and shoulders to move freely, exposing porcelain skin. She was so pale, Rachel felt sure she could see through her if she looked hard enough.

Clotho masked her surprise, smiling slowly, and waved an arm graciously. "Then by all means, come and seek my dear."

Rachel stood fast. She knew that to cross the inner threshold without the proper welcome would result in her spontaneously combusting. The Fates were bound to allow entrance since she'd paid the minimum toll and it was leap day. They couldn't change the Earth's revolution around the sun! Even *they* had to follow the rules set at the beginning of time, but if she entered without the proper invitation, all would be lost.

Clotho's composure cracked. She growled the first sentence required to dissolve the invisible, deadly barrier in front of Rachel. "Enter thee, if it is thy will."

Atropos, dressed in a long, sagging black peplos gown with a matching himation cloak that dragged on the ground as she stepped forward, spoke the second sentence contemptuously, spitting her words. "Hear your destiny, you've paid the bill."

Lachesis had returned to lounging on her chaise. In Rachel's opinion, she looked more humanlike than her sisters. Lachesis had buttery skin and round pink cheeks. Her plush features were enhanced by crisscrossed ropes looped around a long gossamer peplos gown that draped over her curves. She said her part in a pout, her mouth pursed in a bow. "To you, we give our service." All three of them chanted the last line in unison, filling the atmosphere with energy. "Your fate and fortune are our purpose."

A soft whisper of air brushed past Rachel's and she knew the barrier had blown away. She stepped over the threshold before it could return, quickly taking stock of the room since she wasn't wearing a blindfold this time, or bawling her eyes out. The space was a large, lavishly decorated regal throne room separated with workstations for each Fate. At the far end, a deep crimson curtain big enough for several stage performances was drawn closed. It had intricate gold embroidery sewn all over, covering it in shapes, drawings and ancient runes. Rachel's arms sprang into goosebumps when she looked at them. She felt a pleading pull from the massive drapes and assumed the actual tapestry hung just behind them.

In the center of the room, a dark chasm in the ground sucked away Rachel's hope. She recognized it from her visions and shook away the mental image of monsters crawling out of its depths. Floating in the middle of the gaping hole was a large pearlescent sphere swirling inside with creamy liquid. Around this were four sturdy, high backed marble thrones. One had a depressing grey statue sitting in it. Rachel gasped; the statue was Arka!

Arka's inner glow was gone. She sat ashen and lifeless. Her clothes were a washed out grey and her hair marble white. All her essence had been drained away. She looked like a horrible stone carving of a tortured prisoner Medusa would love to display. Arka wasn't moving, but her arms and legs were shackled to the chair and a heavy chain looped around her middle, locking behind the tall chairback.

Enormous baskets stuffed with coarse wool fibers sat on the floor around Arka's feet. Some had been spun onto a large bobbin and Rachel noted Clotho's huge spinning wheel nearby with thick thread twisting around it. She'd been spinning the fibers into thread for the tapestry. It had a faint glow, but nothing like the light Rachel thought it should have.

They were draining Arka to light the wool, but it wasn't right. If they wove that thread into the tapestry, who knew the havoc it would cause! Bile rose in Rachel's throat and she swallowed hard. She couldn't get sick now!

Clotho spoke in a deep sinister voice, giving Rachel the willies. "Welcome, Rachel." She lifted a pointed chin, calling to the Arka statue. "Arka say hello to your *friend*. She's come to visit you. Isn't that sweet?" Clotho let out a throaty laugh when Arka made no movement or sound.

Rachel fought to squash down her rising panic. Arka is still alive, she assured herself, she's immortal. I need to focus. Rachel stood tall, remembering her plan. "I am here to seek wisdom, but I can also give some in return," she said, laying the bate.

Clotho arched an elegant eyebrow and the other two Fates scoffed. "Is that so, little girl?"

"Yes, it is," said Rachel, ignoring the jibe. She crossed her arms protectively over her chest and felt the cuff, safe inside her jacket. "I am a seer."

Atropos barked a dismissive sound and bent to pick up the shears she'd dropped, her stringy black hair sweeping the floor.

Clotho laughed out loud. It was the most absurd thing she'd heard in a thousand years! If there was a seer, she would surely know about it.

Lachesis looked thoughtful, pulling on a red-gold ringlet. Her hair was piled high on her head and she fussed with little ropes, intertwining them throughout the curls. "I think she tells us the truth," she chimed in absentmindedly. The charming voice danced in Rachel's ears, but it no longer clouded her mind.

Clotho whipped her head in her sister's direction. "Do you?" she demanded, surprised at the revelation. Clotho did not like being surprised, and this was the second time she'd been taken off guard within a few minutes. Her lips curled back, baring square teeth in a fake smile. Clotho teetered on the verge of coming unglued, and Rachel battled an impulse to bolt out the doorway, climb down the cliff and row the raft as far away as she could.

Lachesis nodded, tapping a delicate finger at her rouge covered cheek. "I sensed something was amiss when I questioned her before, but I wasn't certain what it was. This girl resisted me, I think. An ability no other has ever had." She stuck out her bottom lip.

"And you just now tell us your charms weren't fully effective? AFTER this girl escaped and AFTER she has returned?" Clotho boomed. She advanced on Lachesis, who flinched at every other word and shrank back on her tufted chaise. It didn't make a difference to Clotho. Seething with fury she upended the couch with Lachesis still on it, dumping her on the floor, knocking down her coiffed creation.

"Now look what you've done!" wailed Lachesis, catching part of her tumbling tower of curls. The Fates dissolved into a heated argument and Rachel used the opportunity to slide stealthily toward Arka. She was within arm's reach when Clotho stepped between them.

"Ah ah, not too close *Seer*," she sneered, blocking Rachel. Clotho was terrifying face to face. Little words moved in and over her translucent skin. She saw Rachel glance at them and smiled smugly. "They are the names of all the people and gods to whom I have, or will grant life." Some names flitted over her unblinking eyeballs, sickening Rachel.

"You do not give life. The Creator does."

Clotho stepped back as if slapped.

Encouraged by Clotho's reaction, Rachel set her terms with confidence. "I will grant you a vision in exchange for Arka's freedom."

Lachesis righted her couch and perched on a corner. "How about you give us a vision to *spare* her life?" she purred, fixing her fallen hairdo, staring Rachel down, willing her to agree. Atropos stopped sharpening her shears and grinned darkly. All her teeth were black, matching the hair that hung heavy with grease down the sides of her face.

Rachel nearly fell for the lie, but she fought the compulsion, breaking eye contact. Exasperated, Lachesis stamped a sandal covered foot, puffing a gaudy purple rug lined with gold tassels that carpeted her area of the room.

Rachel dismissed her tantrum, speaking truth against the corrupt Fates. "You cannot kill Arka. You need her. She is the light of the universe and more valuable than the three of you combined. Without her power, you would be reduced to nothing." Arka's head rose slowly while Rachel spoke, her blank eyes taking in the scene. "Arka's purpose is greater than even *you* three can know."

The three Fates were quite shaken at this turn of events. They had never encountered a seer, or a mortal who didn't cower with fear in their presence. A child ambassador of the Creator was an anomaly. Clotho snapped her fingers, taking the reins of negotiation. "Very well. A vision, and we will unshackle her save but one leg," she chuckled then, "and perhaps we will let *you* live."

A hint of color returned to Arka's stone face. She heard parts of what Rachel was saying and the doubt in her sisters' responses. Her mind felt clouded, and she fought for clarity. Was she made for more than this? The thought gave her strength. Arka tried lifting her arm to scratch the side of her nose and was surprised to find her wrist fastened. That didn't seem right. It was uncomfortable too. She shook her head, trying to clear it.

Rachel noticed Arka's drowsy movements and stole a glance in her direction. A subtle enhancement of color in the shackles attached to her stirred hope in Rachel's belly. She stepped into Clotho's personal space, raising her voice. "I believe in Arka! I believe in the Creator, and His power is stronger than yours Clotho. I am here on his authority!" It didn't seem possible that Clotho could pale any further, but any color left in her drained away. The names that floated through her skin skidded and stopped moving. "Without Arka's light, the tapestry and the universe will cease to exist!"

Fear clouded behind Clotho's eyes.

"And you know that, don't you?" whispered Rachel, almost nose to nose with Clotho. They both blinked at a sudden flash of light. Rachel glanced at Arka. Her head wasn't hanging, and her shoulders weren't slumped anymore. Instead, she sat regally staring straight at Rachel. Tears brimmed in her eyes and she was glowing. The chair, shackles, and all the baskets around her were shining brightly. "She is also my friend," said Rachel, smiling. "No matter what." Arka's glimmering tears spilled over and in that instant, Rachel sprang at Clotho with the cuff she'd been concealing at the ready.

The Cuff of Capture touched Clotho's skin and screamed, pulling her arm back as though touched by fire before Rachel could press it on fully. "NO!" Clotho knocked the cuff out of Rachel's hand, sending it skidding across the stone floor toward the red curtain.

Lachesis squealed and jumped up onto her chaise, bumping a table that held a giant scroll. It fell, unrolling in a river of parchment as she grabbed a spool of thread the size of a filing cabinet and threw it at Rachel. Rachel ducked out of the way, rolling clumsily to the ground.

Arka struggled against her chains, but Clotho grabbed them hard, pinning her back against the sturdy chair. Arka grunted from the pressure but still fought to get her hands free of the iron shackles. Clotho swooped behind the chair, twisting the chains in a binding tourniquet, holding them taut. "No, you don't! You'll stay right where I've put you, Arka."

Rachel crawled frantically toward the cuff. She snatched it and tried standing but her shoes, still wet from rock climbing, slipped. The rubber soles screeched against the ground as she flailed upright, sprinting toward the red curtain. She made it two steps when Atropos close-lined her in the abdomen, knocking the wind out of her, sending her flying backward. Rachel crashed to the ground, aching with the need for air. She kicked at Atropos who lifted one of Rachel's legs, dragging her easily across the floor. From this angle, Rachel could only reach the Fate's legs. Wheezing raggedly, she reached down, grabbed Atropos' calf and pinched the cuff onto her ankle!

Atropos instantly collapsed into a convulsing pile, her grimy limbs thrashing, and then she went completely still. Rachel inhaled deeply but didn't have time to enjoy the victory. In a flash, Clotho had a hold of her ponytail. She punched Rachel in the stomach, knocking her into the monster pit. Rachel screamed wildly. She never wanted to be in a pit again and knew this one was teeming with nightmares.

"Shut up, girl!" snapped Clotho, shaking Rachel by her ponytail. She kept the girl from falling, gripping her hair and wadding up the hood of her sweatshirt in the other hand. "Remove the cuff, or I toss you in."

Howling at the blazing pain in her scalp, Rachel's toes scraped at the edge of the pit as Clotho pulled her up. Clotho shoved her to the floor next to Atropos' lifeless form. With uncooperative fingers, Rachel managed to twist the cuff off her ankle. It left behind a singed branding of its design on the Fate's sallow skin.

Atropos roared to life, on a hunting rampage. "You dare entrap me?!" she spat, scooping up a horror-stricken Rachel and dumped her at the foot of Arka's chair. Atropos whipped her freshly sharpened shears from a heavy leather holster that sagged on her hips. They scratched free and Atropos flicked them open, crouching next to Rachel, pressing the blade to her throat. Atropos' brutal nature radiated a coldness the sheer opposite of Arka's comforting light. "Give me that cuff mortal, or I'll end you," she said, her voice breaking in raspy, quakes. The rotten stench of her breath made Rachel's eyes water, but she kept her head up, tense against the thick blade and handed over the Cuff of Capture she'd worked so hard to retrieve. Rachel's heart sank. She wished she could somehow drain the cuff of its power. She hated to think of what the Fates would do with it.

A triumphant laugh gurgled from Atropos' throat like slow, burning lava, but the moment she touched the cuff, it tarnished. Her laugh turned into a snarl and she stared, dumbfounded, at the useless rusty cuff in her palm.

Did I do that? wondered Rachel, shocked. She felt the sharp edge of the sheers drift off her throat and taking advantage of the moment, leaned back, and kicked the cuff out of Atropos' hand. It skid across the floor, disappearing into the hole at the center of the room. "Ha!" shouted Rachel, pumping her fist as if she'd just kicked the winning goal at a soccer tournament. She was the star player, and Atropos was the stunned goalie.

Chapter 34: Don't Blow A Fuse

Atropos grabbed the front of Rachel's hoodie, yanking her upright into the air, leaving her feet dangling. Atropos bore her black eyes into Rachel's, locking her in a death stare, coagulating her from the inside out. A trail of breath escaped Rachel's lips, and she looked down her nose, watching it curdle in the frigid evil that engulfed her.

Atropos smirked, leaned close, and inhaled it. Her dead eyes rolled back in her skull as she savored the flavor.

Atropos ate soul boogers? Rachel was too stricken with fear to be grossed out. She jerked her frozen joints against Atropos' clutches, and held her breath.

Atropos bared her rotten teeth and pulled Rachel's face so close, their foreheads touched. "Delicious," she rasped. "The essence of a seer is a rare delicacy."

Clotho finished fastening another chain around Arka's chest, securing her tightly, mumbling uncouth noises. She feathered back her disheveled, dishwater brown hair and straightened her gown, pushing the decorative ropes back into place. She looked up, noticing the scene, and scolded her sister. "That's enough, Atropos! If you take all her essence, how will she give us a vision?"

"Very well," grumbled Atropos, smacking her lips. "But after the vision, I will finish her." She dropped Rachel, who crumpled to the floor, and snapped her shears shut, shoving them back in their holster.

Lachesis, who hadn't dared get close to Rachel or the cuff, moved to hover behind Atropos. A few tendrils of her hair had come loose in the commotion and she was tucking them up again. "If she doesn't honor her promise for a vision, I can pull her life strand apart, string by string," she offered, in her deceptively sweet voice.

Clotho let out an exasperated sigh. She needed to gain control over the situation. Marching over with an air of authority, she stood in front of her two sisters facing Rachel. "Can you hear me girl?" she asked.

Rachel lay silently on the ground, still stunned by the trauma of having her life force sucked out. Clotho poked her with a toe, as one might check roadkill to see if it was still breathing. "You will give us a vision, or we'll pull you apart in more ways than you can imagine. We'll start with your darling brother and sister," she half shouted. "If you don't cooperate, we'll move on to your parents. That's before we even get to you."

Terror pulled Rachel out of the stupor. With the cuff gone, Arka still bound, and her entire family threatened, what choice did she have? It was enough to mollify the fiercest of warriors, and she was just a middle school girl! Rachel's heart hammered against her ribcage as she tried thinking up a new plan. She couldn't bargain with them; all she could think to do was respond honestly. "I can't give you a vision," she said simply.

Three identical frowns glowered down at her.

"Seriously. I have visions, but I don't control them. Usually, the person I have a vision about doesn't even know I've had one."

Clotho, Atropos, and Lachesis looked at one another. It was evident they desperately wanted a vision from a seer, but they didn't know how it worked. They were bound to stay in their lair and use their eye to see the destiny of mankind. They had to use a tangible item, like a spinning wheel, sheers, or measuring staff to bring their abilities to fruition.

Rachel suddenly had an idea of how to use their knowledge and power against them. "In order to *force* a vision, the seeker must stand on the Plate of Conductivity, and I must touch them. After I wake, I am bound to tell the person standing on the plate my vision. Without the plate I can't control my power, the visions are sporadic, and I am not required to reveal what I have seen." Rachel touched her temples for dramatic effect.

The Fates murmured to each other in excitement. The names in Clotho's skin swirled faster, some fading in and out, while others had letters breaking off and conjoining again. "Where is this plate?" she asked.

Rachel tossed her head in the direction of the cave's entrance, her dark curls bouncing. "I left it in my bag outside. I didn't want you to steal it," she said truthfully.

"Lachesis, go fetch the plate."

"Why me?" Lachesis whined, shifting from foot to foot.

"Now!" roared Clotho, her patience with Lachesis gone. Lachesis shrieked and hopped to get the plate, bustling out of the lair in a dainty tiptoe run. Clotho turned her disconcerting eyes back on Rachel. "You will cooperate, Seer. If not, you know the consequences." She held her arm up to show Rachel her name, along with those of her family members floating to the surface, pressing against the skin of her forearm in a protruding tattoo.

--RACHEL-MORGAN-LUKE-EMILY-LAWRENCE--

"Believe me, watching someone being unraveled is messy," said Clotho in a low menacing tone. She gloated with power, grinning wickedly when Rachel shivered. She enjoyed toying with visitors in the lair before deciding their fate. With the cuff gone, she was in command, and having fun.

Rachel could tell Clotho enjoyed scaring her. It was the behavior of a common bully. It showed in the way she treated her sisters, bulldozing them and maintaining an atmosphere of fear. Thinking of Clotho as a basic bully helped Rachel steady her churning stomach. She'd been taught how to deal with bullying every year of school since fourth grade! If she couldn't avoid a confrontation, she was to stand up to them. If they didn't back off, she had to neutralize the situation. How was she supposed to do that?

Arka snorted out her nose and pulled at her restraints. She didn't know what the Plate of Conductivity was, but she hated how Clotho intimidated Rachel.

"No Arka, no vision for you. We already know how to control you. It's Zeus and the One we want to know how to control," her thin lips smiled charmingly, "and your little friend here is going to show us."

Rachel looked from Arka to Clotho and back again, realizing Arka hadn't said a word since her color returned. "Why can't Arka talk?" she asked, hoping her voice didn't waver.

"I removed her voice," said Clotho, shrugging. "It was for the best. She shouted the worst insults at us and after I let

Atropos take her essence, she still whispered the rudest things."

Arka gave a wry, weak smile that lifted Rachel's spirit. If Arka could fight back in her state, then so could she.

Clotho noticed the smile too and said rather loudly, "We will have to drain her essence again, after your vision." She looked down at Rachel like she was an insect needing squashing. "Her power regenerates and we can't have her escaping again. By weakening her, we can use the pair of you, as the tools you are." Clotho's gaze shifted upward, imagining the future. "I will finally have dominion over the universe." She said it as a matter of fact, not a threat or bluster, making Rachel doubt her resolve for a second.

Arka blew out a breath with horse lips and snapped her teeth at Clotho, who only laughed at her sister.

That's why Clotho said it, Rachel thought, she's trying to gain the upper hand, to keep me scared and compliant. "You can't use me," said Rachel defiantly, straightening her shoulders. "I challenge you to step on the plate first, Clotho. You'll get your vision, but the only way for me to tell it to you honestly is if I choose to."

Clotho's laugh caught in her throat.

Rachel stood up, her spirit on fire. "I'll only do that if you agree to let Arka go. Otherwise, I can make up anything and you wouldn't know the difference. I'll be bound to tell you a Vision, not to tell you the truth."

Clotho rubbed her chin. Her own sisters rarely challenge her, and she was intrigued.

Atropos spat on the ground, her dingy saliva landing at Rachel's feet with a *splat!* She'd rather devour the mortal girl and be done with it.

"I'll stay in her place," Rachel offered, refusing to back up from the spit blob. She knew any movement would be seen as yielding. "I won't try to escape, as long as you don't harm my family of course," she said. "You'd have access to all my visions. You have my word on that."

Clotho thought about it, running a hand over her spinning wheel, touching the rough strands. Having a seer at their disposal was enticing. They could capture any number of gods and have the girl read them after Lachesis questioned them. But what of Arka?

Atropos spoke as if reading her mind. "If I drain all of Arka's essence and we release her empty into the mortal world, she wouldn't be able to make gateways or operate as a Fate anymore."

Clotho nodded, following the train of thought. "To be able to see the strands of fate, but unable to use them? How fitting for our little weaver." She clicked her nail together. "The tapestry would stay damaged, but that is of no real consequence. Once we rule all the realms, we can make a new one." The deal was too enticing to pass up. "You have yourself a bargain mortal," said Clotho.

Atropos grunted.

On cue, Lachesis glided into the massive chamber with Rachel's bag pinched between her thumb and forefinger, her arm outstretched like she held a ticking time bomb. "You could have said you hid it," she fussed, flinging it at Rachel, careful not to get too close. Lachesis was afraid of the seer and after the cuff fiasco, didn't want to risk losing her powers. "I also found this," she said and sang out, "come in my sweet!"

In trotted Chris, his eyes glazed over and his mouth slack. He stood soaking wet with seaweed dangling from an ear. Rachel gasped. He was in a trance and looked like a zombie.

"He'd was trying to climb the rocks and fell in the ocean when I appeared. I sang to him though, and waited for him to climb up again under my persuasion." Lachesis clapped her hands. "Isn't he cute?"

Atropos circled Chris, sniffing at him. "I'd like to dine on satyr tonight and add his horns to my trophy necklace." She pulled a necklace out of her gown that had twenty or so little horns threaded on it. Rachel paled at the sight of it.

"You will not! I found him, he's mine!" Lachesis pushed Atropos away and cooed at Chris. "Aren't you, my pet?"

"Of course," said Chris, under her charms completely. He bowed regally, causing the seaweed to plop onto the floor. "I am at your service."

Rachel's heart raced. She pulled the flattened metal plate from her bag and unfolded it, sliding it onto the stone floor in front of her. All three of the Fates retreated a step, not trusting her.

Rachel looked at Clotho expectantly. "Well?"

Not to be cowed by a mortal child, Clotho strode forward and stood upon the plate with a fist on her hip. Rachel held out her hand, and Clotho flinched.

Arka wheezed with laughter, her face lighting up, and Clotho scowled at her. Atropos stomped over and yanked Arka's braid, forcing her head up. "You think that's funny, Arkaeivahina? How about this?" She grinned and sucked the very light from Arka, dimming the color in her face.

Arka tried to headbutt Atropos. "Get your filthy hands off me!" she mouthed, still unable to speak.

"Stop it you two!" Clotho hollered. She rested her eyes on Rachel, who was shaking from head to toe.

Rachel vibrated with anger, forcing herself not to claw

271

Atropos's eyes out. She had to focus on the plan. Clotho mistook Rachel's tremors for fear.

"Continue Seer," she said soothingly.

"You must take my hand," Rachel said, and she stuck out her hand like a shark fin. Clotho didn't move. She was wary Rachel had some other artifact to entrap her with. Rachel reprimanded her like a little kid. "How can I force a vision, Clotho if you won't follow my instructions? Don't we have an agreement? You aren't going to back out of it now, are you?"

Arka made puffing sounds, laughing again.

Infuriated, Clotho tossed her hair and forcefully grabbed hold of Rachel's hand. An electric shock powerful enough to collapse the cavernous lair around them jolted through the Clotho. Fortunately, it was contained inside her body. All the names inside her dissolved, and she threw back her head, screaming in agony. Both Lachesis and Atropos leapt forward to pull Clotho away from the seer. The moment they touched their sister, the electric current shot through them too, the power of the bolt electrocuting them in a deafening triumvirate explosion.

Chapter 35: The Greatest Gift

Rachel's hand remained attached to the trio of electrified Fates, and she was blasted into another vision. The immense curtain to the tapestry blew open, revealing the faded tapestry hanging behind it, covered in dark blotches spreading over the weave. Rachel saw the Fates, paralyzed in the current. She pulled her hand free of Clotho's incinerating grip as if moving outside of time.

Rachel ran to unfasten the chains around Arka. Arka weakly tossed her head toward the arm of her chair. A key hung just outside her reach next to a shackle chaffing her wrist in a cruel form of psychological torture. Rachel snatched the heavy key and jammed it into the locks, twisting them open with both hands. She pulled the bonds off and dragged Arka to her feet, hugging her tightly.

Arka's full light returned in a flash! She carefully tested her voice. "What possessed you to return here?"

"I had to free you!"

"I was angry you came back here at first, but now I see it

was meant to be. I understand why you were chosen to be a seer, and why I needed you." Arka stood back and smiled warmly. "It was to help me realize my worth. All those things you said; thank you, my friend. I know what I must do now."

"Arka, I think this vision is somehow real," said Rachel, growing worried that she hadn't snapped out of it yet. "It's happened before, in this room."

"It is real. This is a powerful place, but look, the power has shifted." Arka pointed to the monster hole. The seeing eye had gone dark and was, slowly dropping into the abyss. "We are inside your vision but simultaneously outside of it, in front of time."

"How is that possible?"

"I do it all the time with my weaving. I think for you, it comes from your desire to do the right thing. With the faded tapestry, the separation of our worlds has also been fading. That is why you, a mortal girl, could become a seer and use your power to help me. Isn't it something?"

"What?"

"That in the darkest hour there is always something or," she tilted her brow toward Rachel, "someone sent to help. It was the only way either of us could defeat the corrupted Fates and right their wrongs. And now, your belief has given me the strength to complete our quest."

"What else is there but going home?"

"Exactly. Let me weave a gateway to send you and Chris home." Arka gave Rachel another hug. Her strength flooded back, sparked by Rachel, and she and wove her friend a beautiful gateway embedded with the power of the moment, carefully bending the strands of space and time. Arka turned and spoke to Chris, breaking his hypnosis. "Chris, wake up."

Chris blinked and looked around, bewildered. How did he get in here? Why was he drenched? He was beside himself when he saw Arka and Rachel, safe and whole.

"Chris, you've been more courageous than any satyr in history. I want you to know that. Goodbye, my friend," said Arka. Her words registered, and Chris burst into tears.

"Goodbye," he said, dabbing vigorously at his eyes with a colorful green striped hanky, smushing it up under his warped spectacles. It was his spare, pulled from yet another pocket in his adventure vest. Arka smiled and hugged him too.

Rachel grabbed Arka's shoulder. "Hang on. What do you mean goodbye? Aren't you going through the gateway with us?"

"Not this time, Rachel. I have to finish what we started." Arka took Rachel's hand away and strode toward the tapestry. As she drew near, the threads came to life, glowing brighter and brighter, thirsty for light. The dark blotches faded, shrinking as she approached, and suddenly Rachel knew what Arka planned.

"There has to be another way!" Rachel cried out, tears stinging her eyes. "Chris! Tell her!"

Chris sniffed and shook his head. "It is the greatest gift."

Rachel's tears streaked down her cheeks. "Arka wait!" she sobbed. "There has to be another way! We need you here. I don't know how to fully use my abilities. I'm terrible at communicating, I'm afraid and," her face crumbled, "what am I supposed to do without you?"

Arka paused, turning back. Her face was serene, her eyes peaceful. "Don't view yourself from all you lack Rachel, view yourself from all you have, from all you've accomplished! You proved yourself today." She smiled proudly. "You must return to your own world and grow into who you're meant to be. There is so much to do and see!"

"Is that a compliment?" Rachel sniffed.

"No." Arka smiled. "I was merely stating a fact."

"But what if I mess up?" Rachel sputtered.

Arka held up a hand. "Mistakes are okay, Rachel, they don't stop the design. I'm repairing the tapestry so your thread can weave on, creating a beautiful pattern in each phase of your life. I'll make it whole; you go make it great." Arka placed a fist over her heart. "It has been an honor. I will not forget you, Rachel Soarenson."

Rachel mimicked her, placing a fist over her own heart and watched Arka, walk into the tapestry with purpose. It didn't burn or swallow her like in Rachel's nightmares. Her face and hands shone like the sun and Arka gracefully drifted into it, transcendent, both she and the tapestry shining brilliantly until Arka was no more.

Crack! Lightning blasted through the air as time caught up to itself. Rachel grabbed Chris, diving to the floor. The air warped, growing thick and the immobilized Fates exploded into ashes! A blast of wind blew the ashes around them in a cyclone, circling the useless eye and the violent storm drained into the monster pit, pulling the eye down with it. Chris shuddered and Rachel held him tighter.

The heavy curtain used to hide the tapestry and cover the Fates' evil machinations whumped to the floor. The tapestry shone in full glory, whole and magnificent, stretching on beyond the lair through another gateway that had been obscured behind the curtain. Rachel blinked at the light and the shining gateway leading to another realm. It was so beautiful! The illumination warmed her soul and a wave of peace washed over her.

"She's gone," whispered Chris, standing up and staggering at her elbow.

Rachel placed a hand on his slumped back, steading him. "She's not gone, Chris. She has become one with the tapestry, repairing it from the inside with her love and spirit." There was nothing left but for her and Chris to go home. Rachel gazed at the brilliant tapestry. "I'll never forget you either, Arka."

* * *

"Perhaps we'll see each other again," said Chris, bowing nobly to Rachel.

Rachel pulled him up and hugged him, knocking his spectacles askance. She didn't know if satyrs were supposed to blush, but Chris did. She giggled at him. "Friends?"

Chris straightened his vest and nodded. "Friends."

"You've done well, Chris. If I ever need a navigator, I'll know who to call."

Chris smiled brightly and gave her a quick salute, clicking his hooves together. He was eager to return home and write about his epic adventure with the new seer. There would be an entire chapter about how he was her trusted best friend and daring mariner. Feeling quite accomplished, he stepped through the gateway, head held high in dignified status.

Rachel grabbed the bag she'd borrowed and collected her metal plate, stuffing it inside. She looked around the quiet lair. It felt empty without the hovering eye or wicked Fates slinking around. She knew they weren't dead, but hoped they'd be stuck in the Underworld for a long time. Rachel slung the haversack across her chest. She had to keep her word and return it. More importantly, she had to get home! With one last look at the repaired tapestry, she swallowed fresh tears, took a deep breath, and stepped through the gateway Arka had made for her.

Rachel stepped right onto her front lawn, her shoes crunching on frosted grass. It felt like a lifetime since she'd seen her house and her heart skipped. It looked so cozy and warm, a juxtaposition to the crisp winter air filling her lungs. She inhaled deeply. It smelled like snow.

Just then Rachel's father opened the front door wearing his parka, hauling out a bulging trash bag, and saw her standing there. "Hey Bright Eyes! You're Home!" He tossed the heavy bag into the bin next to the porch and called into the house. "Emily, come see who's here!" Her dad held out his arms in a welcoming wingspan. Rachel ran up the front steps, falling into them. He squeezed her in a big bear hug and Rachel hugged him back with all her might.

Her mother appeared on the porch next to them. "Oh, my stars!" she exclaimed. "How was your weekend, honey? We've missed you! Are you crying?" She joined in, hugging her daughter in a family reunion sandwich, not caring if all the neighbors saw them standing outside in the cold with fluffy snowflakes drifting around them.

"Just happy tears, Mom," Rachel said, burying her face in the embrace of her parents. "It was good, but not as good as this."

Thank you for reading The Fourth Fate!

Please add a short review on your favorite digital platform and let me know your thoughts!

Keep your eyes open for book two!

ABOUT THE AUTHOR

Rebecca Casselman was raised in North Pole, Alaska, and as a military spouse she has traveled all over the United States. She is a writer, actor, and director. She believes in the power of storytelling and encourages all bookworms and artists to share their stories with the world.

Instagram: @rebecca.casselman
casselcore.com

CPSIA information can be obtained
at www.ICGtesting.com
Printed in the USA
LVHW090803010621
689024LV00002B/124